JUL 1 4 2020

P9-DMM-988

DATE DUE

Books by Rachel Dylan

CAPITAL INTRIGUE · 1

END GAME

RACHEL DYLAN

BETHANYHOUSE

a division of Baker Publishing Group
Minneapolis, Minnesota

© 2020 by Rachel Dylan

Published by Bethany House Publishers
11400 Hampshire Avenue South
Bloomington, Minnesota 55438
www.bethanyhouse.com

Bethany House Publishers is a division of
Baker Publishing Group, Grand Rapids, Michigan

Printed in the United States of America

Library of Congress Control Number: 2019949496

ISBN 978-0-7642-3430-9 (paper)
ISBN 978-0-7642-3545-0 (cloth)

This is a work of fiction. Names, characters, incidents, and dialogues are products of the author's imagination and are not to be construed as real. Any resemblance to actual events or persons, living or dead, is entirely coincidental.

Cover design by Faceout Studio
Cover photography by Vanessa Skotnitsky/Arcangel

Author is represented by the Nancy Yost Literary Agency.

20 21 22 23 24 25 26   7 6 5 4 3 2 1

CHAPTER ONE

"**I think they might** be keeping dead bodies in their condo!"

Bailey Ryan sat beside her friends in an Arlington, Virginia, diner and took a big bite of salad as Layla Karam continued to tell her animated story.

"Bailey, Viv, I'm telling you." Layla lifted her hands. "I have to find a new place to live. My neighbors are insane. I'm not joking about the dead bodies."

Bailey laughed at her friend's ridiculous accusation.

Vivian Steele's hazel eyes glistened with excitement. "Dead bodies would be Bailey's territory. She's the hotshot FBI agent."

Bailey shook her head. "I don't think anyone has ever called me a hotshot."

Vivian laughed. "In law school they just called you the gunner."

Bailey placed a hand on her chest. "No way. Layla was the gunner."

"Lies. All lies." Layla grinned as she twisted her long black hair around her finger. "We have to decide if we're going to the five-year reunion."

"It'll depend on my schedule," Viv said. "Things are crazy at work right now." She looked down at her smartwatch. "That's why we're eating dinner at ten p.m." To the outside world, Viv and Layla both worked for the State Department, but though Viv was a lawyer for State, in reality Layla actually worked as an analyst at the CIA. Only a very tight circle of people knew the truth about Layla's career. She and Viv were currently working on a joint project that called for some overnight assignments. "I think I'd like to go to the reunion—but only if we *all* go."

"Georgetown Law reunions are supposed to be fancy affairs," Layla said.

Bailey groaned. "Just what I need. We've stayed in touch with the people we actually liked. I'm not interested in schmoozing with anyone else."

"It's DC—everyone has an angle to play," Vivian said.

Bailey understood that point all too well. Even in her career at the FBI, she had to deal with internal and external politics and power plays. She just wanted to do her job and solve crimes.

She'd just taken the last bite of her salad when her cell phone rang. "Sorry, ladies, I have to get this."

"We know the drill," Viv said.

They all had high-pressure jobs that called on them 'round the clock. It was another reason they got along so well. There was never any guilt over having to deal with work issues. Just the opposite—they were all very supportive of each other and stepped up to the plate to be there. To Bailey, these women were her family.

Bailey stood and answered her phone. "Agent Ryan."

"We've got one," Connor said. "Meet you at the DC morgue."

"See you soon." She had a no-nonsense but strong relationship with Special Agent Remy Connor. Known to everyone as

Connor, he was five years her senior. They had grown very close, and he was like the big brother she'd never had.

She walked back over to her friends. "Sorry, I've got to run."

"An actual dead body this time?" Viv asked.

Bailey nodded. "Yeah."

"We should be getting to work too." Viv looked at Layla. "We're working some late nights these days. I don't think I'm cut out for the night shift. At least this assignment will be over soon."

"You'll have me there for moral support." Layla smiled.

Bailey's heart warmed watching her friends. "Be good. I'll catch up with you two later." She never asked questions about their work but understood they were working on an important project.

She exited the restaurant and got on the Metro. Then she hopped off at L'Enfant Plaza and made the short walk to the DC medical examiner's office. As an agent in the Criminal Investigative Division working out of the DC field office, her days and nights were often filled with things most people would rather avoid, but she did important, fulfilling work. Much more fulfilling than taking a traditional lawyer gig at a huge firm. Although she'd had a ton of offers to do so.

Having a law degree gave her a unique perspective many of her colleagues didn't have. Most of the agents who did have JDs had chosen to work in other divisions at the FBI. Not her. She thrived on the challenges that came with working violent crimes.

No stranger to the medical examiner's office, she flashed her badge at the security guard and made her way to Connor, who stood in the lobby.

"Thanks for waiting on me, or is it that you didn't want to visit the body alone?" She enjoyed giving Connor a hard time, but he always took it in stride.

7

He smiled. "You know I'm a team player."

"So what have we got?" They started walking down the hall-way to the elevator that would take them to the basement morgue.

His blue eyes met hers. "DC police called us in because this is the second murder in three days with a similar MO. The first murder was in Arlington, but this victim was killed in Foggy Bottom. Arlington and DC police stay in close communication, and they put two and two together."

The elevator dinged, and they exited to see Jessie—or Doc Phillips, as she was known—as the coroner on duty. She was one of Bailey's favorite people to work with.

The short, gray-haired woman greeted them both warmly. "Good evening, agents. I'm glad you're here."

They followed her into the morgue, and Bailey was ready to jump in. "Connor tells me the victim is similar to one from just three days ago?"

"That's correct. I got the autopsy report from the Arlington ME's office. The prior victim is Michael Rogers. And while I can't say with certainty, there is a striking resemblance in what was done to the two bodies."

Doc Phillips removed the sheet covering the new victim lying on the table. The first thing that struck Bailey was the man's ultrastrong physique. Given his size and muscle tone, this made the crime all the more perplexing.

"Do you notice his build?" she said. "For someone to get the drop on him, he must have really been caught by surprise."

Connor nodded. "I'm not an expert, but from the angles of the cuts it looks like someone came up on him from behind and maybe caught him off guard." He ran his hand through his short blond hair. "Am I right, Doc?"

"You're right that the wounds were inflicted from behind." The ME pointed toward the body. "As you can see, there are multiple stab wounds. I can tell you they are in the same direction and depth as Rogers's." She walked over to her desk and picked up some papers. "Take a look for yourself. This is the report for Rogers."

Bailey and Connor both took a few moments to study the report.

"So we're possibly looking at the same killer," Bailey said flatly. "Only three days in between, same MO. No cooling-off period. This could be the makings of a spree case."

"It is my opinion that this could be the same killer, but for the rest of it, I'll leave the investigating up to the FBI." Doc Phillips looked away.

Something was up. "What are you not telling us, Doc?" Bailey asked.

Doc Phillips shifted her weight from side to side. "Well, it might not be *just* the FBI."

"What do you mean?" Connor asked.

Doc looked at him. "We ran his prints, and the results came back a bit ago."

"Who is he?" Bailey asked.

"I know exactly who he is," a deep male voice said behind her.

Bailey turned and saw a tall black-haired man standing in the doorway. He sucked all the air out of the room with his commanding presence. "And who are you?" she asked.

"Special Agent Marco Agostini, NCIS." He walked toward them.

That explained Doc's behavior. They wouldn't be working this case alone. "And that must mean he's one of yours?"

Marco's dark eyes locked on to hers. "That's need to know."

Marco eyed the blonde wearing the dark FBI jacket with skepticism. There was no way he was letting the FBI take the lead on this case.

"You'll have to do a lot better than that, Agent Agostini," the blonde said. "We *do* have a need to know."

The ME took a few steps back. "I'm going to get some coffee while you all sort this out. I'll be a back in a few." She quickly exited, obviously not wanting to get involved in a turf war, and he couldn't blame her.

"And who are you?" Marco asked.

"FBI Special Agent Bailey Ryan, and this is Supervisory Special Agent Remy Connor."

Marco stood firm. "I know you're just trying to do your job, but so am I. NCIS is taking this case."

Bailey's bright green eyes narrowed. "We both got called down here. You know you can't waltz in and act like you own the investigation. This is the second murder of its type in less than a week. For all we know, this could be a serial killer, and then FBI has to be involved."

Marco thought he heard Agent Connor let out a little laugh. He tried to size up the two of them. Given their titles, Bailey was the junior of the two but not by a whole lot. Regardless, he had to protect his case. "I'll say it again, ma'am. NCIS is taking charge here."

"I haven't gotten that direction from my boss." She turned to her partner. "Have you, Connor?"

"Nope. Why don't I make a few calls and see if we can get some clarity on the situation?" Connor stepped outside the room with his phone to his ear.

Marco took a moment to study Bailey Ryan. She had straight blond hair that almost hit her shoulders. Her sun-kissed skin was probably a sign that she spent a lot of time outdoors. Above average height, but still stood below his six-one frame. He figured he should take the high road and try not to agitate the situation any further. "Agent Ryan, I have only the utmost respect for the FBI."

"You sure have an interesting way of showing it," she shot back. "What happened to the directive that we should all work together for the common good?"

She had him there. "That's true, but there are still possible security issues present. I just want to be buttoned up here, and we can't afford to take any chances."

Bailey crossed her arms. "If you're worried about security clearances, I worked a joint operation with FBI counterintelligence a few months ago. I have top secret SCI clearance. So that shouldn't be an issue."

He appreciated her zeal, but he wasn't going to give in—it didn't matter that she seemed more than competent. In truth, he didn't have a leg to stand on with the security clearance argument. He was just trying to stall and hopefully get a grip on this situation ASAP.

Bailey stepped toward him. "As far as I can tell, this crime happened while the victim was off duty."

"You know that doesn't preclude NCIS from taking the lead. He's still one of us. That means this is our case to run if we want it."

Bailey placed her hands on her hips but didn't say anything. Probably because she knew he was right. NCIS routinely took the lead in felony cases involving a Navy servicemember. Yes, they had to work with other agencies all the time, but he would like NCIS to be at the helm on this one. Everything about this scenario felt wrong to him.

His phone rang, and he looked down to see who it was. "Sorry, ma'am. This is my boss, and I need to take this."

Bailey smiled. "All right."

She was probably smiling because if the NCIS director was calling right now, that couldn't be good. "This is Agostini."

"Agostini, it's Director Mercer."

"Yes, ma'am. How can I help you?" He dreaded her response.

"You're at the ME's office, right?"

"Yes, ma'am." He swallowed hard, waiting for her orders.

"I know we talked about this being an exclusive NCIS operation, but we have to play nice in the sandbox. I've gotten some pressure from my colleagues at the FBI, and they want in on this too, given the possibility that we might have a serial or spree killer on the loose and the first victim was a civilian. So this is how it's going to go. We work the case jointly, but for now NCIS is still lead."

"Why do you say 'for now,' ma'am?" He feared he already knew.

"Because you know things could change at any minute. But you need to work *with* the FBI and not against them. Am I clear, Agent Agostini?"

There was only one answer. "Crystal, ma'am."

"Agostini, I have a bad feeling about this. Get to the bottom of what's going on here ASAP."

"Roger that, ma'am." As he hung up, he saw that Connor had joined Bailey and they were huddled up talking in the corner of the room. No doubt they'd just received the exact same message from their leadership. Now he had to welcome them in. It wasn't the first time in his career he'd eaten crow, and it certainly wouldn't be the last.

He walked over to where the agents stood. He expected Bailey to rub it in, but she didn't say a word. "I'm guessing you talked to your boss too. My directive is that this is a joint investigation with NCIS taking lead. Is that your understanding?" He looked at Bailey and then Connor.

"Yes," Bailey said. "But given our resource constraints, you're going to be stuck with me. Connor will be monitoring the case but not working the day to day. We're spread very thin, as I assume you are at NCIS as well."

"Yeah, it's the reality these days for all of us. More budget cuts and hiring freezes, but the bad guys never let up." Marco prepared himself to be spending a lot more time with Bailey. He wasn't blind to the fact that she was attractive, but he also put his job first—always. That was probably why he was thirty-one and still single. "Then I guess we need to get to it. We should head to NCIS headquarters and bring in some others on my team to assist. In the meantime, I can get you up to speed on the second victim—Petty Officer First Class Sean Battle."

"What's really going on here? Why all the intense focus on a petty officer?" Bailey asked.

Marco took a deep breath. "Because this one was special. He was a Navy SEAL."

CHAPTER
TWO

By the time Bailey arrived at NCIS HQ at Quantico, she had a lot more questions than answers. But she couldn't help being a bit preoccupied with the cocky NCIS special agent she had to work with. She hadn't personally worked a case with NCIS during her tenure at the FBI, but she'd heard that how smoothly it went all depended on the NCIS agent involved. This should be just like any other joint operation between agencies, and she had done those before, just not with NCIS.

Bailey thought she might have her hands full with Agent Agostini. He'd owned up to the directive from his boss and had been cooperating ever since, but he still seemed a bit overconfident to her. Although, in her line of work, that had been her experience with most men she dealt with. Luckily for her, she wasn't fazed by it.

Marco ushered her into a small conference room where a petite dark-haired woman with big blue eyes greeted her.

"Special Agent Bailey Ryan, meet NCIS Special Agent Isabella

Cole, aka Rookie. She just started about eight months ago. She works for me and will be assisting us on this case."

Bailey shook Isabella's hand. "Nice to meet you."

Isabella gave her a warm smile. "This is going to be an interesting one."

They all sat around the conference room table.

Marco pulled a couple of folders out of his bag. "I've already told you that this matter is sensitive. Given who we're dealing with here, we can't take any chances. I trust you will handle it accordingly."

Bailey knew he had to confirm it, so she didn't take offense. "Yes, of course."

Marco's smoldering dark eyes focused on her. "Petty Officer First Class Sean Battle was a member of SEAL Team 8. What we don't know yet is whether these two murders were the act of a possible serial or spree killer, random acts of violence, or something more sinister—like a link between any of Battle's missions and his death. SEALs have a way of making enemies. That's one of the reasons we try to keep their identities under wraps while they are active duty. There are terrorist groups and others who want to work against the security interests of the United States that would relish the opportunity to take out a SEAL."

"So far there's no claim of responsibility by any terrorist group," Isabella said. "Don't you think that if they were doing this to make a point, they would advertise it and plaster it all over social media?"

Marco jotted down a couple of notes. "I do, but it's still early. We'll have to monitor social media for any claims of responsibility."

Bailey understood why Marco was being cautious on the terrorism angle, but she thought he was definitely barking up the wrong tree. "I understand why you're exploring that option, but since our first vic is a civilian, I think that pokes holes in that theory. We have to determine if there's any link between the two victims. And if there's any chance this is the start of a spree or serial killing, we need to act fast before another dead body turns up. Only three days between the first two kills. That means we could be on the clock."

Marco tapped his pen on his notebook. "I get your train of thought and approach, and you're most likely right. But given that Battle was an elite member of the SEALs, we can't just accept everything at face value."

"But how do you explain the civilian connection? Rogers was the first murder. In serial killings, usually the first murder has special significance." They couldn't overlook that critical fact.

Marco nodded. "I'm just trying to make sure we keep our eyes open."

"Have you alerted the other members of SEAL Team 8?" Bailey knew this was going to be tough news for those SEALs to hear.

Isabella eagerly jumped in. "That's in process. We're going to interview his teammates and see if we can find any useful information."

Bailey thought through the scenarios. "If there is a connection, then don't those SEALs need to be on high alert? If one of them was murdered because of a mission, then all of them could be at risk."

Marco nodded. "Yes. His platoon is stateside right now, stationed in Little Creek, Virginia."

"That's a ways away. Why was Battle in the DC metro area?" Bailey asked.

"Little Creek is just over three hours from Foggy Bottom," Isabella said. "He could've made the trip for a number of reasons. There's nothing suspicious about that, in my opinion."

"Do you think a person acting on his own could've taken down the SEAL?" Bailey asked. "And I say *he* because I think the probability of a female killer here, given everything we know and the physical capabilities of the victim, is very low."

"We can run simulations to help determine the most likely scenarios of how the attack played out," Marco replied.

Bailey thought of something else. "If these killings are not connected, then don't we also have to consider the fact that this could be personal? Maybe he did something to tick someone off, or worse."

Marco leaned back in his chair. "Possible. Like I said, at this point, all theories are on the table."

Bailey felt like Marco was holding out on her. "So where do we start?"

He rose from his seat. "We get all the files on the Rogers investigation from Arlington police and start our review, and then we bring in the other members of SEAL Team 8 and question them."

The next morning Marco took a sip of his coffee and watched the frown spread across Bailey's lips.

"What is it?" he asked.

"The preliminary ME report for Battle is so strikingly similar to Rogers, I just don't see how we can say that the same person isn't responsible. Add to that the time in between the killings—just three days."

After sleeping on it, Marco had come to the same conclusion. "I agree with you. If this was done because of any mission connection, then we've got bigger problems, because Rogers is a civilian."

"And we have no link yet between the two. The more probable

theory is that we're dealing with a cold-blooded killer who is still out there, waiting on his next victim. Time isn't on our side here."

He nodded. "I know." He flipped through the papers in front of him. "Rogers worked construction. I think we should talk to the last guy he worked for and see if that leads anywhere."

"Any progress on video footage?" Bailey asked.

"The rookie is on it. I've tasked her with canvassing all area businesses for any video. She'll gather that up, and then we'll have it reviewed."

"Good. Maybe that will give us something to go on."

Marco wasn't so sure. "Unless the killer is a pro and knew where to strike so he wouldn't be caught on camera."

She gave him a slight smile. "A bit too early in the investigation for pessimism, isn't it?"

Now it was his turn to grin. "I prefer to be realistic, but yeah. I just don't want us to get our hopes up that we're going to catch the perp red-handed. I have a feeling it's going to be a lot more complicated than that."

"Then we'll tackle it one step at a time."

Maybe he *had* become too cynical. It was nice that Bailey was more upbeat about the whole thing. "Do you want to keep our noses in these papers any longer, or get out there and shake things up? Get some answers."

"I'd much rather be out in the field than stuck inside, but are you sure we've gone through everything in the files that we need to?"

Marco shrugged. "The files will be here when we get back."

Bailey leaned back in her chair. "Hey, I'm all for fieldwork, but my training has shown me time and again the importance of details. Being an FBI agent often entails the mind-numbing work of reviewing documents and building a case. I'm sure your job is no different."

He chuckled. "I think we'll get more of the answers we're looking for if we find out who this Rogers guy really is. We'll get all the info we could ever want on Battle from the Navy. Rogers is the wild card. If we can track down what Rogers was all about, then that will give us the best chance of seeing if there are any links between the two, and that in turn could help us know where to look to find the answers."

She closed the folder in front of her. "Or let us know if we have a deranged serial killer out there who just happened to pick these two men and is ready to strike again." She paused. "But you're in charge. We'll do it your way. For now."

"Good." He couldn't help picking up on her skepticism, but he was determined to break open this case, and he didn't think that would happen while knee-deep in paper work. He was more of the take-action type, and it was an approach that had served him well in his career.

"Well, what are we waiting for?" she challenged him. She got up and walked toward the door.

He got there before her and opened it. "After you."

"Thanks."

An hour later, they were pulling up to CXP Construction Management. Bailey exited the SUV, and he quickly caught up with her.

"I guess we'll see if Frank Haddad knows anything that could help us," she said.

A couple of men were outside smoking as they walked past. They entered the old, worn-down warehouse full of construction materials. A few men were milling around on the first floor.

"Can you tell me where I can find Frank Haddad?" Marco asked one of them.

The tall, dark-haired man with olive skin eyed him with skepticism. "Who's looking for him?"

Bailey took a step forward. "We just need to ask him some questions about one of his employees."

"You from ICE? Because if you are, I've got all my papers in order. All of my men are legal. Completely, one hundred percent, and I told you ICE guys that the last time you visited a month ago. I'm going to complain about harassment if you don't stop."

"So you're Frank?" Bailey asked softly.

Marco watched as she continued to try to disarm the situation.

"I am, but like I told you, I'm by the book, and I'm done with ICE. So you can get off my private property."

Marco spoke up. "We aren't from ICE, so you can relax."

"FBI." Bailey flashed her badge.

Marco decided to leave his connection to NCIS out of the conversation to avoid any confusion.

"We just want to ask you about Michael Rogers." She pulled a picture out of her bag and held it up.

Frank bit his bottom lip. "Yeah. I know him."

"Rogers works for you?" Marco asked.

Frank stared off to the side. "He did a little less than a year ago. Haven't seen him since, though."

"Are you sure?" Bailey asked.

Frank turned back to her. "Yeah. I can check my records and show you the last paycheck, if that would help."

She smiled. "Actually it would, thank you."

Bailey's charm offensive seemed to be working. Marco usually preferred a tougher, more direct route, but everyone had their own way, and he appreciated that.

Frank motioned to them. "Let's go to my office."

They walked through the warehouse floor to the back right corner, where there was a small office with a couple of chairs, a desk, and some old file cabinets. The musty smell was even stronger in the office.

"Let me see." Frank pulled out a drawer, and it made a creaking sound. "I have everything in alphabetical order." He seemed to take pride in his organizational efforts, even though they didn't seem that great. After a minute of rummaging around, he pulled out a file. "This is everything I have on Rogers."

"Do you have a copy machine here?" Bailey asked.

"I do, but it's broken."

Bailey flipped through the small folder. "I can just take pictures with my phone. There aren't that many pages. I don't want to take your originals."

As Bailey got to work, Marco turned to Frank. "Tell me what you remember about Rogers."

Frank's brown eyes met his. "He was a loner. Hard worker. Very strong. Definitely flew under the radar. But he only worked for me for about a year."

"Any coworkers he didn't get along with? Skirmishes? Anything like that?" Marco asked.

Frank shook his head. "I wouldn't know. If it did happen, I didn't hear about it. Like I said, I remember him being quiet. Really quiet."

Marco kept pushing. "What about vices? Gambling, addictions, anything?"

Frank laughed. "'Bout all my guys have some type of vice, but I have no idea about Rogers specifically."

"Do you have guys here now who worked with him?"

Frank crossed his arms. "Maybe just a couple. There's high turnover in construction, as I'm sure you know."

Marco was going to get as much from this visit as possible. "We'd like to talk to them before we leave."

"Sure." Frank paused. "If you don't mind me asking, what type of trouble has Rogers gotten himself into?"

Bailey handed Frank the folder. "He's dead."

"Dead?" Frank's voice cracked.

"Murdered, actually," Marco said.

Frank's face paled. "You can't think I had anything to do with this!"

"We don't, unless there's something you're not telling us," Bailey said. "But if you hold back on us, even one iota, you will move up on our suspect list."

The way Bailey expertly handled Frank was impressive—and all without raising her voice.

Frank sank back in his grimy chair. "There were a few rumors."

Marco's pulse thumped. Now maybe they were getting somewhere. "About what?"

"Some of the guys thought Rogers was into something shady, but they didn't know what. Like I said, he was a real lone wolf. Guys get to the site, and as they work, they talk and talk, and their imaginations go wild."

"What was the wildest rumor out there?" Bailey asked.

Frank looked up at them. "I don't believe it at all."

"You don't have to believe it. Just tell us what you heard," Marco nudged.

Frank leaned forward across the desk. "Okay, I'm just the messenger here. That's it. I don't have anything to support this."

"It's okay, Frank. Go ahead," Bailey said.

"All right. The rumor was that Rogers could've been some type of killer for hire."

Marco was starting to think this was even messier than he had imagined.

"And to be clear, you didn't think that rumor had any truth to it?" Bailey asked.

Frank threw up his hands. "Guys have vivid imaginations on a work site. I doubt it, but since you told me to tell you everything, there you have it."

"Thank you," Bailey said. "Point us to the guys who knew Rogers, and then we'll get out of your hair."

They followed Frank out of the office and back into the main warehouse area. "Those two in the corner, unpacking those boxes. Those are the only guys here right now. The rest of the crew on-site are new."

Bailey pulled out a card. "If you can think of anything else that might help us, then please give me a call. We appreciate your help." She gave him a warm smile that easily melted Frank's rough exterior, and he headed back to his office.

"That was quite impressive, Agent Ryan," Marco told her. "You had him eating out of the palm of your hand."

Bailey looked up at him. "I find being nice usually gets you a lot more information than trying to drop the hammer."

He smiled. "I'm more of a hammer-dropping kind of guy, but you're on a roll, so why don't you take the lead with these guys?"

"Sure."

Marco watched as Bailey strode confidently over to the two men. He estimated that they were in their forties or early fifties.

"Gentlemen, I need a minute of your time."

At the sound of Bailey's feminine voice, the two men stopped their conversation and turned their attention to her. Fully.

Immediately Marco felt his protective instincts kick in, and he moved closer to her. He knew Bailey was a seasoned FBI agent and was more than capable of taking care of herself, but he also had her back completely.

"What do you want?" one of the men asked in a gruff tone.

But it didn't appear to faze Bailey. "You worked with Michael Rogers, correct? What do you know about him?"

"Who are you?" the man asked.

"Law enforcement," Marco responded. "We've already talked to Frank, and we hope we can get your cooperation here."

"Rogers was bad news," the other man said.

"Why do you say that?" Bailey asked.

"You couldn't read him. It was like you were talking to a blank piece of paper, but I'm telling you there was ice in his veins. That's one of the reasons he got his reputation for being a contract killer."

"And do you believe any of that?" Bailey asked. "Just because someone is a loner doesn't mean they're a killer."

"True enough," the first man said. "But there was something different about him. It was like he was trying to be invisible. He would pop up when you least expected it, then"—he snapped his fingers—"the next moment he'd be gone. I just don't trust men like that. What's he done?"

She looked at Marco, and he responded. "Rogers has been murdered."

The shorter of the two men whistled. "Well, maybe we weren't too far off. He was up to something, I tell you."

"But you don't have anything more to go on than your suspicions?" Bailey asked.

They both shook their heads. "Nah. It was more of a gut feeling than anything."

The other man looked down. "And I wouldn't have wanted him dead. He always treated me all right. It's just that men that quiet make me nervous. I always worry about what they're hiding."

Bailey gave each of them her card and thanked them before she and Marco exited the warehouse.

"That was a lot more than we bargained for," Bailey said.

He patted her on the shoulder. "Told you we had to get our head out of the sand. Those stacks of papers would never have told us what we just learned."

"True, but the stacks of paper, as you call them, do hold

valuable intel of a different kind. We have to use all the resources at our disposal."

They were quiet for a few steps, both lost in their thoughts. "Who is this elusive Rogers? Could his killing be a coincidence?" Marco wondered.

"I'm not a fan of coincidences."

Marco wasn't either.

CHAPTER
THREE

The next afternoon Bailey sat beside Marco in one of the NCIS interrogation rooms. Isabella was observing from the next room. Marco had said it would be a good learning experience for the rookie.

After the interesting day they'd had yesterday, getting the lowdown on Rogers, now it was time to turn to the SEAL element of the investigation. They'd made their way through multiple interviews, and this was the last one of the day.

The SEAL who sat across from them was all business.

"Lieutenant Alvarez, how long have you led this platoon?" Marco asked.

"A little over a year, sir," he responded calmly.

Bailey was content to let Marco take the lead for this interview. They had switched back and forth with the others. The SEAL team leader's dark eyes met hers, and then moved back to Marco.

"Do you know if Battle had any enemies?" Marco asked.

Alvarez looked down and then back up. "If you're asking if anyone would want to kill him, yes. There are plenty of whack jobs out there who would love to kill a Navy SEAL. But if you're asking if I knew if anyone had a personal beef against him, well, it's no secret that sometimes SEALs get into it with each other, but that's to be expected. I might have witnessed a few skirmishes with team members, but I didn't see anything that would explain what happened here."

Bailey studied Alvarez carefully. He carried himself like a leader—full of confidence, no-nonsense. And she wasn't surprised that they didn't see an emotional reaction from him. He probably kept his grief private.

Marco shifted some papers in front of him. "Why don't we talk about your last few ops. Anything stick out there? Any missteps, any actions that could cause retaliation?"

Alvarez shook his head. "No, sir. The last few missions have gone off without a hitch."

Did Alvarez know more than he was letting on? She decided it was time for her to speak up. "Lieutenant Alvarez, sometimes in these situations even the smallest detail can help us."

"I understand, ma'am, but it's pretty much been SOP over the past few months."

Standard operating procedure. "You mentioned skirmishes among team members. Can you elaborate?"

Alvarez raised an eyebrow. "We're family. There's a fight here and there, some rivalries along the way, but I can guarantee as I'm sitting here today that there is zero chance another member of the teams killed Battle. Zero."

"Any personal disputes that Battle had outside of the teams?" she asked.

Alvarez kept his expression neutral. "Not that I'm aware of."

"Any personal problems? Money, family, drugs?" she pressed.

"No, ma'am, not that I know of." Alvarez looked her in the eyes.

Marco cleared his throat. "Was Battle a by-the-book kind of guy or more of a live-on-the-edge type?"

That question made Alvarez laugh. It was the first show of emotion he'd given. "Sir, we're SEALs. We all live on the edge, or we wouldn't be doing this. That isn't to say he wouldn't follow orders. He stuck to orders. That's what we're trained to do. But sometimes you have to think outside the box to get the job done—or take risks. Risks that others wouldn't take but can end up saving lives."

After another half hour of questioning, Isabella escorted Lieutenant Alvarez out of the interrogation room, leaving Bailey alone with Marco. "Well, we didn't get much from these interviews."

Marco shook his head. "No, but something felt off."

"You think Alvarez was hiding something, don't you?"

"More like protecting someone." Marco shifted in his seat.

She agreed. "He said it—they're family. He will protect his own. They all will. And to hear Alvarez tell it, Battle was a man with no issues or problems. We all know that can't be true."

"We're just at the beginning. There's a long way to go in this investigation." He paused. "How many years have you been with the FBI?"

She raised an eyebrow. "Are you trying to determine if I have enough experience for this case?"

He lifted his hands. "No need to get your hackles up. I was just trying to get to know you better, that's all."

She smiled. "Coming up on five years at the Bureau. What about you?"

"Eight years at NCIS. Spent almost two years in the Virginia State Police first. Did you go into the FBI straight from college?"

Bailey shook her head. "I actually went to law school at Georgetown."

Marco laughed. "Wait. You're telling me that you're a lawyer? You're just bringing that up now?"

She gave him a sly grin. "You worried?"

He leaned back in his chair. "Sounds like I should be, but now I understand why you're into the paper work. It makes a lot more sense."

She needed to set him straight. "I have a JD, but I'm not a practicing attorney."

"Still, you went to law school, which means the lawyer thing is now in your DNA. But hey, I think it's good you're like that, because you can be my counterbalance. As you could tell, I don't have much patience for going through tons of evidence, looking for needles in a haystack."

"Sometimes that's the only way you find the truth," she said.

"It's clear you're into that stuff, and you're obviously really smart. Why become an FBI agent instead of a lawyer and raking in the big bucks?"

This wasn't the first time she'd been asked that. A lot of people thought she was crazy. Especially given the money she'd left on the table by not going to a big DC firm. She'd received some amazing offers with a lot of shiny objects waved before her eyes—the big house, the fancy cars—but at the end of the day, her heart wasn't in it. She knew that money alone wasn't going to fulfill her. "By the time I got through law school, I realized I wanted something different. But what I learned through that process was indispensable and makes me an even better agent. The critical thinking skills you learn from being put through the law school wringer really help."

Marco stood up. "So, how am I doing at playing nice?"

"Fine." She wasn't sure what he was going to say next.

He lightly punched her arm. "Don't be so uptight, Bailey. I won't bite."

She held back a laugh. This assignment was going to be anything but boring.

"How about we get some coffee and plan our next move? Follow me." Marco headed for the door.

"Has anyone ever told you how bossy you are?" she asked.

He grinned. "You would not be the first."

◆

Marco was starting to think it wouldn't be so bad working with the FBI after all. Bailey was the type to roll up her sleeves and get to work, and for that he respected her. They'd quickly put the turf battle behind them and were solely focused on the case. In his experience, sometimes the FBI had a chip on its shoulder when they had to work with others, but not this agent.

They both had large cups of coffee and were seated in one of the conference rooms that he had turned into their war room. The room was equipped with a few computers and plenty of table space for them to spread out the paper files.

"Okay, now we get to do some of the work you love. Why don't you review Battle's personnel file, and I'll take a crack at the mission reports?" Marco suggested.

"I'm on it." Bailey flipped open one of the folders sitting in front of her.

They worked in silence for a while before Bailey spoke up.

"Says here that Battle has an ex-wife and a child."

"Where does she live?" he asked.

"Fairfax."

"Wanna take a road trip?"

She raised an eyebrow. "Why am I not surprised that you'd want to do that?"

"C'mon. Work with me here."

She smiled. "I actually agree with you. We need to talk to her. It's a good lead we need to run down."

About an hour and a half later, they pulled into the driveway of the small ranch-style house. As Battle's ex-wife and mother of his child, Ms. Battle would have already been notified of his death. So at least they wouldn't have to have that incredibly difficult conversation.

He rang the doorbell and waited. A moment later a tall, pretty brunette woman opened the door.

"Can I help you?" she asked.

"Are you Ms. Tiffany Battle?" Marco asked.

"Yes. You must be here about what happened to Sean."

"Yes, ma'am. I'm Special Agent Agostini with NCIS, and this is Special Agent Ryan with the FBI. Could we come in and ask you a few questions?"

She nodded. "Come on in. Would you like some coffee?"

"That won't be necessary," Bailey answered.

"Please, I insist. Have a seat in the living room, and I'll bring it in."

Marco and Bailey walked into the bright and cheery living room decorated in spring colors.

A few minutes later, Ms. Battle returned with the coffee. "I spoke to some agents briefly already."

"And we're sorry to bother you again, but we have some questions. The two of us are the lead investigators on the case, and we want to make sure we have all the information," Marco said.

Ms. Battle lifted her coffee cup but didn't take a sip. "You know, I realized that, given what Sean did, there was a chance he could get killed. But I never, ever thought he would be killed right here at home." She paused. "They said they think it was a robbery?"

"That's our job to find out," Marco responded.

"Ms. Battle, how long were you married to Sean?" Bailey asked.

"We had a whirlwind romance. We started dating and fell so hard for each other. We were married three months later. It was like a fairy tale, but when reality set in, especially with his deployments, it was all just too much. Once Jaden was born, things got even worse. We divorced when Jaden was two. That was two years ago."

"And how would you describe your relationship with him now?" Marco asked.

"We weren't like those couples who fought. It was more like he knew how miserable I was, and he didn't want to see me like that. We were on good terms. I had no idea what I was signing up for to be a SEAL's wife. I was ill-equipped to handle everything, and unfortunately Sean didn't know how to help me through it. He really loved Jaden, though." Her voice started to crack. "Jaden's too young to really know what's going on. His father didn't see him as much as I would've liked, given his schedule, but when they did see each other, it was quality time."

"I assume Sean was paying child support?" Bailey asked.

Ms. Battle nodded. "Yes, and spousal support too. He always paid, although sometimes he was a little late, but nothing major. It was never an issue, because I could always count on him. I knew he was doing the best he could, so I didn't push it. Like I said, Sean was a good man." A few tears slid down her cheeks.

"Ms. Battle," Marco said, "do you know of anyone who would want to hurt Sean?"

She didn't immediately respond.

"Please, we need you to be completely honest with us so we can help," Bailey said.

"He was really tight with his SEAL buddies, and he had a

few friends in other military branches. Sean was a bright light entering a room. People liked hanging around him. It was one of the reasons I was drawn to him from the start. He was always an eternal optimist. Saw the best in people." Her voice started to waver again. "But there was one SEAL who didn't see eye to eye with Sean. I know they had gotten into fights quite a few times."

Marco leaned forward. "And what's his name?"

"Tobias Kappen," Ms. Battle said softly.

"How well do you know him?" Bailey asked.

"I've met him a few times at various events, but since I knew he and Sean weren't on great terms, I purposely didn't get too close. However, I have a hard time thinking that he'd stab Sean to death, no matter their disagreements." Her voice cracked as the last words came out of her mouth. "But you should know that Sean told me Kappen has struggled with PTSD. I almost felt sorry for the guy, because I know what being on the teams can do to someone."

"Your ex-husband lived in a small apartment a few miles from base. Do you know if that's the only place he lived?"

Ms. Battle nodded. "It is. But Sean also had a storage area. He did one of those monthly rental things. His apartment was a studio, so he placed a few things in storage."

"Do you have any of the information on the storage facility?" Bailey asked.

"Yes, I do." Ms. Battle rattled off the name and general directions to the facility, which Bailey wrote down.

Marco thought they had pushed her enough for one visit. "Thank you so much. We're still at the beginning phases of the investigation, so we might need to visit you again."

"I understand. Whatever I can do to help." Ms. Battle sighed loudly. "I have to come to the realization that my son will never see his father again, and honestly, I don't think I've fully processed that yet."

Bailey reached out and patted her hand. "It's going to take time. Grieving is a process. You aren't expected to just turn your emotions on and off."

Ms. Battle squeezed Bailey's hand. "Thank you for saying that. I don't think everyone understands what this is like. Even though we were divorced, I still loved him. Always will."

Bailey nodded. "You're not alone in this. The Navy provides resources."

Marco pulled a business card out of his jacket. "Here's the number to someone who can connect you with Navy grief counseling."

Ms. Battle took the card. "Thank you for that. I'll definitely be calling."

Once they were back in his SUV, Marco turned toward Bailey. "Thoughts?"

"She didn't have anything to do with his death."

"Because she cried? You do realize that killers can put on the crocodile tears when they need to."

Bailey shook her head. "She would've had to hire someone for the hit. Why would she be motivated to kill him? She was getting support from him. In my opinion, she still loved him, and it was clear to me that she was broken up because of her son. I'm telling you, Marco, that woman did not put a hit out on her ex-husband."

He pulled out of the driveway. "I agree with you."

"You just wanted to push me a bit?" She quirked an eyebrow.

"Exactly. We should push each other. Keeps us sharp." And he enjoyed sparring with her.

"Sounds like we need to track down Kappen."

"Yes, we do, but we'll close the loop on Ms. Battle too. We'll still run down her financials, along with Battle's, and do a full work-up just to make sure she hasn't tricked us both. We should also visit Battle's storage facility, but we have to start thinking about other options, including Kappen." They had blank spots to fill in. Marco thought for a moment, then said, "Kappen could also be the person Alvarez was trying to protect. Maybe Alvarez knew that if he told us about the bad blood between the two men, that would put a target on Kappen's back, and he wasn't prepared to do that to one of his own. Especially if you consider any PTSD issues Kappen has had."

"We'll follow up with Alvarez again. Also, even if Kappen has something to do with this, how would he fit in with Rogers?"

"I'm not sure," Marco said.

"The evidence still indicates that the same person is responsible here. If that turns out to be right, then you're talking about a Navy SEAL killing two people—one a civilian."

"You're not hiding your skepticism."

"I'm not trying to," Bailey said.

He looked at her. "You were really good with her back there."

Bailey smiled. "Thank you. That kind of thing is always tough."

"You showed empathy. Not everyone can do that."

She nodded. "And that's a shame. Just because we're federal agents doesn't mean we don't have emotions."

He laughed. "I've never heard it put quite that way before."

"Admit it. You felt it too. You're not heartless."

"Oh, I agree. That was rough. I feel really sorry for the kid. Dad's a SEAL and gets killed stateside. What are the chances of that?"

"Too low. Something is wrong here, and we have to figure out what we're missing before it's too late."

CHAPTER
FOUR

The next day Bailey was anxious to hear what Petty Officer First Class Tobias Kappen had to say. They'd brought him into NCIS for questioning and were now sitting across from him in the interrogation room.

"Do I need a lawyer?" Kappen asked.

"That depends," Marco said.

Bailey felt she had to step in. She wasn't one for playing fast and loose when it came to someone's legal rights. "It's your right to obtain legal counsel. So if you want a lawyer, you need to tell us now before we start the questioning."

Marco shot her a look, but she knew she was doing the right thing. She took the right to be represented by counsel very seriously, and in this case especially she wanted to make sure the Navy SEAL understood his rights.

Indecision filled Kappen's light blue eyes. "I assume this is about Battle's death?"

"Yes," Bailey answered. But that wasn't all it was about. They'd get to Rogers in a minute.

Kappen sat quietly for a moment. "Yes, ma'am. I think I'd like to have a lawyer present."

"That's your right." Marco looked at Bailey as he said it. "You hang tight, and we'll see what we can do."

An hour later, JAG lawyer Lieutenant Lexi Todd sat to the right of Kappen. The JAG attorney wore her dark hair pulled back in a bun, and she pulled a legal pad out of her briefcase. "You all can start your questioning, but my client is here voluntarily. He's cooperating because it's the right thing to do. But I'm warning you, don't take advantage of this gracious offer. You'll find that I may not be as accommodating as my client."

Bailey appreciated Lexi's tough tactics. It was at moments like this that she couldn't help but wonder how she would have been as a practicing lawyer. She knew she'd made the right decision by going to the FBI, but there would always be that fleeting question in her head of what kind of lawyer she would have become.

"We appreciate your cooperation, Lieutenant Todd," Marco said. "And yours as well, Petty Officer Kappen. Why don't you tell us about your relationship with Petty Officer Sean Battle?"

Kappen looked at his attorney, and she nodded for him to continue. "Battle and I are on SEAL Team 8, but we work in different platoons. I met him a few years ago. We got off to a really rocky start. A bar fight that went way too far. We were both the stubborn type, and it became a running feud that pretty much everyone on the team knew about. Our rivalry was almost part of the fabric of the team." He leaned forward. "But I did not kill him, and I would've never wanted him dead. We're brothers. I might've had my issues with him and given him a lot of grief over the years, but when push comes to shove, we all have each other's backs and would die for one another. That's what we signed up for. I take that duty very seriously."

"Where were you on June tenth?" Bailey asked. Best to get right to the point, as she wasn't sure how much time or leeway the JAG lawyer was going to give them.

"I was on base all day doing some paper work. Since this is our downtime, I drove up to DC. I grabbed dinner with a friend. After that I went to my parents' condo in Arlington. I stay there when I'm hanging out in the city. They live in Florida now."

"Were you alone?" Bailey asked.

Kappen nodded. "Yes, ma'am. After dinner I was alone for the rest of the evening. Was back up early the next morning doing PT."

"Who did you go to dinner with and where?" Bailey asked.

"A woman I just started seeing a few weeks ago. We went to a swanky place in Georgetown." Kappen shrugged. "I forget the name. That's the only time I've been there. It was her choice. Not really my scene."

"You were trying to impress her?" Marco asked.

"Yes, sir. But I don't think it worked."

"As evidenced by the fact that you went home alone?" Marco asked.

Bailey shot him a look. He was pushing things a bit too far.

"No," Kappen answered. "I just don't think she was ready to handle all the baggage that comes with a guy like me."

Even with Marco's jab, Kappen hadn't lost his cool.

"What's your area of expertise on the team?" Bailey asked. She didn't have all the military lingo down, but that didn't matter. All she was concerned about was getting the information.

"Sniper, ma'am."

"Are you aware of the details of Battle's death?" Marco asked.

"What do you mean, sir?"

"Like how and where he was killed."

"I heard that he was killed in Foggy Bottom, supposedly stabbed to death, and that authorities are saying he was robbed."

"Why do you sound skeptical?" Bailey asked.

Kappen looked down before making eye contact. "I'm sorry, ma'am. I'm at a loss. I have no idea why this happened or how I fit into it. But my first thought, knowing Battle like I do, is how would one man do that to him? I say it's unlikely. Battle was one of the strongest men on the teams. He would've put up a heck of a fight."

Now they were getting somewhere. If Battle had fought back, his killer would be bruised or wounded. "Would you to submit to physical examination?"

"Why? What does that have to do with anything?" Kappen looked over at Lexi.

"I'd like to discuss that further with my client and get back to you," Lexi said firmly.

Bailey kept pushing. "All right, but back to your point. You think more than one person is responsible?"

Kappen nodded. "Based on the facts that I've heard, yes. Battle was one of the most highly trained SEALs. I don't see any other logical explanation."

Bailey thought he might be telling the truth. She hoped he would submit to an examination and that it would shed some light, although she wondered if his attack-dog lawyer would let that happen. She would have done the same thing as Lexi, though. Protecting the client was the utmost responsibility of the attorney.

But now they had to go down another road. "Where were you on the night of June seventh?" Bailey asked.

Kappen looked off to the side. "Let me think." He paused. "I was at my parents' condo by myself."

Lexi cleared her throat. "I think we're done here. Unless you have any evidence against my client you want to present, this interview is over."

Bailey shifted in her seat. "Actually, we need to ask about a few more things."

Lexi gave her a slight nod to proceed.

Bailey looked at Kappen. "Do you know a man named Michael Rogers?"

Kappen frowned.

"Do you?" Marco asked.

Kappen shook his head. "No. That's not ringing any bells. Definitely not someone on the teams, that's for sure."

"What about outside the teams?" Bailey asked.

"No. It's a pretty generic name, but it doesn't mean anything to me." Kappen paused. "Is he a suspect too?"

Bailey made eye contact with him. "No. He's another victim."

"Don't know him," Kappen said.

Bailey wasn't done. "The last topic, and I realize it's a difficult one, is about whether you've had any issues with PTSD." She hated asking about it, but they had no choice.

Kappen's eyes widened. "I thought my medical records were private and confidential."

"I haven't seen your medical records. I was just asking a question," Bailey answered honestly. She wasn't going to reveal that Battle's ex was the source. It wasn't necessary.

"It was over a year ago." Kappen's voice started to shake. "I'm good now. Solid."

Lexi shot up out of her chair. "Okay, the interview is really over now."

"We'll be in touch," Marco said.

They didn't have anything to charge Kappen with at this point, so they had no choice but to let him go.

Once it was just her and Marco, Bailey turned to him. "I think there's more to this feud than he let on."

"Isn't there always?" Marco ran his hand through his thick dark hair.

"I felt like a complete jerk for bringing up PTSD, but you saw his reaction." She looked away. "Unfortunately, I know it's a bigger problem than any of us would like to admit. Especially with guys who face the toughest battles like Kappen."

"There's definitely something there. And as much as we don't want to think it, we can't pretend like that isn't a factor here. These men are under such pressure, and the things they see and do can take a great toll."

"But is it enough of a toll to make him snap and go on a killing spree?"

Marco lifted his hands. "For a Navy SEAL to kill one of their own . . . I don't want to believe it's possible."

"Now who's being naïve?" she asked.

"I hear you."

"His reaction to the Rogers question seemed sincere to me," she said. "What about you?"

"I tend to agree with you, and if he is telling the truth, that makes this all the more complicated." He looked down at his watch. "It's getting late. Wanna get out of here and grab some food?"

She hesitated for a moment.

"Unless you have something else to do. It is a Friday night."

She couldn't remember the last time she'd had plans on a Friday night that didn't involve her friends. "No, and I'm famished."

Marco suggested an Italian place, and by the time they had ordered and were waiting for their entrees, Bailey felt herself finally relaxing a bit.

"I want to know the real story on why you didn't become a practicing lawyer," Marco said.

"I already told you."

He leaned forward. "No. You told me the result, but you didn't tell me the why." He picked up another breadstick and took a bite.

"I thought, going into law school, that I would be some big shot corporate lawyer. But once I understood more about what being a lawyer was and about the justice system, being an attorney at a large law firm didn't seem to fit me. I wanted to make an actual difference."

"You could've made a difference as an attorney. Just look at Lexi in JAG. Or you could've become a prosecutor."

"You're pushy, you know that?"

He laughed. "Yeah. I know." He smiled warmly. "You don't have to tell me. I'm just giving you a hard time."

"Sometimes in life your priorities shift. Things become more clear, and what you might have thought you wanted isn't what you want anymore. I went to a recruiting meeting for the FBI on campus during my first year at Georgetown Law, and I was immediately drawn in. It's hard to explain, but everything just started to click."

"I do understand. I always knew I wanted to be in law enforcement, but if you'd told me years ago that I'd end up at NCIS, I wouldn't have believed it. I didn't even know what NCIS really was."

"How did you end up here, then?" She took a sip of her tea.

"The former NCIS director was close friends with my boss at Virginia State Police. The two of them got to talking about me one day, and my boss asked if I would be interested in applying. NCIS had a couple of people retiring, and they were in search of replacements. I interviewed, and the rest is history."

"You're glad you made the switch?"

"One hundred percent. Can't you tell what an amazing NCIS agent I am?"

She laughed. "You're really too much." Marco had a way about him that she liked, easygoing and fun.

He lifted his hands. "Hey, I don't take myself too seriously. You can't in this line of work, or you'll go mad. There's too much real life-and-death stuff to sweat the small things."

She knew all too well about life and death.

"What is it?"

"Nothing." She didn't want to have a heavy discussion right now. "What do you do for fun?"

"I don't have a lot of free time with this job, but I love working on cars, watching eighties movies, and I'm pretty good in the kitchen. What about you?"

"Spending time with my friends. I also enjoy outdoor stuff, especially hiking and anything on the water."

His eyes lit up. "Oh yeah, me too. Too bad I don't have a boat."

She smiled. "I don't either, but I wish I did." As their eyes locked, a totally unexpected spark shot through her. She couldn't deny that she was attracted to Marco, but that was where it needed to end.

"I have a Navy buddy who has a place on the water. He's got Jet Skis, a boat, the whole nine yards. Maybe when this case is over, we could hit him up."

"That would be fun." The words came out of her mouth before she could even measure them. Marco was just being friendly, but she wondered if there was something different brewing inside of her. She couldn't remember the last time she'd felt this type of connection to someone. But it didn't matter. She had a job to do, and that didn't entail having a crush on her handsome NCIS counterpart.

Thankfully she was rescued by the arrival of their entrees. She was foolish for even allowing thoughts about anything happening between them. Bailey was used to being all business, and she planned to keep it that way. Protecting her heart was always her primary mission.

◆

The next afternoon Lexi Todd sat with Tobias Kappen in the back corner of a coffee shop. She eyed the SEAL and his blond buzz cut, wondering how he would respond to her.

"I need you to tell me the truth. I'm your lawyer. I can't help you if I'm in the dark." In her job, she'd seen it all. While she would be disappointed with his guilt, she wouldn't be shocked. Nothing shocked her anymore.

"I'm telling you. I didn't do it." Tobias sighed. "I know the PTSD thing sounded bad."

Yeah, that had taken her off guard, but it wasn't an unfamiliar topic. "Tell me about that."

"I had issues when we came home from a deployment. I saw someone about it, and I'm okay now. It was a little over a year ago, but I guess it's going to follow me around for the rest of my life. I haven't had any issues since, but I'm branded forever. And we wonder why guys don't speak up. Now it could make me look like I've lost it and gone on a murder rampage."

Lexi shook her head. "I won't allow that to happen. There is absolutely nothing for you to be ashamed of. You did the right thing. You sought help. You said yourself that you haven't had recurring issues. That shouldn't dictate how this case is viewed. If you do need any help, though, because I can imagine the toll these allegations are taking on you, please let me know. We can get you the help you need."

"I appreciate that. But I promise you, on that front I am fine.

Yeah, I'm worried about all of this, but it has absolutely zero to do with what I faced before."

Something else was bothering her that had nothing to do with PTSD. "What is it that you're *not* telling me?"

Tobias lifted his chin. "There's a reason I didn't immediately say yes to a physical examination. They're going to find out that Battle and I got into a knockdown, drag-out brawl on base last week. And I've got a few bruises and scrapes from it."

Great. Just another negative fact they didn't need. "What was the fight over?"

Tobias crossed his arms over his chest. "I told him I was going to ask out his ex-wife. I had no intention of doing that. I was just messing with his head. But the next thing I knew, we were on the ground in a wrestling match."

"I assume other members of your team saw this?" She already knew the answer to that.

"Yes, ma'am. Multiple guys. They ended up having to separate us."

"In situations like these, guys take sides. Who had more support, you or him?"

"Him," he answered without hesitation. "I'm known to be a bit difficult. I'm a member of the team, but I'm also a loner. I don't hang with the guys like everyone else, but it's what makes me good at my job."

"As a sniper?"

"Yes, ma'am. It's better for me that way, but it hasn't gained me many friends. Most guys know not to push my buttons and just leave me alone. But not Battle. He was the worst at getting me riled up, and I did the same to him."

It was time for her to play hardball. Her entire legal strategy would depend on whether he was actually guilty or innocent. "Tobias, look me in the eyes and tell me that you didn't do it."

He looked away for a moment before making eye contact. "I did not kill Sean. As much as he drove me up the wall, I would've never wanted him dead. You have to believe me."

She considered his response and his body language. As she studied him carefully, she thought he might be telling the truth. "I believe you. We also need to talk about this other victim. I've done some digging and talked to local PD about the other murder. It appears Rogers worked in construction and lived in the DC area. Are you sure you don't know him?"

Tobias nodded. "Yes, ma'am. I can't swear as I'm sitting here that I've never met a man named Michael Rogers, but I sure don't *know* a man by that name. If he was killed right before Battle, does that mean they're thinking the two murders could be connected?"

"Yes, and that's why it puts you in the double hot seat. The good news is that if we can show you absolutely had nothing to do with the Rogers murder, that helps you if they are trying to pin both killings on one guy."

Tobias let out a heavy breath. "So what do we do now?"

"If they had anything on you, they would've detained you. That tells me they are still fishing around and trying to put together the evidence. Unfortunately for us, you do have a possible motive for Battle's murder, but if you're telling me the truth, they won't be able to link any forensic evidence to you."

He nodded. "And I'm telling you the truth."

"NCIS and the FBI will want the right person to pay for this."

"Do you really believe that? Or will they just want a fall guy?"

She could understand his skepticism. "I know why you might be cynical, but I really do believe they will search for the truth." She paused, hoping her words were true. "Do you think Battle could've been killed because of any of the missions you've been on? I know you are in a different platoon, but have you heard of anything that might be possible?"

Tobias shook his head. "Not that I know of. Like I said, I keep to myself. Maybe if you talk to some of the other guys, they can give you a better feel for that."

She made a few notes for herself.

"Give it to me straight, ma'am. Am I at risk here?" Tobias asked.

"Yes, but I'll do my best to make sure we contain that risk. As long as you're honest with me, we won't have a problem. If you lie to me, though, that's when things will get much worse for you."

"Understood, ma'am."

She hoped this wasn't going to get out of control. She wanted to believe Tobias, but it wouldn't be the first time a client had lied to her.

◆

A few hours later, Lexi sat across the dinner table from prosecutor Derek Martinez. But tonight's dinner wasn't about work. This was her seventh official date with Derek—not that she was counting or anything. She'd been shocked when he asked her out two months ago, but so far everything had been falling together for them. They clicked on multiple levels, and she had to fight hard to keep her expectations in check. But she was the type of girl who was always waiting for the other shoe to drop.

"Something's bothering you." Derek's dark brown eyes studied her.

She finished her last bite of chocolate cheesecake and set down her fork. "Sorry. I think I'm a little preoccupied with work."

"Anything you can talk about?" He understood, since he was

a lawyer too, that certain topics were off-limits if they dealt with confidential client information.

"Did you hear about the stabbing death of the Navy SEAL?"

Derek nodded. "You're working that case?"

She shook her head. "No, but I'm representing another SEAL who is a person of interest in the investigation."

He leaned forward. "They don't really think that another SEAL did this, do they?"

"You're a prosecutor. You know how they like to keep all their options open."

"Hey, now. As a JAG attorney, you've worked both sides. So don't hold it against me that I'm a prosecutor," he joked.

She smiled. "I don't. I actually prefer that side myself, but I think it's important that we have lawyers on the defense side who care about the truth and representing their clients to the fullest."

"I only wish more defense lawyers were like you," he said quietly. "Enough about work, though. I've had a great time tonight. Thank you for coming to dinner with me." He reached across the table and took her hand.

Her stomach did a little flip. She hadn't felt this way about a guy in a long time. Finding herself at a loss for words, she squeezed his hand instead.

"You have no idea how nervous I was to ask you out." He laughed. "It was like high school all over again."

"Did you seriously think I'd say no?"

He smiled. "I thought it was a distinct possibility. I'm not exactly known for my mojo with the ladies."

She found that hard to believe. Not only was he good-looking, he had a great personality and smarts to go with it. Which was why she couldn't help but wonder if this was too good to be true.

He leaned in toward her. "I can tell you're trying to overthink this. Overthink us. Don't do it. I'm the same way, so I completely get it, but can't we just agree that we have the start of something good here?"

"Counselor, I think I can agree to that."

She would have to be careful, or she would really start falling for this guy.

Her cell buzzed loudly, and she groaned. "You know I have to get that."

"Of course."

That was part of Derek's appeal. He fully got that as an attorney, you were always on call.

"This is Lieutenant Todd," she answered.

"It's Agent Agostini, NCIS."

"What can I do for you this evening, Agent Agostini?"

"We need to talk to your client again."

"Why?" Were they really going to keep pushing this fishing expedition? "I need more than just your request."

"We have some follow-up questions."

"Let me make some calls, and I'll get back to you." She ended the call.

Derek smiled at her. "Hey, at least we made it through dessert. I'll take that as a win. I can tell that you need to go."

"Yeah. They want to talk to my client again."

"Well, if there's anything I can do, you know you just have to ask."

Her heart felt full as she looked into his eyes and wondered if this could be the real deal. They walked out of the restaurant, and he took her hand in his.

"There is one thing," she said.

"Name it."

"Let's look at our schedules and figure out when we can see each other again."

"Now that's an easy request." He pulled her close and leaned down to kiss her.

Derek was definitely the bright spot in her life right now, and she was going to make sure not to mess this up.

◆

The next morning, Marco and Bailey arrived at the storage facility, armed with a warrant to see Battle's unit.

As it turned out, they probably wouldn't have even needed the warrant. Once Bailey flashed her badge and a smile, the young guy named Chuck who worked there had practically melted. Marco couldn't blame him. Bailey seemed to have that effect on people. He was enjoying her company, and he thought there might even be some chemistry forming between them. He wasn't sure what to do with that, so for now he was just making sure his head was in the game on the investigation.

Despite Chuck's eagerness to help, Marco wanted to be by-the-book for evidentiary reasons, so they handed over the warrant and followed Chuck down a long line of units until they reached the end.

"Here it is," Chuck said. "Unit two-twenty." He opened the lock. "Just let me know when you're done so I can lock back up."

"Thank you for your help," Bailey said. The young man walked away, and she turned to Marco. "Let's check it out."

"Maybe we'll find something useful." Marco hoped the contents wouldn't just be old college furniture and would actually provide some clues that they couldn't get elsewhere. He lifted the sliding door to the storage area and let Bailey go in first.

She flipped on the light and coughed as she moved farther inside. He followed, brushing a spider web off his shoulder. His eyes went to the center of the area, which included an old beat-up futon and dresser. But there were also a lot of boxes and paper files.

"We'll just have to dive in and see what we can find. There's no easy way to do this," Bailey said.

"Wait." He grabbed her arm, pulling her back. "Do you hear that?"

They were silent for a moment, and he heard it again. A very faint beeping noise coming from the back corner.

"Yeah, I do," Bailey said.

They both walked toward the noise. When he got to the back of the unit, Marco's stomach dropped. There was a black box mounted on the wall along with a keypad and a chunk of C-4. It was an alarm system—a rigged one.

The beeps started to come in rapid succession. If they didn't input the security code, that thing would blow.

"Bailey, get out of here now. Run!"

She didn't question him and started to run. He was right behind her.

They'd barely crossed the threshold of the unit when the boom thundered behind them. He threw himself forward onto Bailey, trying to protect her body with his own from the flying debris.

"Bailey, are you okay?" He lifted himself off her and tried to catch his breath.

She nodded, her green eyes wide. "What was that?"

"I think Battle set up a security system. If we didn't put in the code within a certain amount of time, it was set to blow."

"Wow," she said. "He really didn't want anyone in there. We'll have to see if anything is salvageable."

"I'll call and get an explosives team out here to do a thorough cleanup and forensic analysis." Marco let out a low whistle. "I hope key evidence didn't just get incinerated." He stood and offered his hand to help her up.

"How did you know that's what was going on?" she asked.

"I had a case a few years ago where someone had rigged something very similar. Man, I'm glad I did." He hated to think what would have happened if he hadn't realized what was going on. He quickly made the phone call to NCIS and asked them to coordinate with FBI.

Bailey grabbed his arm. "You saved my life, Marco. I owe you. We were so close to the bomb. We never would've made it if not for your quick thinking."

He smiled. "I'm sure you'll return the favor at some point."

Chuck came running around the corner, out of breath. "Are you two okay?"

"Yeah. I've called in a team to investigate. And just as a precaution, I need you to close this place down until we can confirm that there aren't any more explosives."

The color drained out of Chuck's face.

"You understand?" Bailey asked him.

Chuck nodded. "Yes." His voice cracked. "I'll get right on it." He turned and jogged away.

"We need to help secure this place until the team arrives. I think our young friend is in shock," Marco said.

Bailey agreed. "Yeah. Let's make sure no one else is down in this area, and then clear the building from there."

Marco looked down at her. "We've learned one very important thing this morning."

"What's that?"

"Guys don't just randomly put explosive fail-safes in their storage units. Battle had something to hide. Something so big, he was willing to kill to protect his secret."

CHAPTER
FIVE

That afternoon Bailey sat in the NCIS interrogation room with Marco. She was a bit shaken up after the close call at the storage unit, but beyond a couple of bruises, she'd be fine. She was thankful that Marco had had the presence of mind to know what was happening. If it wasn't for him, she wouldn't be sitting here right now.

They were about to question Kappen again, with his JAG attorney present.

"Petty Officer Kappen, did you and Battle have any physical altercations recently?" Marco asked.

Kappen looked at his attorney, and she leaned in and whispered in his ear before he responded. "Yes."

"Do you care to elaborate?" Bailey asked. They had found out through their follow-up interview with Alvarez that the two men had gotten into a brawl. It bothered Bailey that Kappen had not admitted to that initially, but putting on her lawyer cap, she understood why he hadn't. Lexi had probably advised him not to offer up information at this point. To make them work for everything. It was how she would have approached it, so she couldn't blame them.

Kappen glanced at Lexi before responding. "I was picking on Battle. I told him I was going to make a move on his ex-wife. As you can imagine, that didn't go over well. He was still completely in love with her."

"Had you ever approached his ex-wife before?" Bailey asked.

"No, ma'am, and I had no intention of doing it. I was just trying to rile him up. I miscalculated, though. I didn't anticipate he would fly off the handle. Next thing I knew, we were on the ground, throwing punches. Some of the guys separated us."

"And this was?" Marco asked.

They knew the answer. They were just trying to establish if Kappen was going to tell the truth about all the details.

"Last week," Kappen answered. "But I hope you see that that's just how he and I operated. I would've never really hurt him, and definitely would not have killed him."

"Is the fight the reason you were hesitant about the physical examination?" Bailey asked.

Kappen nodded. "Yes, ma'am. We got after each other pretty good, so I still have some scrapes and bruises."

Lexi cleared her throat. "But those are from his fight with the victim, not—and I repeat, *not*—from any other altercation and certainly not from Battle's murder. I hope you can see that this forthcoming statement from my client is just another indication of his innocence."

"We appreciate the explanation, but I do have some additional questions. Do you often have problems controlling your anger?" Bailey asked.

"No," Kappen answered quickly. "I'm usually cool, but as I told you before, there was just something between Battle and me. But I didn't kill him."

"I'd like to shift gears. There's something else we'd like to follow up on. Here's a picture of Michael Rogers." Bailey opened a folder and slid the picture in front of the SEAL. "Does this jog your memory where he is concerned?"

Kappen took a moment and studied the photograph. "No, ma'am. I don't think I've ever seen this man in my life."

Lexi leaned in. "And I think NCIS and the FBI can understand why we're done here. Unless you have something more?"

Marco shifted in his seat. "We understand your client's concern about the physical exam, given the altercation, so instead we'd like your client to voluntarily submit a DNA and hair sample."

"No way," Lexi responded quickly.

"If he's innocent, what better way to prove it?" Bailey challenged.

"Let me talk it over privately with my client." Lexi shot Kappen a look that clearly told him to keep his mouth shut.

"We'll be in touch," Marco said.

Once Bailey and Marco were alone, she turned to him. "What do you think?"

"We'll keep digging to see if Kappen is lying about not knowing Rogers, but I think it's doubtful he did this."

"Unfortunately, a lot of criminal activity doesn't make sense."

Marco leaned back in his chair. "Now you're starting to sound like a profiler or something."

She lifted her hand. "Just trying to make a point. Can we go talk to your analysts and see if they have anything?"

"Yeah. I know they were working really late last night. Let's head down there."

A few minutes later, they entered the NCIS forensics lab, where Bailey met the chief analyst, Ryder Cooke. The tall and lanky man with light blond hair was probably in his forties.

"What do you have for us, Ryder?" Marco asked.

"We're analyzing all the physical evidence from both scenes. We know the victim's blood is present, but if there's any other blood, we'll have those results today. I've also pulled some hair follicles and other materials that we're testing as well. The only prints we've been able to pull came from the victims."

"Which meant the perpetrator knew how to cover his tracks," Bailey said.

Ryder nodded. "Yes. Most likely he—or they—were wearing gloves."

Marco frowned. "We tried to get Kappen to hand over a DNA and hair sample voluntarily, but I'm highly doubtful that will happen."

Ryder laughed. "Would you do it, if you were in his shoes?"

Marco leaned against the table. "I'd like to think I would, if I didn't have anything to hide."

"We could get a sample another way, but then we'd have admissibility problems," Bailey said.

"Spoken like a lawyer," Marco teased.

"Agent Ryan, are you an attorney?" Ryder asked.

"Please call me Bailey. I have a law degree, but I've never practiced."

"The FBI is more appealing?" Ryder quirked an eyebrow.

"Actually, it is." She paused. "Do you have anything that can help us take next steps?"

"I can tell you that I have matching hair follicles at both crime scenes. The question is who they belong to. By comparing samples, we know it's not the victim's hair. I can also tell you the person is Caucasian, and if I had to guess based on physical examination of the hair specimen, I'd say it's from a male."

"All of this still keeps Kappen in play as the chief suspect," Marco said. "But I wish we had more to go on."

"I'll keep you posted on my progress," Ryder assured them. "Hopefully, I'll know more soon."

◆

"I want to do it," Tobias looked at Lexi.

"As your lawyer, I strongly advise against submitting a DNA swab. They're asking for a hair sample as well. That means they have evidence they're attempting to match you to." Lexi was trying her best to talk some sense into her client, but she wasn't having much success.

Tobias shook his head. "You don't understand. I can't go on with my life under this cloud of suspicion. The guys are looking at me and wondering if I killed one of our own. I've even heard them making killer-sniper cracks about me."

Lexi sighed. "They're just giving you a hard time. If they actually thought you were guilty or a serial killer, I highly doubt they'd be making flippant jokes about it—especially in your presence."

Tobias's eyes met hers. "I still don't think you believe me. That's a problem."

"I do believe you, but I've been a lawyer long enough to know that things aren't always black and white. And if you didn't do it, someone else did, and what if they wanted to put a target on your back? Have you ever considered the possibility that you were framed? You said yourself that you have a lot more enemies than friends."

He frowned. "You're right. I get that, but I'm telling you that I don't have a choice. I have to clear my name. The teams are my life. My entire life. If I don't have that, I have nothing."

She leaned in closer to him. "You're telling me that you

57

fully understand the risks involved here. If they have evidence tying you to the scene, they will come after you hard. You'll have it coming from both angles—both military and civilian." Everything was telling her this was a complete and utterly idiotic decision. But part of being a lawyer was listening to the wishes of her client. "I'm just urging you to sleep on it, okay?"

Tobias nodded. "I can do that."

She had a sick feeling in the pit of her stomach that this wasn't going to end well for either of them.

———◆———

The next morning, Isabella Cole tapped her foot as she waited to escort Bailey into the building. She was still sizing up the blond FBI agent and wondering if she would be friend or enemy.

"Good morning, Isabella." Bailey smiled.

She took a step forward to greet her. "Please call me Izzy."

"I've never heard Marco call you that."

"That's because Rookie is his favorite name for me. He claims it's all part of the process." Izzy wasn't so sure. Marco pushed her really hard. Much harder than she'd seen him when he dealt with others.

Bailey tucked a strand of blond hair behind her ear. "So you've been here at NCIS eight months?"

"Almost nine. I worked Arlington PD for one year and then made the jump. Although sometimes Marco acts like I have zero experience." As the words came out of her mouth, she wondered if she'd been too open with her feelings, but that was just how she was. Tact was not her strong point.

"If Marco is hard on you, I bet it's because he sees potential in you. Believe me, if he thought you weren't talented, he wouldn't put forth the effort. You should see it as a good thing."

"Sounds like you speak from experience?" Izzy asked.

The two women started to walk down the long hallway. "Yeah. I'm not going to lie to you. Being a woman in law enforcement can be tough, and it doesn't necessarily get easier as you progress."

"It is tough." Izzy had learned that the hard way. She'd had an experience with a powerful man in uniform while at Arlington PD that still impacted her. She hadn't told a single soul and instead tried to keep those painful memories locked in a box.

Bailey kept talking. "It helps to have some women in your life who can support you through it."

That wasn't Izzy's life. "I've always had more guy friends than girls."

They turned a corner, and Bailey continued their conversation. "I've always been a bit of a tomboy. As you can probably tell by looking at me, I'm very low-maintenance. When girls in high school were putting on makeup, I was thinking about how much I would hate to have that junk on my face. I'll never forget the time in eleventh grade where my mother gently insisted that I needed a bit of mascara and lipstick if I was going to the prom." Her voice trailed off for a moment.

Izzy thought there was more behind Bailey's story, but she had noticed that Bailey seemed low-frill. But Bailey was pretty even without makeup. Izzy, on the other hand, felt like she had to put on two coats of mascara, eyeliner, and lipstick before she'd even consider leaving the house in the morning. "I wish I could pull off the natural look like you, but I don't think I was made for it."

Bailey raised an eyebrow. "I think you might have an un-balanced view of yourself. It's something we all face and strug-gle with, especially in today's society. We're told we're never thin enough, pretty enough, or stylish enough. That's another reason it's important to have positive female influences in your life. In law school I was fortunate enough to meet two other women who have become my best friends. I know sometimes as women we can be our own worst enemies, but it doesn't have to be that way. My door and phone are always open for you."

Izzy was used to Marco's gruff style. Bailey's different ap-proach was a breath of fresh air. She knew that Bailey was right about all of it, but Izzy had a hard time connecting with other women. She always felt like she was being judged, and she didn't even know for what. She put up a lot of walls. "The police academy was pretty brutal. There were five women in my class, and I didn't connect with any of them. It's like you said. I think we all saw each other as the competition."

Bailey shook her head. "There's enough room for all of us to succeed. You seem like a dedicated and hungry agent. That's what is needed to excel."

"I'm glad to be working this case with you. As awful as the facts are, it's the biggest case I've been exposed to so far. I can't afford to make any mistakes." Izzy knew Marco wasn't very forgiving. He constantly demanded the best from his team.

Bailey placed her hand on Izzy's arm. "We all make mistakes, Izzy. It's part of learning and growing, and that's why we're part of a team. Just work hard, ask questions, stay engaged. The rest will come with experience."

"I hope so." Izzy's self-doubt was always present.

Bailey led her into the war room. "Let's get to work."

Izzy might put up a tough front, but she had struggled with

confidence since she was a little girl. It might have been one of the reasons she gravitated toward law enforcement, to try to overcome those fears and insecurities. But she knew that wasn't the biggest driver for her career choice. She was passionate about catching bad guys, and for good reason.

CHAPTER
SIX

That afternoon in the war room, Bailey looked into Marco's dark eyes as she tried to unravel this puzzle.

"What's the latest?" she asked.

"I got bad news from the team. They couldn't salvage anything of use from the storage unit. The documents and any tech in there were obliterated by the blast."

"Battle was willing to go to great lengths to keep his secrets. We have to figure out what he was hiding. We've got people claiming Rogers is an assassin, and Battle willing to blow up storage units. There has to be something big going on here."

"Big enough to get them both killed," Marco responded.

"I just don't get the motive for Kappen to kill Rogers. They don't appear to have known each other, and I can't put together anything that makes logical sense."

Marco nodded. "You're right on face value, but we have to look further in case there's something that isn't apparent."

He had a point, but her gut was saying that Kappen didn't kill Rogers, and it was telling her something else even more illuminating. "If Kappen didn't kill Rogers, then he most likely didn't kill Battle either. We have to be open to that prospect, especially since all we have now is bad blood and a brawl between them. I'm not ready to jump out and say he's guilty—especially since he's a Navy SEAL. I think we owe him more respect than that."

"I understand that the rocky relationship is all we have to go on, but men have killed for a lot less. I'm not trying to lock him up without due process. I just want to make sure we're fully considering all options, even if we don't like what it means. As an NCIS agent, unfortunately, I see the dark sides of these military members sometimes. And to compound matters, we have Kappen's history of PTSD. Even if he's been doing well recently, he could've had a setback."

The lawyer in Bailey made her want to get this right even more. "We don't have anything to even detain him on right now. I just want to make sure we don't rush to judgment."

Marco placed his hand on her arm. "I'm not doing that, Bailey. I promise you. The last thing I want is to have the wrong guy. Please don't take my pushing him as a suspect as anything but trying to make sure we aren't blindsided. And the good news is that if we clear his name, then we can move on."

"I understand. But there's still a distinct possibility we're dealing with a spree killer who could strike again at any moment."

Izzy walked into the conference room. "Ryder says he has something for us, and we should go down to the lab."

Marco stood. "I like the sound of that."

They made their way down to the lab in the basement of HQ, and Bailey clenched her fists as she anxiously waited to hear what Ryder had to say. Maybe this would be the break they were looking for.

"Ryder," Marco said, "what do you have for us?"

"Well, hello to you too, Marco." Ryder smiled. "I can tell you definitively that no other blood is present and no prints. The hair follicles are the only other evidence. You connecting the dots?"

Bailey was. "You're saying that if someone goes through the trouble to make sure no blood and no prints are left but leaves hair . . ."

"That the evidence could've been planted," Marco finished for her. "Professionals are just that. They take precautions to make sure nothing is left behind."

"Is that all?" Bailey asked Ryder, hoping for a bit more.

The analyst grinned. "I see I haven't earned your confidence just yet, Bailey, but I will. We were able to run a few computer-generated simulations of the attack. I'd like to play those for you."

They had high-tech stuff at the FBI, but in most of the crimes that Bailey worked, they didn't use these types of tools. She was interested to see what this simulation could tell them.

"Roll the tape, Ryder," Marco said.

Ryder turned to his computer and started typing. A video popped up on the large screen for them all to see. "We ran a few different scenarios—the first one is a single attacker."

Bailey's eyes were glued to the screen as she watched a male figure come up behind Battle and grab on to him before he began stabbing him. "This looks very awkward," she said, thinking out loud.

"Is this even possible in real life?" Izzy asked.

Marco moved closer to the screen. "Replay it, Ryder, can you?"

"Sure thing."

They all watched the simulation again. It became apparent

that it would have been very difficult for one person to physically accomplish this feat.

"Even though the computer makes it happen, in real life, it seems unlikely," Marco said, expressing all of their thoughts.

Ryder chuckled. "That's exactly why we run these simulations. One attacker is possible but not probable. He would've had to have amazing strength, especially since we tailored this to Battle's specifications."

"Like another Navy SEAL," Bailey couldn't help but say. "This simulation doesn't make the one-attacker theory impossible. And with Kappen's size and strength, it still has to be on the table."

"Show us the next simulation," Marco said.

Ryder proceeded to run the program with two attackers. One subdued Battle while the other stabbed him.

"That's more like it," Bailey said. "Based on these simulations, the two-killer theory makes more sense."

Marco stepped back. "This is great work, Ryder."

"Yes," Bailey added. "This will really make a difference in cracking the case." But she knew they still had a long way to go.

◆

Marco watched in amusement as Bailey scarfed down the Thai food that was spread out in the war room thanks to Izzy making a necessary food run before Marco had sent her home for the evening.

"I realize now that I haven't been feeding you enough," he said.

Bailey grinned. "Yeah, I have a big appetite. It's a joke among my friends. They get a little jealous that I seem to be able to eat anything I want. My mom and dad were both the same way."

"Were?" he asked, fearing the answer.

She looked down at the plate of noodles in front of her. "Yeah. They died in a car accident my first year of college."

Marco felt like he'd been punched in the gut. "I'm so sorry."

"Thanks. It was a test, that's for sure. If I didn't have my faith, I don't know how I would've gotten through it, and it was still the biggest challenge of my life—and my faith. Even now, years later, there are some days when I cry because I miss them so badly." She stared off into the distance, the Thai food now forgotten.

"I honestly can't imagine." The pain of that idea was too much for him to fathom.

She looked back up at him. "You're close to your parents, then?"

He laughed. "We fight like cats and dogs, but I love them like crazy. We fit the stereotypical Italian family in a lot of ways. My mom would love you since you actually enjoy food. She's always complaining that my female friends don't eat her special lasagna based on her grandmother's secret recipe, and she takes it as a personal insult."

Now it was Bailey's turn to laugh. "Got a lot of female friends, huh?"

He was glad that the mood had lightened, but he felt terrible about Bailey's loss. "Yes, I do, but my mom constantly reminds me that I don't have a girlfriend. Or a wife. Or kids. She's champing at the bit for grandkids. It's basically a continuous topic of conversation on her part every single time we talk. I've learned to give her the stiff-arm in the most loving way I know how."

"It's good that you're close with your family. I know it's easy to take them for granted. I think I did many times in my life." Her voice started to shake. "Then, with one phone call, everything changes."

Their conversation at dinner the other night started to make more sense to him. She had been holding back then, but he'd seen the sadness in her eyes. He was glad she'd decided she could open up to him now. "It's at times like that when your faith is really put to the test," Marco said quietly. He'd certainly had tough times in his life when he wondered if God still loved him.

She looked up at him. "It sounds like you speak from experience?"

His family had seen the darkness, and it was a place he never wanted to go again. "My little sister was diagnosed with cancer years ago. She beat it and is in remission, but it rocked my entire family. My dad's a quiet guy, but his faith is rock solid—he helped us all get through it. I put on a brave face for my mom and sister, but at the time, I was questioning God a lot. Wondering how he could subject a young girl to such pain and disease." He took a moment, remembering those days.

"How did you get through that?"

It had been a struggle day by day. "A lot of prayer, a lot of questioning. The thing is that even in the darkest hours, seeing the faith that my dad put in the Lord and the example he lived out for me really put things in perspective. If his little girl was going through this and he could put it all in the Lord's hands, then shouldn't I be able to? I tried to push aside the anger I felt, because at first the anger almost consumed me. I asked God to walk with me through it. To pull me through the roughest of days. To give me a purpose for living."

Bailey took another bite of noodles. "Faith and family is really what life's all about."

Marco looked at Bailey and for the first time felt an inkling of attraction that went beyond the external. It was easy to be drawn to her. Way too easy. He didn't really have a type, but Bailey was beautiful, and she did it without trying. The real

Bailey he was coming to know was a whole lot more than a pretty face. But unfortunately, they had murders to solve right now, and he couldn't get distracted. "And we have work to do to give these families answers."

"Any word from the JAG attorney?" she asked.

"I expect to hear from her tomorrow morning. I think she's feverishly trying to talk Kappen out of voluntarily submitting the sample."

"If I were her, I'd do everything in my power to stop that from happening. If he's that adamant about doing it, though, that also speaks to his state of mind. Guilty men don't voluntarily submit to DNA tests. Has Izzy found anything yet linking Rogers and Kappen?"

Marco shook his head. "Nothing yet."

"Izzy's been here less than a year, right?" Bailey asked after a short pause.

Marco laughed. "I see she must have gotten to you if you're calling her Izzy."

"Is that a problem?"

He could tell that Bailey had taken a liking to the rookie. "Izzy is green. Very green, but she has great instincts and a killer work ethic. Those two things are worth their weight in gold to me." He paused. "Has she told you that she hates me?"

Bailey shook her head. "No, not at all. But I get the sense that she thinks you're being extra tough on her."

Then he was succeeding in his job. "Good, because I am."

That made her smile. "Because she's going to be really good if you do."

He nodded and decided it was time they got back to work. "Izzy left her research here so we can go over it too. I always like to have multiple eyes on things."

"I've got all night."

Marco figured there would be many long nights until they solved this case.

◆

Two days later, Lexi's pounding headache had just gone from bad to worse. Tobias had not only decided to submit the samples, but she'd just gotten word from NCIS that they wanted to interrogate Tobias again ASAP. She didn't know if they had the DNA results back yet, but they most certainly would have the hair analysis.

As she waited to meet Tobias and escort him into NCIS headquarters, her phone rang. It was Derek. It wasn't the best time to talk, but she really wanted to hear his voice. She'd had such a nice time with him at dinner the other night, and she was hopeful for what could be next for them. It wasn't that often she was this excited about her romantic prospects.

"Lexi, hey, it's Derek."

Just hearing his voice made her stomach do a flip. "Hey," she said. "It's good to hear a friendly voice." She was met with silence. "What is it?"

"I've got some news I have to share with you, and you're not going to like it." His voice sounded somber.

And just like that, her excitement was doused. "What is it?" Her pulse sped up.

"I got a call from local PD. They want to talk to your client."

"What? What do you mean?"

"The murder of Michael Rogers," Derek said.

"And how are you involved in this?" she asked, fearing the answer.

"I've been assigned the case," he said quietly.

She couldn't believe how this had turned south so quickly. "You've got to be kidding me."

"Yeah, it's not ideal. The police are still in the investigation stage, but it's going to be mine. I think we'll have to postpone our personal plans until this gets sorted out. I know you understand."

She wanted to ask why he didn't just have another prosecutor take the case. But she wouldn't want him telling her how to run her career, so she did the only thing she could. "Okay. I get it."

"I can't really say anything further, but between NCIS and the locals, you're going to have your hands full. And I'm sorry about how this worked out."

Again, she held back what she really wanted to say. "Thanks for the call."

She hung up and tapped her foot impatiently as she waited for Tobias. She only had to wait a few more minutes before he got there.

"What's wrong?" he asked her.

"We've got problems."

Tobias raised an eyebrow. "Bigger than me being accused of murder?"

"They're going after you hard for both murders now."

"But how?"

"I don't know, but if I had to guess, they matched your hair to both crime scenes."

Tobias shook his head. "But, ma'am, that is impossible. I wasn't there. I didn't do it. I did not kill either man."

"Then it's even worse, because you're being framed, and we have no idea by who or for what reason." She'd dealt with some trying cases before, but this one had the most troubling fact pattern. She wanted to believe Tobias, and yet all the physical evidence was mounting against him in the worst possible way. Putting all that together made her fear for what was to come.

She wondered if she was fully equipped to handle a case like this.

"Ma'am, we have a name for a situation like this, but I won't say it in polite company."

Being around military guys her whole life, Lexi knew exactly what he was talking about. She wondered how in the world she'd be able to get him out of this mess.

◆

Bailey stared at the computer screen in Ryder's lab. "So we're certain the hair follicles are a match to both crime scenes?"

"Yes," Ryder answered. "And that they belong to Tobias Kappen. I can confirm that as well."

"If there were two attackers, wouldn't you expect to find the other man's hair as well? Also, what's the likelihood of the hair of only one of them showing up at both scenes?" Bailey was skeptical about this entire thing, but the problem was that this hair evidence, the only concrete piece of evidence they had, pointed to Kappen, even if there were a lot of unanswered questions.

"All good points," Ryder said. "All I can do is tell you what I've found. I could hypothesize, though, if you'd like?"

"Go right ahead," Marco answered.

"If someone was trying to set up Kappen to take the fall, planting hair evidence at both scenes would do the trick. It would point to there only being one attacker, and that it was him. Even if our simulations say that a two-attacker theory is most probable, the physical evidence points to a different scenario—one in which Kappen is the single guilty party."

Marco looked at his watch. "Kappen should be here any minute. We'll get another run at him and see if anything changes when we present him with the evidence. But I also want to make sure we are first in line here. Local PD will be coming after him for Rogers's murder now that there's physical evidence tying him to the body."

"What a mess," Bailey muttered. Something was wrong here. She worried about a potentially innocent man being put in the cross hairs, but she felt a bit helpless in stopping this train. And by cooperating and providing the sample, Kappen had just unwittingly put himself on the fast track to prime suspect—right now the only suspect.

About half an hour later, she sat beside Marco and across from Kappen and his attorney. Marco had told her that he was going to push hard, and she waited to see how this would play out.

"Petty Officer Kappen, you need to start explaining yourself—and quickly. Your hair was found at both murder scenes," Marco said.

Kappen shook his head. "Sir, I have no idea how that is possible. I was nowhere near either scene. I didn't do this. If I had done it, why would I give samples voluntarily? If I was trying to hide, wouldn't I have stonewalled you? But no, I've done everything you've asked. I've answered all your questions truthfully and have been completely upfront with you. Someone is trying to make me the fall guy here."

"And do you have any idea who that could be?" Bailey asked.

"No, ma'am. I'm racking my brain, but this is all very strange to me. I don't know why I would be targeted."

"You still stand by your claim that you didn't know Michael Rogers?" Marco asked.

Kappen's blue eyes focused on Bailey. "I definitely did not know Rogers. The first time I saw him was the picture you showed me. Never met him. Don't know him. I'm certain of that."

Bailey looked at Lexi. The worry showed on the attorney's

face as she frowned. This was a tough case. There was no doubt about it. But Bailey wanted the truth more than an easy conclusion. She was willing to keep pushing to find it, because getting it right was most important. Lexi was in an impossibly difficult position, trying to prove her client's innocence. She wasn't sure how Lexi planned to try to exonerate Kappen. Right now everything seemed stacked against him.

Marco slammed his fist on the desk, causing Bailey to jump.

"You need to do a lot better than that, Petty Officer Kappen. There are two dead bodies, one of them belonging to one of your teammates. Your hair is at the crime scenes—both of them. This is *game over* unless you have something else to say for yourself."

Kappen looked at Lexi and then back at Marco. "I can only tell you the truth, sir."

"And what is the truth?" Marco asked.

Kappen blinked. "That I'm an innocent man. That I'm a loyal SEAL. That I lay my life on the line day in and day out for this country. My country. The country I love."

Frustrated, Marco stood up and started pacing. Bailey wasn't sure if this was theatrics or if he was really that wound up. "Agent Ryan, why don't you see if you can talk some sense into this man. I've had enough." He slammed the door, leaving her alone with the two of them.

This felt like a calculated move by Marco, and she was willing to go along with it. Seemed like good cop, bad cop to her.

"Petty Officer Kappen, I want to help you, but to do that, you've got to give me something to work with. Think. Think about who would want your teammate dead. Even if you didn't know Rogers, stick with what you knew about Battle."

Kappen didn't immediately respond but instead stared off into the distance.

"As I'm sure your lawyer told you, it's only going to get worse for you from here."

Bailey was pushing him because as she listened to every word out of his mouth, she really didn't think he had done this. But her gut feelings would only get them so far in the face of hard evidence.

CHAPTER
SEVEN

To say Lexi was bummed was an understatement. Not only had her promising romance with Derek come to a screeching halt, she had to somehow figure out a way to prove Tobias's innocence. She was meeting fellow JAG attorney Nolan O'Brien for coffee and advice. He had about ten more years of experience than she did and was one of her trusted mentors.

She laid out the case for him. His light gray eyes narrowed, and a frown pulled down on his lips.

"You've got yourself a mess here, Lexi," he said.

She couldn't help but laugh. "I didn't need you to tell me that. I need your help. I'm out of my depth."

He leaned forward in his seat. "Your instincts are right on. Something is amiss. The issue is how you go about getting evidence to prove it. I assume you don't have anyone who can put Kappen somewhere else at the time of the murders?"

She shook her head. "No. And unfortunately, he was up having dinner in Georgetown on the night of the second murder. He says he went home to his parents' condo alone afterward, but there's nothing to corroborate that once he left the restaurant. His parents are in Florida. He stays at their condo in Arlington when he's on leave."

Nolan gripped the large blue mug holding his hot chocolate. "Why in the world did he submit to the voluntary DNA and hair sample?"

She still couldn't get over that fact herself. But Tobias's actions told her a lot. "Doesn't exactly sound like a guilty man, does it?"

"No, but it sounds like a stupid one." Nolan shook his head. "You've got to push as hard as humanly possible for that kind of thing not to happen. As lawyers, it is sometimes our jobs to protect our clients from themselves. Use your powers of persuasion to convince him to take the right path. It's as big a part of the job as anything else."

She didn't take his scolding in a negative way. She knew he was just trying to help her advance as an attorney. "I did push. But I wonder if there's anything else I could've done to stop him." It was something that kept her up at night.

"It's over now, but in the future, dig in as hard as you can on things like this. They can be game changers when you're dealing with hard forensics. You need to find a way to discredit the evidence. Think chain of evidence, tampering, anything like that."

"And to top all this off, I've now got the civilian side breathing down our necks."

He took another sip of his drink. "But NCIS should get priority. Locals will bow to pressure on that. Especially if there isn't anyone on Rogers's side pushing hard and fast for prosecution."

Lexi frowned. "We'll have to see how that plays out. You know, maybe I need to look harder at Rogers. He could be the key to finding the real killer . . . or killers. I didn't tell you that part. I believe there are two people involved."

He sighed. "This is starting to sound more and more like a cover-up. I know you're a naval officer, but I wouldn't be a good friend if I didn't remind you to watch your back."

A chill shot down her spine at his warning. "Someone wanted Rogers and Battle dead, and they were willing to frame Tobias for it."

Nolan leaned in. "Dig and push as hard as you can. Just trust your instincts. You always have good ones." He paused. "What's your feel for how NCIS is handling the case?"

"They were aggressive in their interrogation, but I got the feeling the FBI agent jointly working the case has her reservations about whether Tobias is guilty. I was going to reach out to her. I want to use any angle I can, even if it's not the norm. The last thing I want is for an innocent man to be put away for this—and to think he's a Navy SEAL is beyond my comprehension." After all Tobias had done in service to his country, it was time for Lexi to step up her game.

"I have faith in your abilities. And if you need me, I'm just a phone call away."

She thanked Nolan again for listening, and they said their good-byes.

Later that evening, Lexi looked down at her watch and saw it was almost ten o'clock. She had waited this late in the hope that Bailey Ryan would be finished working for the day. Lexi wanted to talk to her one on one, without NCIS interference. She didn't need Marco the Alpha Male making things more complicated than they already were. She wanted to find out if she was reading Bailey correctly.

Lexi dialed Bailey's number and waited. After a couple of rings, Bailey answered.

"Agent Ryan, this is Lieutenant Lexi Todd. Sorry to call you this late."

"It's not a problem. I actually just got home. What can I do for you?"

So far, so good. Bailey wasn't the least bit hostile and, if anything, seemed friendly.

"I got the sense in the interrogation room that you might have some reservations about whether my client is guilty."

"Do you have any new exculpatory evidence since we spoke?"

"That's a very lawyerly response," Lexi said.

Bailey laughed. "You caught me. Sometimes my lawyer side comes out."

"You went to law school?"

"Yeah, Georgetown. But I went straight into the FBI."

"I didn't know that." No wonder Bailey wasn't taking things at face value. This new development might end up working in Lexi's favor, and she planned to use any advantage she could muster.

"My legal background isn't really the point, though," Bailey said. "I'm guessing your answer to my question is no, because if you did have the evidence, this isn't how you would've approached me."

"You're right, Agent Ryan. I don't have anything. Yet. But I'm working on it, and I had the feeling you might be as well." She waited to hear how Bailey responded, hoping she hadn't misjudged the situation.

"I can guarantee that we are working as hard as we can to gather evidence to prove who the murderer is. I'm going to go wherever the evidence leads me. That's my job, and one I take very seriously. I don't have any specific agenda here except the truth," Bailey said firmly.

Lexi didn't want to push too hard, but she did want to keep the door open. "I'm just asking you, as a law enforcement officer, to continue to have an open mind. I've seen how expediency sometimes wins out over the truth, and I don't want that to happen here. Especially to a man who has done nothing but serve his country honorably for years."

Bailey sighed. "I understand your point. We have a lot of open questions, but unfortunately for your client, the physical evidence is stacked against him."

"You have no real motive, though—especially for the first murder."

"I don't think you called me at ten o'clock at night to debate motive."

Lexi needed to turn this conversation around quickly. "You're absolutely right. I think I've made my point. I believe strongly that my client has been set up, and if I'm right, then there is something much bigger and more dangerous going on here. I believe you want the truth and for justice to be served. That's all I'm asking."

"I'm doing my best, Lieutenant."

"Thank you. And I'm sorry once again for the intrusion, but I get the sense that you understand the importance of zealously advocating for your client."

"Good night, Lieutenant."

Once the call was over, Lexi groaned. She hoped she'd made an okay impression on Bailey. The last thing she needed was to tick her off, but she had to make the case. No one else was going to advocate for Tobias. That was her job. And now her prospective boyfriend was also nipping at Tobias's heels.

She picked up the pillow on the sofa and threw it across the room. Having a temper tantrum wasn't going to help anyone, but her frustration was through the roof.

There was no way she was ready to sleep yet, so she made a cup of decaf tea and powered up her laptop. The answers were out there, and she intended to find them.

◆

That Saturday night Bailey sat in the living room of her apartment with Vivian and Layla. The ladies had insisted on coming over to discuss their plan for the upcoming Georgetown Law reunion scheduled for the fall.

They'd already destroyed the Chinese takeout Layla had brought with her, and now they were devouring the warm chocolate chip cookies that Bailey had just pulled out of the oven.

"You're just afraid you're going to see Hunter if you go." Vivian shot an accusatory glance at Layla.

"I'm not," Layla insisted. "Hunter and I are a thing of the very distant past. I don't have any issue seeing him."

Bailey looked at Layla and then Vivian. "Does anyone here actually believe that—including you, Layla?"

Vivian shook her head as she bit into another cookie. "It's okay. We know what happened. You don't have to put up a front with us."

Layla let out a groan. "I should be so completely over him by now. It's been over five years since we broke up. But I admit the possibility of seeing him has me a bit nervous. I have this idea of him walking into the party with a gorgeous woman on his arm—someone who is everything I'm not."

Bailey couldn't take her friend putting herself down like that. "Layla, you are beautiful inside and out. Hunter was an idiot." Hunter had infamously cheated on Layla during law school with a blond bombshell undergrad. Or that was the rumor. His cheating and betrayal still impacted Layla to this day.

"You all are so sweet. Just what I need—takeout, cookies, and my girlfriends telling me lies." Layla laughed, and the others joined her.

"We're not lying. The reunion might actually be fun," Viv

said. "I know I was skeptical the other day, but the more I think about it, why not? It's just one night. We could even go shopping."

Now it was Bailey's turn to groan. "No. You two can shop till you drop, but you know I hate it. I'll wear something in my closet. I have plenty of cocktail dresses that only get worn to Christmas parties and charity events. And we still have a few months before the reunion. They haven't even sent out the formal invitations yet, just the save-the-date."

"We won't subject you to shopping," Viv said. "But, Layla, I know you'll be up for some serious retail therapy."

Layla threw up her hands. "All right, you two. You've worn me down. Assuming work doesn't interfere, I'm in, but if you two end up bailing because of work, I'm not going alone. No way."

"We wouldn't send you in without backup," Bailey said. "It's settled. Make sure everyone has it on their calendar."

"You're one to talk. Who gets called out the most for work? That would be you," Viv pointed out.

"Yeah. Murder has a way of happening at the most inopportune times."

"Like the case that called you away the other day. What happened there?" Viv asked.

Bailey bit her bottom lip. "I can't give you all the details. It's need-to-know right now."

Layla laughed. "You know I have the highest clearance of all of us, but I get it."

They were all hyperserious about confidentiality with their work. They only chatted about what they could and never crossed any lines. "It involves the military. I'm actually working with an NCIS agent."

"Really?" Layla asked. "Man or woman?"

"Well, both actually. I'm working directly with a guy, although he has a larger team."

"Is this guy cute?" Viv asked.

Bailey felt her cheeks get hot, because Marco was a lot more than just cute. She couldn't tell her friends that right now, though. "You two are the worst. I'm working with him. Not dating him."

"Is he boyfriend material?" Viv pushed. "How old is he?"

Bailey took a moment before relenting. "I think he's about our age. Maybe a tad older."

"I think he's cute," Layla said.

"You have no idea what he looks like." This was quickly escalating. Her friends loved to give her a hard time about her nonexistent love life.

Viv lifted her hands. "All right. We'll back off."

"Good." Bailey smiled at her friends. She was so happy to have them in her life. They'd met their first year at Georgetown Law and had formed a study group, since they were in the same section. They all had very different backgrounds but had grown together in ways she'd never thought possible.

"I want more cookies," Viv said.

"I'll get them." Bailey stood and walked into her kitchen. When her phone rang, she sighed, because that meant her Saturday night was probably over.

"Agent Ryan," she answered.

"It's Marco."

"What is it?" she asked, fearing the answer.

"We've got another body."

◆

Izzy hightailed it down to the new crime scene in Arlington, following Marco and Bailey in her own vehicle. As the rookie, she often felt like the odd one out, but she told herself just to keep her head down and focus on the case.

They'd gotten a call about an hour ago from Army CID, which was basically the Army counterpart to NCIS—although from what she understood, most of their agents were active servicemembers. NCIS agents were majority civilian.

Izzy grabbed her gear and jumped out of the car, running to catch up with Bailey and Marco. She'd actually taken the Army CID call, so she knew they had a dead Army Ranger on their hands. The news about Battle's death had made its way through the special-ops community, so this Ranger death set off alarm bells and caused Army CID to call NCIS. But that was where her information stopped.

Izzy joined the others and saw a man dressed in an Army uniform standing near the body. He was probably a good twenty years older than her. He stood well over six feet and was sporting a light brown buzz cut.

"You all must be from NCIS," he said. "I'm Army CID Special Agent Jay Graves."

Bailey stepped forward. "I'm Special Agent Bailey Ryan with the FBI. These are NCIS Special Agents Marco Agostini and Isabella Cole."

Jay shook their hands. "My boss told me you'd be joining us. Unfortunately, this is one of ours. An Army Ranger."

"Thanks for looping us in," Marco said.

Bailey crouched beside the body. "So you know we're investigating the stabbing death of a Navy SEAL."

"Yes, ma'am," Jay said. "I was briefed on that."

Marco also squatted by the body. "We just want to make sure there's not something bigger and interconnected going on here."

Jay nodded. "You think someone could be coming after our special-ops guys?"

"We don't know," Marco said. "Hopefully we can work together as needed."

"I'm all about getting this right," Jay said.

"COD?" Izzy asked, figuring it was as good a time as any for her to jump in.

Jay turned toward her. "Gunshot wound to the head. Kill shot. I'd say by a sniper."

She frowned.

"What's wrong, Agent Cole?" Jay asked.

She hesitated a moment, but Marco gave her a nod. "Our suspect in the two murders we're working is a Navy SEAL."

Jay's light brown eyes widened. "What? No one told me that part. I only heard about the victim."

"The thing is, we think there's a possibility he was set up," Marco said.

"So what's the rub?" Jay asked. "This COD is different than yours."

"Our suspect is not just a SEAL. He's a sniper," Bailey answered.

Jay let out a low whistle. "Seems like you need to figure out where your sniper was this evening, and pronto."

Marco pulled out his cell. "On it." He walked away, leaving Jay with Izzy and Bailey.

"What makes you think the sniper was set up?" Jay asked Bailey.

She looked down at the body and then turned her attention toward him. "Both men were stabbed, and the simulations we've been able to run make it look like it most likely had to have been done by two people. Our second victim was a very large Navy SEAL in top physical condition."

"What if the attacker was another trained SEAL, though?" Jay asked.

Izzy wanted to answer, but she let Bailey take the lead.

"It's not impossible, but we looked at the simulation and included both men's physical specifications. It's a much more plausible scenario with two attackers."

Jay stepped back from the body. "And do you have any leads on motive for the setup?"

Bailey nodded to Izzy, giving her the opening. "Not yet. We're also struggling to find a link between the two victims, but we haven't given up yet."

Jay frowned. "The more I hear, the less I like it."

"Then you can probably understand why we want to include you on this," Bailey said.

"Completely. Sounds like we have a lot of work to do."

Marco came back, his face red. "Kappen's lawyer hasn't heard from him today. She's waiting on a call back from him." He ran a hand through his unruly dark hair. "I hope we didn't make a mistake by letting him go. If so, he could be long gone by now."

CHAPTER
EIGHT

Early the next morning, it was all hands on deck in the NCIS war room. Bailey was surrounded by Marco, Izzy, and Army CID agent Jay Graves. She was impressed by Jay so far. He'd been more than willing to collaborate and work with them instead of trying to take his case and run it in isolation. They had a solid team of people who wanted to get to the truth, and she was convinced they could do it.

"We need to divide and conquer," Marco said.

Jay nodded. "Agreed. Also, for everyone's benefit, we have a positive ID on our victim. Army Ranger P. J. Wexford. His family has been notified."

"Married?" Bailey asked.

Jay shook his head. "No, but both his parents are still alive, and he has a brother." He looked at Marco. "I think I need to take a trip down to Fort Benning in Georgia. That's where Wexford was based."

"Good," Marco said. "How about you take the rookie with you?"

"Works for me. Why don't we pack up and get transport?" Jay stood.

Marco agreed. "The sooner the better. Bailey and I will stay here and keep working from this end."

Jay and Izzy gathered up their things and left Bailey and Marco alone in the war room.

"What's our plan?" Marco asked her.

"I'm going through these phone records today. Trying to find any linkages."

He placed his hand on her shoulder. "Did you sleep any last night?"

She laughed. "Do I look that bad?" She almost feared what his answer would be. She had learned quickly that Marco had no problem speaking his mind.

He shook his head but kept his hand on her shoulder. "Bailey, I don't think you could ever look bad, but you do look tired."

She hadn't been expecting that response. It hit her that she cared how he saw her. Could she be crushing on him? She thought she'd successfully kept any budding feelings in check, but right now she was acutely aware that Marco's hand lingered an extra moment on her shoulder before he moved away.

The feelings bubbling up inside scared her. Thinking he was cute was one thing, but developing any real connection to him was another matter. Marco was in a high-risk profession much like her own. The idea of starting to care about someone only to lose them was too much for her to think about. Loss was something she knew all too well, and the best way she'd found to protect herself was by not letting a man near her heart.

"Yeah, sleep isn't coming easily these days," she said. "I just lie in bed and keep running through the case. I can't be a part of convicting an innocent man."

"I feel the same way, but no matter what our feelings are, we can't ignore the evidence in front of us. And right now, that evidence says that Tobias Kappen killed two people in cold blood, and we can't rule out a third victim."

She looked into his eyes. "And you know as well as I do that people can be framed. We just have to figure out why and who." That was one of the many questions keeping her up at night.

Marco took a seat beside her. "At times like this, do you wish you were Kappen's attorney instead of an FBI agent?"

She considered his question. "You know, I do have those moments, but one of the reasons I love being an FBI agent is the chance to forward the cause of justice. I think, in the bigger picture, I get to do that more in my current role—by catching real bad guys and helping put them away. The issue here is that I don't think Kappen is a bad guy, and that's what has my stomach churning."

Marco tapped his pen on the table. "And now we have to figure out how Wexford fits in."

"Do you think Kappen's going to have an alibi this time?" she asked.

"If he fled, we're going to be in a serious mess. And it will tell me that we might have discounted the psychological angle too much. I'm still waiting to hear back from Lexi."

"Kappen didn't flee."

"How can you be so sure?"

"Because SEALs don't cut and run." Of that much she was certain.

Marco quirked an eyebrow. "Even if they are still struggling with PTSD? Kappen's a sniper. That means he's taken a lot of lives in his career. Sometimes that is just too much for any man, no matter his strength."

"I know," she said quietly.

"You sure seem to have a lot of confidence in him."

She wanted to push Marco. "Admit it. This third murder only decreases the chances it's him."

"Gunned down by a sniper rifle? I don't know. You could argue just the opposite: It seals his guilt."

Bailey shook her head. "I disagree, but let's get back to it and see what else we can find."

They sat at the large table, poring over documents for several hours. As she continued to scour the phone logs, Bailey had to reread the document in front of her a few times. She highlighted several call entries in bright yellow.

"Marco," she said loudly.

He looked up from his stack of papers. "You have something?"

"Yes." This could be the break they were looking for. "You're not going to believe this."

He stood and came around to her side of the table to sit beside her. "Tell me."

She slid the highlighted pages in front of him. "Battle and Rogers knew each other. These phone records show that they called each other at least three times over the past four months."

"How did Izzy miss this?" Marco's elevated voice was filled with frustration.

"Cut her some slack, Marco. I think she ran an electronic search. Sometimes, depending on how the data is stored, there can be misses. That's why I wanted to double-check the hard copies. Remember, that's why we have a team—to make sure we cover all our bases."

Marco ran his hand through his hair. "So Battle and Rogers were communicating, but about what? And how do they even know each other?"

"That's what we need to find out."

"And you didn't see anything showing that Kappen called or was called by either man?" Marco asked.

"Nothing." Bailey groaned. "Maybe Battle and Rogers got into trouble together and were killed for it. We need to take a harder look at their financials. Maybe there's some sort of gambling debt angle or something like that."

"But why frame Kappen? If this was an organized crime hit, they usually don't care about these things as long as they can't be directly connected to the murder."

Bailey didn't have an answer to that. Nor did she have answers for the million other questions floating around her overworked brain.

◆

When Lexi finally got ahold of Tobias, she had chewed him out for making her sweat out the night. Now, a couple of hours later, she was meeting him in person at a diner. He claimed he had to drive from the base back up to DC, but she was suspicious. After everything she'd done so far, sticking her neck out for him, he'd better not be lying to her.

"Do you realize how much trouble you're in right now?" She looked right into his blue eyes.

He hung his head. "I'm sorry, ma'am."

"I don't need apologies. I need the truth. Now." She picked up her coffee mug and took a big drink.

"I was on base until I drove up here to meet you. The reason I didn't answer your calls is because I was assisting in an extensive training exercise, and we weren't allowed to have our phones with us. After the training was over, I completely crashed. I wasn't purposely evading you. I hope you realize I wouldn't do that."

His explanation made her feel a little better. "Just to be clear, last night between the hours of seven and eleven p.m. you were still on base?" She'd expanded the range a bit to make sure she had the full picture.

"Yes. I didn't leave until I came here today. You can verify that through the base entrance and exit records."

If that was true, it would be the best news she'd heard in a long time, but she wasn't going to let him off the hook that easily. "Can anyone else verify your whereabouts?"

He shook his head. "Probably not. I was alone at my place on base."

It was time to break the news. "There's been another murder. This time an Army Ranger. And he was shot by a sniper."

Tobias shook his head. "It wasn't me. That much I promise you, and this time I can prove where I was."

"I'll talk to base security right away." This might just be what she needed to clear his name once and for all. "I've also got to call NCIS. They've been hassling me."

"At least now maybe this thing can be over. Right?"

"If we can get the information from the base showing you were there, it will go a long way toward making the case for your innocence."

She needed to start making phone calls ASAP.

◆

"Why did Lexi call you instead of returning my call?" Marco asked Bailey that evening.

Bailey smirked. "I don't think she likes you very much."

He shook his head. "She thinks she can bond with you."

She smiled. "She thinks she can reason with me."

Marco threw up his hands. "And I'm not reasonable? Look at me. I wouldn't hurt a fly."

"Remember the last interrogation?" The comeback rolled off

her tongue, but it was all lighthearted. Marco was just giving her a hard time. He knew full well that he'd been the bad cop. She almost thought he was flirting with her.

"So what did Lexi say?"

"That she's gathering evidence that will clear Kappen of the third murder." Bailey hoped Lexi would come through.

"Sounds like he finally has an alibi."

"Which would clear him of murder number three and provide more ammunition that he was framed for the first two."

"But then we're back at square one with absolutely zero suspects."

That didn't seem like a good alternative either, but at least they wouldn't be going after an innocent man. "We now know there's a connection between Battle and Rogers. I think at the end of the day, we're going to find all three men knew each other."

Marco leaned in. "We also have to consider that murder number three is completely unconnected."

Bailey knew he was right, but it was unlikely. "I think the chances of that are low, but I get your point. Which is why I'm focusing on connecting the dots between Wexford and the other two men."

Marco looked down at his watch. "We worked another long one, but at least I feel like we're making progress. If we can clear Kappen, even if it's just for murder number three, that would be helpful."

Bailey stretched her arms above her head and yawned. "Are we calling it a day?"

"Yeah. I'm beat. I think your insomnia has worn off on me." He grinned and gave her arm a light punch.

Yeah, definitely flirting. She felt like an idiot, unsure how to respond, but she also wasn't sure if this was just Marco's way.

His outgoing and playful personality shined through. She took the easy way out and didn't respond directly.

They said their good-nights and agreed to meet tomorrow at seven thirty to get started. Bailey was a morning person, so that wouldn't be a problem for her.

It was already eight o'clock, but she'd skipped her run for a couple of days, and she refused to let that keep happening. She told herself that she'd run tonight, but first she had to make the hour commute home. At least at this later hour, traffic was more manageable.

As she drove, she thought back to her interactions with Marco. She didn't know how she felt about him, but she'd be lying to herself if she didn't admit that she was attracted to him. *Lord, I'm scared to open up to him. What if I get hurt?*

And what if she was misreading him completely and he wasn't interested in her? She knew she'd never be the one to make the first move. They had a case that needed their full attention, but one day this case would be over.

Her psychoanalysis was starting to tire her. *Why do I have to be so messed up about this, God?*

Her faith had ultimately gotten stronger after her parents' deaths, but it had taken years to get to where she was now. She didn't know what the Lord had in store for her life beyond feeling like she was in the right place as an FBI agent. In the romance department, though, she wasn't sure. She'd been on a date here or there, but her time and energy were focused on her job, and the spare time she did have, she poured into her friendships with Viv and Layla.

She pulled into her assigned parking spot in her apartment complex's garage. After sitting in the car for an hour, she was more ready than ever for a run. *I'll be glad I did it in the morning.*

Bailey grabbed her small purse and workbag and stepped out

of her black Durango. She closed the door and turned around, but she was immediately thrown against the SUV, her back connecting hard against the vehicle. She let out a surprised scream at the unexpected physical contact.

A large man with a black ski mask and piercing blue eyes grabbed her neck and squeezed.

Lord, please help me.

She'd been trained in hand-to-hand combat and advanced self-defense techniques at Quantico, but she was momentarily paralyzed with fear and wondered if she was about to die.

As her attacker tightened his grip on her neck, her survival instincts finally kicked in—along with her training.

Not today.

Bailey jammed her knee up—hard—making contact with her attacker's abdomen, which caused him to loosen his grip. She had two choices: go for her gun or keep fighting. In a split-second decision, she shoved him away from her and started to go for her side arm. A weapon was always preferable when you were weaker.

But her assailant was faster. He picked her up and slammed her down on the concrete garage floor. Her head pounded and her ears rang from the impact. One more punch to the face, and she was barely conscious. She heard herself cry out. Her eyes squeezed shut in pain. *Lord, please, I need you now.*

Bailey opened her eyes, expecting to see the attacker coming in for the kill, but instead she saw nothing. He was gone. She rolled to her right and saw he'd taken her purse and workbag.

She racked her brain, thinking about what was in her workbag. She'd brought home some copies of the phone records in case she wasn't able to sleep. Plus her handwritten notes about the case were in her notebook.

Pain radiated through her entire body. Thankfully her phone was in her jacket pocket and not in her purse. She dialed for help.

◆

When Marco got the text from Bailey that she was being held at the hospital overnight for observation, there was no way he was going to sit at home. He made the drive and arrived at the Arlington-area hospital to search for her. Flashing a smile and his credentials certainly helped get cooperation from the duty nurse.

Marco arrived at room 314 and heard a set of distinctly female voices. The door was open, but he still knocked gently before poking his head in. He saw two women at Bailey's bedside.

"Marco. I told you that you didn't have to come. It's after midnight," Bailey said.

He walked over to the other side of her bed. "Are you all right? What happened?" There was a fresh bruise on the side of her face, and her neck was red. Seeing that made him seethe.

He glanced over at the other women.

"Marco, these are my friends Vivian Steele and Layla Karam."

Vivian, a pretty brunette with big hazel eyes, offered her hand. Then he turned and shook Layla's hand. The petite, dark-haired woman with olive skin and chocolate-colored eyes was striking. "Wish we were meeting under different circumstances," he said.

"Us too," Vivian said.

Layla moved toward the door. "Viv and I will go get some coffee to let you two talk about the details. We'll be back in a bit."

"Thanks," Marco said. He turned his attention back to Bailey.

Anger continued to brew inside of him as he thought about what she must have gone through. "Tell me what happened."

Bailey closed her eyes for a second.

He moved closer to her. "You're in pain. Maybe this should wait." He kicked himself for pushing for information. In situations like this he needed to act, and right now he wanted to make the monster pay for the pain he had caused Bailey. But he couldn't push for that at her expense. He had to keep his emotions in check, which was not one of his strong suits.

Bailey shook her head slowly and winced. "No. I need to tell you." She paused. "I had pulled into the parking garage and into my spot. I got out and turned around, and a man was there, wearing a black ski mask. I'd say right under six foot, but large and bulky—maybe two fifty. Caucasian with blue eyes. He totally got the drop on me. I never saw him coming. He choked me and then threw me to the ground. I tried to get to my gun, but he was stronger and faster. He hit me. Hard. Then next thing I knew, he had vanished."

This was even worse than Marco had expected. "What did he steal?"

She winced again. "My purse and my workbag."

"I'm sorry," Marco said. "I can help in getting your credit cards cancelled and all of that."

"No need. My friends are already on that." Her bottom lip started to quiver.

He realized she was still in shock. Moving even closer, he took her hand in his, not worrying about anything except her. "Bailey, you're safe now. No one can hurt you." As he said the words, he realized he wasn't leaving her alone here tonight.

"You're right. I have my friends. They're pretty tough."

"I have no doubt that they are, but I am too. And I'm not going anywhere."

"You're staying?" Her eyes widened.

"Absolutely. So if your friends need to go home and get some shut-eye, they can rest easy knowing that I'm not leaving you."

This was not negotiable. Bailey had been attacked while they were working a case. *Their* case. *His* case. He couldn't help but feel like he had failed her, even though he knew that wasn't a rational response.

His statement made her tear up. "I'm normally not this emotional. I can't explain why I'm acting like this. It just . . . it really hurts."

"Have they given you something for the pain?" He would track down a nurse.

"Yes, but only a limited dosage. I wanted a clear head." She paused. "Marco, I don't know what happened to me out there."

"What do you mean?"

She looked up at him. "I've trained for years. First at Quantico and then yearly fitness tests, plus my regular training regime. But when I turned and he was standing there . . ." She took another deep breath. "I froze," she whispered. "I can't believe I froze."

Marco squeezed her hand. "Even the most seasoned agents can freeze. You had no expectation of danger. You were at your home."

She shook her head. "But we're taught always to be on alert, and I was too busy focusing on other things instead of being situationally aware. I let down my guard."

The last thing he needed was for her to start psyching herself out. He needed her strong and clearheaded in order to solve this case. "You're being too hard on yourself. I assume you've never had any incidents in your garage before tonight."

"That's right."

"So put that out of your mind." He replayed everything she'd told him. "Did he speak to you?"

"Not a word."

He nodded. "Why don't you try to get some rest. I'll talk to your friends when they get back. Did the hospital staff tell you when they will release you?"

"The doctor is going to reevaluate in the morning, and if everything looks good, they'll let me go."

He watched as she closed her eyes again, his fists clenched by his side. Taking a second to calm himself, he stepped outside her door to make some calls, which included calling her FBI partner, Connor, so he would know what had happened.

Bailey's friends arrived just as he was finishing his calls. "You two can go home and get some rest," he told them. "I'll be staying tonight. Nothing is going to happen to her."

Layla's big chocolate eyes focused on him. "Bailey is really tough, but she doesn't know when to stop and take care of herself."

"And we're counting on you to look out for her. Can you do that?" Vivian asked.

"Absolutely," he responded. "Bailey is fortunate to have friends like you. Are you two in law enforcement?"

Vivian shook her head. "We both work at the State Department. I'm an attorney, and Layla's an analyst. We met Bailey in law school, and we'd do anything for her."

Marco smiled. "Right now I think she'd want you to get some rest, because I'm sure you have to work tomorrow. I promise she will be safe now."

"If there's anything we can do to help, no matter how small, let us know," Layla said.

"We're going to get through this," he responded.

Vivian handed him a business card. "All of my contact info

is on there. If you need anything or if Bailey starts giving you a hard time, contact me no matter day or night. We'll check in on her in the morning."

"Roger that," he said.

The two women thanked him again and then left. He headed back into the room to keep watch over Bailey. He knew the case should be his first and highest priority, but who was he kidding? Right now his mind was focused solely on Bailey.

CHAPTER
NINE

The next day Lexi couldn't believe what she was reading. She sat with Tobias in her JAG office in the Washington Navy Yard. She'd just gotten the entrance and exit logs from Little Creek and was reviewing them with her client.

"These are wrong," Tobias said.

"Base security is adamant that their system is accurate. And these logs show you leaving base at three p.m. and not coming back until after midnight."

Tobias ran a hand over his light blond hair. "Someone really is out to get me, Lieutenant, and I don't have the foggiest idea why."

"So you're saying someone falsified these records?" She fought to keep her voice even. She was on his side, and even *her* patience was starting to wane.

"It's an electronic system. It's hackable."

As exasperated as she was, she had to entertain his crazy theory. "That would require some level of sophistication."

He leaned in toward her. "This whole operation is sophisticated. My hair being planted at the first two murder scenes, the logs being falsified. I don't know how I've gotten into this tangled mess, but I'm ready to find a way out of it."

She had to draw a line in the sand. "I've stuck by you each step of the way, but I have to ask you again, Tobias. This is your last time to come clean without me totally losing it on you, but I need to hear it from you that you didn't do this."

"Ma'am, my answer is still the same. I promise that I am innocent. We have to figure out who wants me to be the fall guy and why they would kill these three men."

"I owe NCIS a call. I already told them I could produce evidence of your alibi. When I have to walk that back, it's not going to go over well. I don't know if they'll be willing to buy in to our conspiracy theory."

Tobias shook his head. "Ma'am, with all due respect, this isn't a conspiracy theory. We're talking about my life here. My career. My future. Please tell me that you're willing to fight for the truth here." His blue eyes pleaded with her.

This man was either the best liar she'd ever met or an innocent man in a world of trouble. "For someone to go to these lengths to cover up these murders, we have to be talking something big. Really big."

"That's exactly what I'm afraid of. Who else is next? Where does this end? At this point, it might be preferable to get taken into custody. Then they couldn't keep pinning things on me."

"There's a very real chance you'll get your wish. Once NCIS and the FBI see these logs, I think you'll be arrested."

"Maybe it's for the best. At least that way they'll know exactly where I am and nothing else that happens will be on me."

"I just don't always trust the system." She couldn't believe she had said that, but it was true.

◆

Izzy thought Jay might end up being a stick-in-the-mud, but he was proving her wrong. He was old enough to be her father, and that comparison wasn't something she could easily forget.

They'd gotten processed through base security at Fort Benning in Columbus, Georgia, the home of the 75th Ranger Regiment. Now they were sitting in a conference room, about to meet the commanding officer. Jay had warned her that Colonel Jeff Hayden was known for his tough-as-nails personality.

"I know I might have unduly scared you about the colonel. I just don't want you to be taken off guard." Jay smiled at her. "He can be gruff."

The door opened, and Jay shot to attention. She stood as well, but not with the same military finesse.

"Sit, both of you," the colonel said.

Well, so much for introductions, she thought.

"What do we have?" Hayden asked.

Jay gave the report. "A Ranger, P. J. Wexford, was shot by what we believe to be sniper fire in Washington, DC, while on leave. His death comes on the heels of the murder of a Navy SEAL. The suspect in that case is another SEAL. There is some feeling that the SEAL suspect could be a setup. We're working with NCIS to determine if there is any link between the cases. If so, we could have a killer out there targeting our most elite military servicemembers."

The colonel finally looked in Izzy's direction. "Ma'am, are you with NCIS?"

"Yes, sir," she said.

"You can't be a day older than twenty-five," he said.

She felt her cheeks redden. Hayden wasn't pulling any punches.

The colonel cleared his throat. "I assume if NCIS really

thought this was a massive threat, they would've sent someone more senior."

"Colonel, there is a senior agent back at NCIS working jointly with the FBI. Everyone is taking this very seriously."

"Terrorism still a possibility?" Hayden asked.

"Only a remote one. Our energy is focused on other areas."

Colonel Hayden sat straight in his seat. "What do you need from me?"

"We'd like to talk to some of the other Rangers and see if we can find any links between the victims. There was also a man murdered in the same way as the SEAL—he was the first victim in all of this. He knew the SEAL, but he wasn't military."

The colonel stood, and Jay shot to his feet again. "You'll have whatever you need." Then he turned to her. "Ma'am."

That was all he said as he walked out of the room.

Izzy turned toward Jay.

"I told you," he murmured.

Another man walked into the room. "I'm First Lieutenant Shi. The colonel has asked me to see to your needs. I'll be available to set up the interviews you want to conduct and get you around base."

"Thank you, Lieutenant. We're eager to start talking to those who knew Wexford as soon as possible."

Shi nodded. "Wexford was a member of the Third Battalion. I've done some initial recon, and I've got a few soldiers lined up to speak with you. I assume you want to talk to them one by one?"

"Yes, sir," Jay said.

"Follow me, and I'll take you to the conference room where you'll do the interviews. Is there anything I could get you, or you, ma'am?"

She would kill for another cup of coffee, but she didn't speak up.

"Coffee would be great, Lieutenant," Jay said. "I'm sure Agent Cole would like some too."

"Yes, sir, coming right up."

A few minutes later, the two of them were in a conference room with Ranger logo mugs filled with coffee, waiting on the first Ranger to arrive.

"Aren't you glad I warned you about the colonel?" Jay asked.

"Yeah. He definitely wasn't the touchy-feely type." She laughed. "But I guess you don't get to his position by showing your emotions."

"Nope."

"How did you end up in CID?"

"Well, I'll let you in on a little secret." Jay smiled.

"What?"

"I used to be a Green Beret."

"Really?"

"Yes, ma'am. But after many years and numerous deployments, my body just wasn't what it used to be. When I turned forty, I decided to apply for CID. I've been doing it now for nine years."

That would make him forty-nine. Her father would have been fifty-one if he were still alive. "I guess it's good to move on to a new challenge in a different phase of life."

Jay laughed. "That's the nice way of saying I got older and needed to take it easier. This job can still be demanding, but obviously not like what I did before. I know the colonel called you out for being young, but I wouldn't let it get to you. Youth has its advantages."

She nodded. "I am young. Something that I get reminded of often. I'm just twenty-four."

His eyes lit up. "You're around my son's age. So why NCIS?"

"I started out in Arlington PD, but when I saw this opening come up at NCIS, I thought I had to try it. I knew it was a long shot, getting hired with only one year of experience, but someone in Arlington PD put in a good word for me. Someone who knew my father," she added softly.

"So your father is Arlington PD?"

Izzy shook her head. "He was. He was killed in the line of duty when I was sixteen." She paused, determined not to cry on the job. "He's the reason I wanted to go into law enforcement."

"I am so sorry." Jay took a moment. "But even though I never knew your father, being one myself, I have no doubt he would be so proud of the path you've taken."

"Thank you for saying that." It did mean a lot. She often wondered what her dad would say about her career choices.

Their conversation ended when a huge hunk of a man entered the room. He was probably six three and all muscle. They made introductions, and Staff Sergeant Young took a seat.

"How well did you know P. J. Wexford?" Jay asked.

"Well. We went through Ranger school together. Bonds like that never break."

"Do you know why he was in the DC area?"

Young shook his head. "We had a week-long leave, but he told me he was going to visit his brother, who lives in Atlanta. He never said anything about going to DC."

Izzy jumped in. "Does he have friends in the DC area?"

Young's almost-black eyes met hers. "If he does, he never spoke about them. He's from Gainesville, Florida."

She glanced at Jay. It was possible that Young just didn't know everything about Wexford, but she was still skeptical. "His brother told investigators that he hadn't seen P. J. this past week. They spoke by phone, and P. J. didn't even mention his leave time."

Young crossed his arms. "Something doesn't add up here. Why would he lie to me and his brother?"

"That's our job to figure out," Izzy said.

Jay leaned forward. "I've got two names for you. Sean Battle and Michael Rogers. Ring any bells?"

Young's eyes lit up. "Yeah, actually. I've heard P. J. on the phone before, talking to someone named Battle."

"Do you know what about?"

Young averted his eyes. "I guess now that he's gone, it doesn't matter," he said softly.

"What is it?" Jay leaned in a little further.

"I really hate doing this. I gave my word."

"You did, but the man you gave it to has been murdered, and there could be something really bad going on here," Jay said. "It's your duty to tell us."

Young sat without saying a word.

Izzy noticed that Jay didn't push anymore, just allowed the silence to hang.

After a minute, Young spoke. "P. J. had taken on a side job. I think that's what he was talking to Battle about. He swore me to secrecy, because you're not allowed to take on any other work unless it's specifically approved by the CO—and for good reason."

"Any idea what kind of work?" Izzy asked.

"No. He didn't get into details. But I had to cover for him once. He promised he would never put me in that position again, and he didn't. P. J. wanted to give me as much plausible deniability as he could, but he told me it was something he *had* to do. I didn't push. Maybe I should have. If I had spoken up, maybe he'd still be alive." Young stared out the window.

Izzy pulled out her phone and texted an update to Marco, letting him know what they'd just found out. This was a major development.

"Did you ever hear P. J. say anything about Rogers?" Jay asked.

"No. But that name is so common, it's possible that it didn't register. Battle seemed unique to me, so it caught my attention."

Izzy gathered her thoughts. "When did this job discussion happen?"

"Maybe six months ago." Young sighed. "I can tell you one thing, P. J. was a straight-up guy. He wouldn't have been doing anything illegal."

"Even if he was desperate and needed the money?" Jay pushed.

"I don't think so. If he'd been in a really bad way and asked me, I would've done what I could. Not that I have money lying around. But he said he had things under control."

"What's your best guess as to what type of work he was doing?" Izzy asked.

"I would be completely speculating, but obviously it could be anything from being a bouncer to things a bit less savory. But I still don't think he would've done anything to break the law. It wasn't his style."

Jay glanced over at her before asking, "Is there anything else you can think of that might help us?"

Young put his head into his hands for a moment. "No. I can't believe P. J.'s gone. If there's anything I can do to help find his killer and make him pay, I'm all in."

"Thank you for your time. We'll be in touch," Jay said.

"Thank you, sir. Ma'am." Young nodded toward her before standing and exiting the room.

They sat for a moment as the information they'd just learned sank in. Finally, Izzy turned toward Jay. "The puzzle pieces have been dropped on the floor. Now we have to figure out how to put them together."

He nodded. "Before it's too late."

CHAPTER
TEN

"**Are you sure you're** up for this?" Marco asked Bailey.

"Yes." After she was released from the hospital, they'd come to her apartment so she could regroup. "We have to get back to work. We can't let this slow us down any more than it already has."

He touched her arm. "You're completely safe now."

"You know you can't make that promise. I'm a big girl, Marco. I know I got emotional last night at the hospital, but my head is on straight now. I'm up for it. Though I can't believe the irony of working these dangerous investigations unharmed and then getting beaten up by some random street thug." She took a breath. "I've never been a victim of theft before. It feels a lot more personal than I could've predicted."

"You gave your statement to local PD. They'll be on the lookout for the guy."

"You and I both know they'll never catch him. A mugging isn't exactly their highest priority. They need to be focused on truly violent crimes."

"Well, I've got your back."

"And I appreciate that. But we have to get focused back on our case. That text from Izzy is huge. We can't just sit on it."

"All right. What else do you need to do here before we can leave?"

"Let me grab a new bag, and then I'm good."

Marco had been exceedingly patient, keeping watch in the living room as she showered and pulled herself together. She wouldn't tell him, but she was still in quite a bit of pain. She would have to find a way to push through it. This new revelation had given her a boost of adrenaline.

Marco's tenderness had shown her a side of him she hadn't seen before, one that made her want to be closer to him. She normally didn't let anyone past her walls, but there was something disarming about Marco. There wasn't time for her to process those feelings right now, but the spark she felt for him had only grown stronger after the way he'd come to her aid last night.

They got into Marco's SUV and left her neighborhood. After a moment, she looked around. "You're going the wrong way."

"We're not headed back to NCIS immediately. We're going to do some recon first."

"Where?"

"I'd like to drive through the last two crime scenes again. Izzy wasn't able to come up with anything useful from the area video cams, which bolsters the argument that the attacker or attackers knew what they were doing and how to hide. But I've got some other ideas today."

She knew where he was going. "You want to see if there's anything in the area that could explain where they might've been working."

He tilted his head. "It's a long shot, but now that we have

this information about them taking on a side job, we have to run down every possibility."

Bailey thought back to her review of the victims' bank accounts. "Based on their financials, I'd say they were definitely getting paid in cash, because there was nothing from an external business source of any kind."

Marco gripped the wheel. "So we have three men. Two elite military operatives and one odd man out. We know that Wexford and Battle were working off book. We know that Battle knew Rogers and Wexford."

"There's something we're not seeing." She tapped her fingers on her leg. "What could these three men have in common?"

"It would be a lot easier if Rogers wasn't in the picture," Marco said.

"I know."

They drove the rest of the way to Foggy Bottom in silence. Once they arrived, they found some paid parking and got out to survey the area on foot.

"I guess I didn't think about the walking. Do you think you'll be okay?" Marco asked, his eyes concerned.

"Yes. It's good for me to move around and keep my muscles loose." Her biggest pain was in her neck and head anyway. "I'm not saying I'm ready to go for a run, but I'll be okay for this. You know it would be much faster if we split up."

"It would, but given you just got out of the hospital, we'll go together."

Four hours later, they were back in the war room at NCIS after canvassing all the businesses within a four-block radius of where Battle and Wexford were murdered, but they had come up empty.

"I guess we know where they weren't working," Marco said.

Bailey had another avenue she wanted to explore. "I'm going

to send their pictures to my contact in Organized Crime at the FBI. We can't presume what they were doing was on the up-and-up, even if their buddies think they'd never go there."

Marco tapped his pen on the desk. "Let's spin that theory out. Say the three men were doing work for some organized crime group. Maybe they saw something they shouldn't, or threatened to blow the whistle, or they just got tired of the work and wanted to cut and run. So they were killed off to make sure there were no loose ends."

Bailey considered it a moment, then shook her head. "But then why the setup of Kappen? That's the thing that throws a wrench into that otherwise good theory. We know they were doing something outside of their sanctioned roles. That something is what tied at least Battle and Wexford together and most likely got them killed."

"Even if this is organized crime, it's not run-of-the-mill. This has to be something much bigger for someone to jump through all these hoops and take these evasive actions."

"I hate to even say this." As the thought formed in her mind, she tried to push it away but couldn't.

"What?" He leaned in closer.

"We don't know enough about Rogers, but we do know about the other two. They would've been a treasure trove of intelligence and operational knowledge." She paused for a moment. But before she could continue, Marco started to speak.

"You think they could've been working for a foreign government?" he asked quietly. "Playing both sides of the fence?"

She balled her fists under the table. "I don't like it any more than you do, but we have to start thinking bigger. It has to be something that would cause such a reaction. Three murders, and who knows if that's the end of it."

"Okay, let's keep the foreign operative theory on the table

but continue to brainstorm. What other job would these two men be suited for?" Marco asked.

"Security or mercenary types?" Bailey answered.

He drummed his fingers on the table. "We need to work all our contacts and figure out the most likely defense contractors they could've worked for. Then we go through them one by one."

A thought occurred to her. "If it was a completely off-book operation, then the company may just deny it."

Marco nodded. "True, but we can question them and make our own determinations. If the victims were working at one of those companies, someone there has to be willing to talk. We can leverage whatever relationship they have with the government."

"We've double-checked with both Battle's and Wexford's commanding officers. Neither of them had approved any side job of any kind." She rested her head on her hand.

"Hey, I think you have pushed it enough for one day," Marco said.

"It's only six thirty," Bailey said.

"Yeah, but you've been through a lot, and then I had the bright idea to walk around Foggy Bottom and downtown Arlington. We should get you home."

"Thank you." She wasn't going to play too tough. She was fading fast. "Maybe we should also talk about logistics, given this investigation is really ramping up, and I'd like to be closer to NCIS. I could stay down here in a hotel."

Marco waited until she made eye contact. "It would be more convenient, but only do it if you're comfortable. A hotel isn't home."

"Given the work we need to get done here, I hate having to drive back and forth. I'll pack up some stuff tonight, and we can figure out the best place for me to stay tomorrow." She exhaled. "I'm sorry if I've been a burden. The robbery threw me for a loop."

"You're not a burden, Bailey." He reached over and squeezed her hand.

And she wondered exactly what she was starting to become to him.

◆

Lexi decided to try Bailey again. She'd called her last night and first thing this morning but never gotten ahold of her. She'd been tied up all day on another case, but now it was time to face the music.

When Bailey's voice answered, Lexi let out a sigh of relief before steeling herself for a difficult conversation.

"Bailey, it's Lexi."

"Hi there," Bailey said softly.

"I've been trying to get in touch with you." Lexi was met with silence. "Bailey, are you there?"

"Yes. I'm sorry."

Lexi wasn't sure why Bailey was acting squirrelly, but she soldiered on. "I know I told you that I had solid evidence for an alibi for my client—namely, records showing entrance and exit onto the base on the day of the murder." She paused.

"Yes, we're eagerly waiting to see those."

At least now she had Bailey's attention. "Well, here's the thing. The records we got, which were all electronically kept, don't tell the story we expected."

"What do you mean?" Bailey shot back.

"The records don't exonerate my client, but I still stand firmly convinced that Tobias is being set up for this. I'm working on determining how the electronic records could've been altered.

I know this isn't what I told you I could provide, but some of this is completely out of my control, and I called you as soon as I knew about this. You can't hold it against me that you didn't respond to my multiple calls." Lexi fought the urge to say something more.

Bailey sighed loudly. "I didn't respond because I was in the hospital."

Lexi's stomach sank. "The hospital? Are you all right?" She felt like a jerk.

Bailey hesitated for a moment. "Yes. I was attacked in my parking garage last night."

"Oh no. Are you still in the hospital? How're you doing?"

"I'm just a bit banged up. They released me today."

"I'm sorry. I had no idea." Lexi's thoughts shifted to concern for Bailey's well-being. "Do they know who did it? Was it just a mugging?"

"I don't know who it was, but he took all my stuff." Another moment of silence passed. "Can you ask Kappen if he's familiar with any defense contractors or private security firms that employ special-operations types?"

"Where is this coming from?" Lexi's antenna immediately went up.

"I can't get into that right now," Bailey said flatly.

Lexi figured she shouldn't push her luck. "I'll see what I can find out from my client. Anything to be cooperative and get to the truth." And she meant it.

She ended the call and dialed Tobias. Maybe he'd have some helpful information. They needed to get on the good side of the FBI and NCIS.

"Please tell me something else didn't happen." Tobias didn't even bother saying hello.

"No. Thankfully not, but I still think you need to prepare

yourself for an arrest. Get your affairs in order. I'm calling because I just got a strange request from the FBI."

"What?" he asked.

"They want to know if you're familiar with any defense contractors that employ special-ops types."

"Why in the world would they be asking that?"

"I don't know. The important thing for us is whether you know the answer to the question."

"Of course. SEALs are very attractive candidates for those jobs. And they pay a heck of a lot more than the government."

"Do you have specific names of companies?"

"Yeah."

She wrote down the names as he rattled off a list. Her mind was still in overdrive. "Maybe they think there's some connection to a defense contractor. Maybe another suspect." She could only hope. But then another option came to mind. "Would it have been possible for Battle to have been working for any of these companies?"

"Possible, yes, but it would've had to be in a limited capacity. Our schedules wouldn't permit anything else."

"This is becoming stranger by the minute," she muttered.

"I'll take strange all day long if it helps exonerate me."

"We need to figure out how to maximize this information. I'm not going to rely on the FBI or NCIS to run this down."

"What're you thinking?"

"Ask around and see if you can track down anything about Battle having done work for a security or defense contractor. I'll start researching on my end." She gathered her thoughts. "Tobias, this is important."

"Lieutenant," Tobias said after a pause.

"Yeah?"

"Uh, I think I've got a more pressing problem."

"What?"

"It looks like the police are at my door."

Lexi's pulse started to drum. "Police, not NCIS or FBI? Are you sure?"

"It's definitely Arlington police."

That meant the locals were flexing their muscles. NCIS hadn't moved fast enough, and now Tobias was going to be arrested. "Cooperate, Tobias. I'll meet you at the station, and we'll figure this out."

◆

Marco hadn't slept well last night. That was two nights in a row, but he was amped up about Bailey. A nagging thought kept popping into his head. They'd all been operating under the perfectly reasonable assumption that Bailey's attack was a random mugging. But what if they were wrong? Questions ran through his head about who could have been behind the attack and what their true intentions were. If Kappen was guilty and this was an open-and-shut case, then his concerns were for nothing. But what if Kappen wasn't guilty? What if someone else was out there, and they had come after Bailey? After all, they had taken her workbag in addition to her purse. What if they'd been looking for something? He hadn't voiced his thoughts to Bailey because he didn't want to frighten her. She was already shaken up enough.

As the questions continued to swirl in his mind, he watched Bailey typing on her laptop. She also had telltale dark circles under her eyes, but she had brought a bag with her this morning and told him that she would be staying at the hotel closest to HQ. That made him feel a little better. Bailey was a seasoned FBI agent who could tangle with the best of them, but he couldn't help but want to protect her.

And it wasn't just about protecting someone on his team—no, with Bailey it was becoming much more than that. When she'd broken down in the hospital, it had taken all his will-power not to wrap his arms around her. The feelings were growing quickly, and he wasn't oblivious to that—or the fact that they needed to keep working well together. He didn't want to do anything to jeopardize that, but he was always true to his heart. And his heart was screaming to him that Bailey was special.

"I just got an email from Lexi, and you're not going to believe this," Bailey said.

"What?" he asked.

"It seems we've been trumped. Tobias has been taken into Arlington police custody and charged with the murder of Michael Rogers."

"You can't be serious. Why would the locals try to get out in front of us on this? And without even telling us about it." He could hear his voice getting louder with every word.

"According to Lexi, they thought we were dragging our feet because we were waiting on the base records. They didn't care. Once the hair matched, they decided to move forward."

"Well, there's nothing we can do about it right now. We just have to plow forward with our investigation."

"On that note, we did get something valuable from Lexi as well. She gave me a list of security and defense contractors she got from Kappen. I'm going to shoot it to you right now."

"Good. We'll figure out how we want to handle it."

"And one more thing. I heard back from my contact in the organized crime unit."

"Any luck?"

She shook her head. "Nothing. No one recognizes them. So that seems to be a strikeout."

A few minutes later the conference room door opened, and Izzy and Jay walked in. "We're back," Izzy said.

Bailey took a moment to get them up to speed on Kappen's arrest.

"Things are moving quickly," Jay said. "Is it unusual for them not to give you a heads-up, since they knew NCIS and FBI are working this?"

"Yeah, and I don't like it one bit," Marco said.

"How was the trip to Fort Benning?" Bailey asked.

Izzy's eyes lit up. "Good. I think the biggest find was obviously about the off-book employment, but we have some other nuggets too."

"Izzy's right." Jay took a seat. "We talked to everyone we could, including the Ranger who had the intel on the side job and overheard the conversation between Wexford and Battle. We pushed him as hard as we could to see if he had any info about the actual nature of the work, but we didn't get that. At least not from him."

"What do you mean?" Bailey asked.

Jay turned to her. "We caught a break in our last interview yesterday. Another one of the Rangers said he heard mumblings about Wexford doing some side job for a security firm. He didn't know which one."

"That's got to be it," Marco said. "These guys were all working for some security company doing who knows what. And whatever that was, it just might have led to them getting murdered."

Bailey tapped her fingers on the desk. "I got a list from Kappen of companies that he knows recruit SEALs. I say we divide that list up between us and start digging. Marco and I went ahead and got DoD credentials for a cover, because they all have DoD contracts. That could be our best way in."

Jay nodded. "Let's give this plan some thought, because we're only going to get one chance. If we blow it, then they'll just lawyer up and we find out nothing."

Izzy frowned. "But if these guys were willing to murder three people, why would they tell us anything? Wouldn't they just stay silent?"

Marco could tell Izzy hadn't fully processed the potential plan. "We don't walk in the door and ask about the murders. We have to be more discreet than that. I think we start by targeting mid-level employees before we head up to the top of the company."

"Ah," Izzy said. "That's what Bailey meant by a cover."

"Exactly." Bailey smiled.

Jay's phone started buzzing, and he stepped out to take the call. Bailey used the brief interruption to do a coffee run, leaving Marco and Izzy alone.

"How was it working with Jay? Did you learn anything?" he asked her.

Izzy opened her notebook. "Definitely. He's a nice guy. And it was really good to witness such a highly skilled interrogator in action."

"Are you saying I'm not?" Marco couldn't help but laugh.

She shook her head. "Sorry. No, I didn't mean it like that."

"It's okay, Rookie. I get it." He paused. "All joking aside, what's your read on all this?"

"You really want my opinion?"

Her reaction made him question if he had been too hard on his rookie after all. "Absolutely."

"I think the off-book employment is key, but I'm still confused as to why they set up Kappen. Why him? Why another SEAL?"

Marco was glad she had thought about this. He was seeing her grow as an agent by the day. "We know there was a personal beef between Battle and Kappen. It also makes sense that to take down a SEAL, you'd need someone equally matched. To that you add his history with PTSD. What better person to frame than someone with a personal grudge and a record of psychological struggles? Kappen makes a great scapegoat—if that's truly what happened here. We obviously don't have all the answers." But he really wanted them. Needed them to be able to bust open the case. There was still a nagging fear in his gut that whoever was responsible would kill someone else and that time wasn't on their side.

"While we have a minute, what's the deal with what happened to Bailey?" Izzy's eyes widened. She had every right to be concerned.

"Unfortunately, we don't know. At this point, it seems like a random crime." He wasn't going to share his fears with Izzy. He needed more to go on before he went down that road.

"Is she okay?" Izzy asked.

"Yeah. Bailey's tough. She'll be fine." He was also a bit shaken up over this, but he'd never show that weakness to a rookie. "We have to keep our heads in the game and determine if Kappen was just a fall guy and if this is all connected to a yet unidentified company the victims worked for."

Izzy looked skeptical. "Don't you find it odd that these guys who put their lives on the line for our country would have gotten into something nefarious? I just can't wrap my head around it."

Marco had asked himself the same question, but Izzy needed a reality check. "One thing you'll learn in this job is that we see some of the hard truths. The darker side of humanity. And there's one fact we have to come to grips with. Even those we believe are heroes can sometimes be villains."

Izzy averted her eyes but didn't say anything.

Bailey and Jay walked back into the room a moment later. It was time to get to work.

CHAPTER
ELEVEN

Izzy had watched while the others debated the best course of action. Did they come up with a cover story and use the DoD credentials? Would they just go in as themselves?

Of course Marco had big ideas about how they should handle things. He always had ideas. But he wasn't the only one. Bailey and Jay did as well. In fact, everyone had them except her. Maybe she was being too hard on herself, but she felt at a loss.

Did she have any good ideas? She sat silently and watched the debate, but she feared to speak up. What if everyone thought what she said was stupid? It wouldn't be the first time she'd been told that.

Around these seasoned agents, she truly felt out of her league. It was better to be silent than to look like an idiot.

"Izzy, you be the tiebreaker here," Bailey said.

"What?" Taken off guard, Izzy wasn't expecting to be called on, but now wasn't the time to freeze. She wanted to provide her best assessment. "I say we go with the audit option."

The audit option, as Izzy understood it, would be for them

to pose as DoD auditors in order to talk to key people at the companies. These companies all had DoD contracts with audit requirements—meaning the DoD could come in at any point and conduct an audit. It was also the option Jay had suggested. She'd only worked with him two days, but she already felt a loyalty and bond that she didn't feel toward Marco.

"I can admit when I'm wrong," Marco said. "Auditors it is. Jay, are you good working with Izzy again?"

"Absolutely," Jay said.

Izzy planned to soak up as much knowledge from Jay as she could. "How are we going to divide the list?"

Marco unceremoniously ripped the piece of paper in half. "You two take the top half, and we'll do the bottom. They're in alphabetical order." He handed her the torn sheet of paper.

"Come on, Izzy. We have work to do." Jay stood.

Izzy grabbed her gear and followed him out of the room.

He walked quickly down the hall. "All right. We need to talk about how we're going to approach this."

Izzy's short legs could barely keep up as she trotted down the hallway.

"You're going to need to put on your game face," he told her.

Her worst fears were materializing in front of her. "Are you worried I can't handle this?"

"No. I'm worried that *you* think you can't."

He'd obviously identified her insecurities in the short time they'd worked together. "Shouldn't we do more preparation first?"

Jay stopped and turned toward her. "You don't want to just walk in there?"

"No," she answered honestly.

Jay frowned. "If we had the luxury of time, I'd agree with you, but we don't. We don't know if more people are in danger.

And this is also a shot in the dark. We can't sit around and pontificate. We need to act."

"You really think someone else could get killed?" Izzy found herself asking quietly.

Jay shifted his weight from foot to foot. "We can't rule it out."

"Then I guess you're right. There's no time to lose." Izzy's heartbeat sped up.

Jay took a step closer to her. "I'm not trying to scare you, but my gut is screaming that something sinister is going on here."

Dread settled into her stomach, and she hoped they could figure this mess out in time.

About an hour and a half later, they were stationed outside BF Solutions.

"I assume you have some sort of plan?" Izzy asked.

Jay gave her a little smile and looked down at his watch. "We're going to do some impromptu questioning of employees as they exit the building."

"But how will we know if we're talking to the right people?"

"We won't, but we don't have an accurate way to prescreen people, so we'll just have to do our best."

"Why do I feel like you're trying to teach me some bigger lesson here?"

"Because I am." He laughed. "Our jobs these days rely a lot on technology and electronic means to connect the dots and solve complicated puzzles. But sometimes you just have to get out there and pound the pavement. Just like what you did as a cop."

He had a point there. "All right. Are we dividing and conquering here?"

"Whatever you're comfortable with."

"I can handle this." If she couldn't question random people

in a low-risk situation, then what good was she? As Jay said, she had been a police officer.

"Looks like our first wave of employees is leaving for the day." He opened his car door, and she followed suit. "Remember, we're DoD auditors. Flash those credentials. You have every right to be here. You can't act uncomfortable or out of place, or they will know something is up."

"Understood." She wanted to demonstrate to Jay that she could be useful and could operate independently without a babysitter.

Izzy focused on a tall black-haired woman walking out of the building. She moved quickly, as if she had somewhere to go. It was now or never. Izzy hightailed it over to her, flashed her DoD credentials, and introduced herself.

Immediately upon hearing who Izzy was, the woman stopped cold. "What's this about?"

"What is your name, ma'am?"

The woman looked at Izzy closely for a moment before responding. "I'm Regina Fairbanks."

Izzy couldn't believe this turn of events. "Are you related to the Fairbanks that BF Solutions is named after?"

Regina tossed her hair over her shoulder. "My father started the company."

The quick internet research Izzy had done on the ride over was paying off big time. Otherwise she wouldn't have known the Fairbanks connection. "And what's your role?"

"I'm VP of human resources." Regina tilted her head. "Maybe if you told me the nature of the DoD audit, I could direct you to the correct person."

"I'm not at liberty to reveal the exact details." Izzy put on a serious face. "See that man over there?" She pointed toward Jay.

"Yes."

"He's my boss, and he will kill me if I say too much. I'm pretty new." Izzy had learned early on that the best lies had threads of truth.

"So it's not just you here?" A frown pulled down on Regina's bright red glossy lips.

"No. The boss doesn't let me venture out on my own yet." Izzy decided to push further. "But I do know this is something big," she said in a hushed tone. She just hoped she wasn't overplaying her hand.

"Why don't we head back inside?" Regina didn't wait for an answer and turned, walking briskly toward the building.

This woman had something to hide. Whether it was related to the case remained to be seen. Izzy shot a glance at Jay and made eye contact. He could see that she was on the move.

Once they got inside the building, Regina faced her. "Please have a seat in the lobby. I'll be back down in a few minutes."

Izzy didn't like the sound of that at all. "I'd actually prefer to be taken up to your office. One of the things we're doing is spot checks on how records are kept." She took a step toward Regina and purposely lowered her voice. "And I probably shouldn't tell you this, but you should make sure you have your employment roster in order."

Regina tilted her head to the side. "My employment roster is always in order."

Izzy had hit a nerve by going into an HR-related topic. The problem with this strategy was that Izzy was having to make all this up on the fly. She hoped she wouldn't paint herself into a corner at some point. "Regardless, the DoD would like to have the full cooperation of BF Solutions in this matter."

Regina blew out a breath in frustration. "All right. Come with me."

Izzy's heart pattered with excitement as she followed Regina down a long hallway to the elevator bay. She couldn't believe she was actually pulling this off. She figured there was no time like the present to start poking around. "I'm not that familiar with your company. Do you hire mostly on-roll or do you also contract employees?"

"That's relevant to your audit?" Regina raised a perfectly arched eyebrow.

They got off the elevator. "Yes, actually, it is. I can't say any more than that, though." Izzy stood firm, a careful balancing act between playing dumb and acting at least mildly competent.

Regina crossed her arms. "We hire a mix of both."

Izzy followed Regina down the hall and into an immaculately decorated corner office. "Former military?" Izzy could feel herself holding her breath, waiting for an answer.

Regina sat down behind her large mahogany desk and motioned for Izzy to take a seat. "Some, yes. But we do a lot in the tech space as well as engineering."

Maybe Izzy should take a step back. "Do you provide actual security services?"

"Very little. I'm completely confused as to how that could be relevant, though."

Izzy shifted in her seat. "I was asking for my own benefit so that when my boss asks, I can give him the information. You must know how hard it is to be a woman in this field." Yeah, she had played that card.

Regina's dark eyes softened. "All too well. And believe me, it's just as bad, if not worse, when your father runs the company."

Good. She'd formed a connection with Regina. Now was the time to go in hard to get to the key issue. "Do you hire any former special-ops types?"

Regina shook her head. "Not on a regular basis. They usually go elsewhere, but we have one or two."

"Could I meet them? Are they here?" Izzy was really jumping in.

"No. They aren't here. They're on assignment."

Izzy needed to do something to divert. "Let's talk about the gender breakdown."

Regina rolled her eyes. "I knew it. This is an employment-related audit. We strictly follow all DoD guidelines with regard to protected classes."

"Any lawsuits in the past year?"

"Related to that?"

"Yes." Izzy needed to push this a little.

"One, but it was settled. Those settlement terms are confidential. I can't discuss them without talking with our legal counsel."

"Understood." Izzy decided to go at it a different way. "This is kind of an awkward question, but I'm afraid I need to ask."

"All right," Regina responded with skepticism.

"Do you believe your company could validate all of its operations?"

"How so?"

"With a paper trail. Either hard copy or electronic."

Regina's eyes widened. "I don't like the sound of where this is going."

Izzy raised a hand. "I promise you this is SOP. I'm asking this question of other companies as well."

Regina didn't seem so sure. "I think maybe I need to call our lawyer."

That was the last thing Izzy wanted. "No. I don't think that's necessary."

"I think it is, given I think you're asking if we're engaged in any off-the-record work that we can't substantiate. Is this about auditing our books? Our financials?"

Izzy was more convinced than ever that BF Solutions had some skeletons in its closet. She had no idea what. But the last thing she wanted was to get into a tit for tat with a lawyer. Other people were much more suited for that. Like Bailey.

"I think I need to circle up with my boss. I've probably already said too much. I've been told I can be too helpful sometimes, if you know what I mean."

A sly smile spread across Regina's lips. "You know, it's important for women in the defense industry to stick together. I've been in this business much longer than you. How old are you? Twentysomething?"

"Yes," Izzy responded but didn't give her exact age.

Regina leaned against the desk. "You'll learn some tough lessons, but I can't tell you anything else without getting our lawyer involved."

Izzy nodded. "I'll head back down to talk to my boss. I doubt anything else is going to happen right now."

"I can escort you."

There was clearly no way Regina was going to let Izzy roam around, although that was exactly what Izzy wanted to do.

A few minutes later, Izzy stepped outside the building and saw Jay standing alone. She walked over to meet him, and they headed to the car.

"What happened?" he asked.

"They're definitely doing something they're worried about, but I don't know if it's our problem. BF Solutions doesn't specialize in areas that would be a great fit for our guys."

Jay patted her on the shoulder. "Good job. I'll want the full debrief later, but we need to make a stop by Arlington PD."

"What?" Her stomach dropped.

"While you were working your magic, I talked to Marco. Since we're already out this way, he wanted us to talk to the detectives working the Rogers case and figure out why they jumped ahead of us."

"All right," she said softly.

He looked closely at her. "Izzy, are you okay? You're getting a little pale."

She had to put on a strong face. "I'm fine. Nothing a protein bar can't fix." She didn't know how she was going to even take a bite of anything, but she couldn't tell Jay what was really going on.

By the time they pulled up to the main precinct, Izzy was fighting back waves of strong nausea. She tried to rationalize with herself that the likelihood her fears were going to come true was very small.

As they walked inside the familiar building, Izzy felt the walls closing in on her. Her fingernails dug into her palms. She fought to keep her breathing steady as her pulse drummed loudly.

"Izzy, what're you doing here?" a friendly, familiar voice called out.

She turned and saw Andrew Leahy. "Hi, Andrew. We need to speak to the detectives in charge of the Michael Rogers case."

"Let me find out who that is. Just hang tight for a sec. The coffee's still awful, but it's hot, and you know where to find it."

"It must be nice to see your old friends here," Jay said when Andrew had left.

"Yes." Andrew had been a friend. But she couldn't say the same for everyone. Not even close.

"Want some of that bad coffee he was talking about? Maybe it will give you a kick of energy."

Coffee was the last thing she wanted. She thought she might get violently ill any minute. She hadn't expected her reaction to be this strong and awful, but it was. "No. I'm good, but I can take you to the break room if you want some."

Jay shook his head. "Nah. Let's just wait here."

Her heart felt like it was going to explode out of her chest, but she remained silent and unmoving. At least she didn't have to wait long before a man and woman walked toward them. She didn't know either of them, and she felt a tiny twinge of relief.

The woman spoke first. "I'm Detective Perez, and this is Detective Sloan. You were looking for us?"

"I'm NCIS Agent Cole and this is Army CID Agent Graves. Are you two working the Rogers case?"

"Ah," Detective Perez said. "That's why you're here."

Izzy straightened. "Yes. My boss wants to know why you went around NCIS. And the FBI, for that matter. You all knew we were working the Rogers case in conjunction with others."

"It actually wasn't our call," Detective Sloan said. His gray eyes met hers. "We were getting pressure from our boss, given the hair evidence belonging to the suspect. We were told to make the arrest."

Jay cleared his throat. "Not even a courtesy call? That's not playing nice in the sandbox. We've got a major case going on here, with two special-ops members killed. I would think our joint investigation would've gotten a little more deference."

Detective Perez lifted her hands. "Don't shoot the messenger. We were just following orders, and we're sorry about the lack of contact. I can take the blame for that. Honestly, once we had Kappen in custody and had dealt with his very incensed JAG attorney, we got pulled onto another hot case that was time sensitive. I blew making the call to NCIS. That's all on me."

Izzy studied Detective Perez. She seemed to be telling the truth, but that meant someone higher up the chain of command was pushing the case against Kappen. They needed to find out who that was.

"Has Kappen spoken to you?" Jay asked them.

"No. He's lawyered up and hasn't said a word. His counsel was insistent on that. She's on a warpath."

Izzy respected that the JAG lawyer was pushing so hard to protect her client. "What's next, then?"

Perez crossed her arms. "Arraignment and turning it over to the DA's office. They'll continue their investigation, and I'm sure they'll be in contact with NCIS and the other agencies involved."

Jay nodded. "Well, if Arlington PD does unearth anything further, I would hope that you'd share it with us ASAP."

"Will do," Sloan said. "We're on the same team here."

They had a funny way of showing it, but Izzy held her tongue.

"Thanks," Jay said.

A hand on Izzy's shoulder caused her to jump.

"Cole, what're you doing here?"

As the words hit her, she knew who the speaker was. She turned and felt like she was staring into the blue eyes of the devil himself.

"They're working a case we're also on," Perez answered.

Izzy took a step back, putting more distance between the two of them, but she refused to look away. She wouldn't give the monster the satisfaction. She'd played this horrific moment over and over in her mind, knowing that at some point in her career after she left the department, she'd face this man. But this wasn't like it was in her mind. It was much worse. She had to fight the real urge to pull out her gun.

"I'm Sergeant Tybee." He stretched out his hand to Jay.

"Agent Graves, Army CID."

"Sounds like you have your hands full. I hope Cole here is pulling her weight."

"Yes, and then some," Jay said.

Jay's words of affirmation made her stand a little taller.

132

Knowing Jay was there right beside her gave her a boost of confidence, but she had no desire to stick around. "We should be getting back. There's a lot of work to do."

"Good to see you, Cole," Tybee said. "And let us know how we can help." He winked at her.

The nerve. She didn't respond to the snake but instead focused on Perez. "Remember, call us if you get anything new."

Izzy turned and briskly walked toward the exit, waving good-bye to Andrew but not looking back.

She steeled herself for the third degree from Jay, but it never came. And that almost made it worse. She feared she wouldn't be getting any sleep tonight.

CHAPTER
TWELVE

The next day, the team continued to conduct their visits to defense contractors. They had looked into BF Solutions but come up empty, so they had turned the investigation over to another set of agents so they could focus on their main case.

Bailey was exhausted, as they had spent the morning conducting interviews under the auspices of being auditors from the DoD. So far they'd come up with nothing, and Bailey could tell Marco was getting impatient. But this was the hard investigative work, and they had no choice but to do it.

"Here's our next stop." Marco put the car in park in a garage in Arlington.

Bailey looked down at the paper in her hands. "Whitfield Security International—otherwise known as WSI, according to my notes."

"You ready to do this?" he asked.

"Yes. Maybe we're one step closer. Everything we rule out helps move us closer to our goal." That was her trying to be positive, but she understood all too well that they were running out of time. She dreaded thinking there could be another phone call at any minute. They couldn't afford to lose someone else. If that meant going through the entire list of security contractors, then they'd do it.

They walked through the garage and up to the front walk. The building had large glass windows and *Whitfield Security International* plastered in block letters on the sign. It was game time, and Bailey straightened her shoulders. She thought they'd been convincing so far playing their role as DoD auditors, and they were getting better with each one.

"I got this," she told Marco.

He gave her a nod before opening the door for her. They walked into the lobby and up to the large white receptionist desk. The building's style was very modern.

"May I help you?" A thin, older blond woman sat at the desk with a smile that wasn't all that friendly.

"Yes, ma'am." Bailey flashed her credentials. "We're here from the DoD. We need to speak to someone in charge."

A flicker of concern washed over the receptionist's face. "Is everything all right?"

Marco stepped in. "Yes, ma'am, there's no cause for alarm." Bailey noticed that he gave the woman a million-dollar smile.

"But we do need to find someone in charge," Bailey added with a confident tone.

"Of course," the woman said. Her perfectly polished red nails tapped on the phone, and she started talking in hushed tones. Bailey was able to pick up that she'd told whoever she dialed that there was a situation with people from the DoD.

Good. Let them think there was a situation. Bailey exchanged a glance with Marco that let her know he too had heard those words.

"Please have a seat," the receptionist said. "Someone will be down very soon to assist you. In the meantime, is there anything you need? Coffee or water?"

"No, thank you," Bailey said. She followed Marco to the bright white couch in the center of the room.

Marco leaned down. "Why do I get the feeling that it's going to be more than just a minute before anyone comes down?"

His words were slow to register because his warm breath in her ear sent shivers throughout her body—not of fear, but of recognition of how close he was to her.

"You cold?" he asked her.

"No. I'm fine." She couldn't believe he'd noticed her visceral reaction to him. She needed to get her head back in the game. Ever since the attack, she'd been in a vulnerable state that made her uncomfortable. She hadn't let down her guard in so long. She couldn't even remember the last time she had.

"You'd tell me if you were still in pain, right?" His dark eyes showed such kindness.

"Yes. I'm fine. It's not the pain, I promise." She couldn't tell him that *he* was the cause of her reaction.

Thankfully, Marco's prediction proved to be untrue, and after another minute, a short and stocky man who was probably in his fifties walked toward them. He wore a nicely tailored navy suit and a lavender tie.

"Hello, I'm Cullen Mink. I'm the VP of WSI. How can I help you two today?" His icy blue eyes said he wasn't excited to have them there, even though he was smiling.

But to get the VP of the company was a much different reaction from the other companies. The highest person they'd gotten at the other places was a senior manager. Maybe they were getting somewhere.

Marco cleared his throat. "We're auditors with the DoD. We're here to do a compliance check."

Bailey naturally inserted herself. "Given your DoD contracts, as I'm sure you're well aware, we have the right to audit unannounced."

"Of course, of course. I'm sorry, I didn't get your names."

They had decided to use aliases. "I'm Tom Weatherby, and this is Jen Franklin." The names matched their fabricated DoD identification.

Mink adjusted his gold cuff links. "Mr. Weatherby, Ms. Franklin, I can assure you that WSI will fully cooperate with the DoD. But for an audit to be efficient, it might help for us to have some time to prepare the records you want to see."

Bailey lifted her chin. "Actually, first we'd like to ask your employees some questions."

Mink raised an eyebrow. "About what?"

"To ensure the integrity of the audit, we need to talk to them without your input. I'm sure you understand the need to make sure we cross all the *T*'s and dot all the *I*'s."

Mink nodded. "Yes. Whatever you need. WSI highly values our relationship with the DoD, and we have robust compliance procedures in place. You tell me who you'd like to talk to, and I'll make it happen."

This might be promising. "Thank you," she said.

"Come up to the executive floor. We have conference room space there, and I can send employees in to meet you." Mink paused. "I have to say, though, I think we were just audited last year. Is it common to be audited again this quickly?"

"We do spot audits for a variety of reasons," Marco responded. "That's what this is. And as we told the receptionist, there's no need for alarm. The sooner we can get started, the sooner we will be out of your hair."

"Perfect. Follow me, then."

They were escorted by Mink up to the tenth floor of the

building and led into a large conference room. "Who can I bring in for you first?"

"We'd like to see someone in your HR department," Bailey said.

"What level?" Mink asked.

"Let's start with a senior manager," Marco responded.

"Okay, sit tight. I'll have my assistant come in and take care of refreshments for you two, as I imagine you might be here for a while today." He left the room.

"What's your read of him?" Bailey asked.

Marco leaned back in his chair. "Seemed a bit shifty, but I imagine auditors would make people feel that way. Kind of like lawyers." He smiled.

"Yeah, I hear you. This is the first place we've been to where we got the upper echelon."

"Maybe they heard the word *audit* and had a knee-jerk reaction. Remember, they could be clean for our case but dirty on something else. That's exactly what I think we're going to find about BF Solutions once the other investigative team digs their teeth into their business activities."

Bailey pulled her notepad out of her bag, trying to be every bit the good auditor.

When a few minutes had passed, the door opened, revealing Cullen Mink and another man. Bailey and Marco stood.

Mink stepped forward. "I want to introduce you to Rex Barnett. He's the CEO of WSI."

Well, wasn't this a nice turn of events for them? Getting to meet the top executive of the company. Bailey offered her hand, as did Marco as they made introductions.

Barnett was taller and older than Mink but just as impeccably dressed, down to the gold cuff links. He still had a full head of gray hair, and his dark brown eyes looked intently at her.

"We want to offer the DoD our full cooperation in these matters," Barnett said. "We take great pride in our relationship. So anything we can do to assist, please let us know."

"We appreciate that, sir," Marco said.

"I must say that, given our long and valued relationship with the DoD, I'm surprised I didn't get a courtesy phone call telling me that you were coming."

Bailey moved a step closer. "Mr. Barnett, auditors in all agencies have been encouraged to buckle down on our unannounced visits, even with our best and most trusted business partners. It's all about audits being a separate and independent function of the organization. So please don't take any offense to our unannounced visit." She smiled at him, hoping to get on his good side.

Barnett nodded. "Thank you for that explanation. I stand behind everything we do here, and if there is anything amiss with our record keeping, I'd like to know about it ASAP. So please keep me informed of any issues you come across."

Bailey nodded. "We will definitely do that."

"Well, then I'll be on my way," Barnett said. "Cullen can help coordinate anything you need during your visit."

A few hours later, they were starting to feel like they were hitting dead ends. They told each other they would do one more interview and call it a day.

"What do you do here at WSI?" Marco asked.

A thin man named Sam who wore wire-framed glasses looked at Marco. "I'm one of the IT specialists."

"Do you ever have to set up employees with special technology needs?" Bailey asked.

"Like what?"

Bailey wanted to be somewhat direct without coming out and saying it. "I'm most interested in things that might be outside the normal channels."

"You mean off-the-grid type stuff?" Sam asked.

He had quickly picked up on her point. "Yes."

Sam cracked his knuckles. "Yeah. We do a lot of classified work, which I'm sure you're well aware of, since you're from the Pentagon. Sometimes that requires setting up tech on an ad hoc basis."

"Is all of that still documented, even if it is ad hoc?" Bailey asked.

Sam nodded. "Yeah. I mean, I have to keep track of things on my end, or it would be a total disaster around here. We have to track our technology assets, for one. But there are other things we care about too. We're very discreet, but there is still a paper trail, if that's what you're trying to get at. I have to make sure my boss and his boss are happy. Sometimes the executives have requests, and if we aren't organized, we'd be fired because they expect answers in real time. That's the nature of the work."

Bailey glanced at Marco. "In regard to the more sensitive work you mentioned, do you know the names of the individuals you do this work for? Would you have that documented?"

"Yes. In a file on my computer."

"Can we get those files now?" Marco asked.

"Yeah. If you give me a minute." Sam pulled out his phone. "As long as someone gives me clearance to do it."

"We're giving you clearance," Marco said in an authoritative voice.

Sam shrugged. "I think Mr. Mink will have to approve it also."

"We were told that WSI would fully cooperate with us." Bailey decided it was time to up the pressure here. "We'll go with you to your office, just to make sure this all goes smoothly. How does that sound?"

"Sure," Sam said. "You'll handle Mr. Mink?"

Marco stood. "Absolutely."

They walked out of WSI an hour later with a USB drive full of data. Bailey couldn't wait to search it and hopefully find some answers.

CHAPTER
THIRTEEN

Earlier in the day, Lexi had watched from her car as Marco and Bailey entered Whitfield Security International. At least the two of them appeared to be acting on the information Tobias had provided. That was a positive thing for her client. But she still had Derek breathing down her neck—and not in a good way. She feared that if the case actually went forward, the two of them wouldn't have a real chance at a future because of the damage this case would do to their relationship.

At first Derek had seemed willing to take a back seat to NCIS, but she worried that he'd soon be under political pressure in his department to push for answers, now that Tobias had been arrested. That was why she had to take on not only the role of lawyer, but also private investigator as she dug into these contractors.

Lexi looked down at her watch as she waited to be escorted in to meet her client in the holding room at the prison.

"Sorry I'm late," she said once she was finally in the same room as Tobias.

"Not a problem. It's not like I can go anywhere." He laughed.

At least he seemed to have perked up some. All they needed was this thin thread of hope to give them both a much-needed boost.

"And I'm sorry about how the arraignment went. The judge wasn't taking any chances with this case. That's why he denied bail."

Tobias nodded. "You warned me that was likely, given the severity of the crime. I'm trying to look on the bright side. If I'm in here, they can't pin anything new on me."

"I'm glad you're keeping your head up. We need you to stay that way. I saw Marco and Bailey go into WSI earlier today."

"Good. Because WSI is on my short list. I used the phone call they gave me to call in a favor, and I learned some really interesting stuff."

"Go on." She couldn't wait to hear what he'd unearthed.

"A couple of people thought Battle might be working off book. I floated a few names of contractors past my guy and found out that WSI is one of the companies most likely to hire SEALs or any special-ops types."

"Were you able to get the inside scoop on WSI?" Lexi asked.

Tobias nodded. "Known as a top-of-the-line contractor. They're one of the leaders in security services abroad. For example, if you need to get a VIP in and out of Kandahar, they're who you'd call. And since they're private, nonmilitary, they can play outside the lines when they need to. People who work for them make big money but also take big risks."

"Does that sound like Battle to you?" Lexi asked.

"Honestly, my head is so messed up right now, I don't know that I can be objective. But if pushed, I wouldn't have pinned him as the type to want just the fat paycheck. The thrill of the danger maybe, but not the money."

"If that's the case, then what're we missing here?" She drummed her fingers on the table.

"Maybe he really needed the money. His kid is getting older, and maybe his ex was pushing him for more cash."

Lexi wasn't convinced. But there was something else she wanted to discuss. "I also have a technical analyst looking into the base records. Hopefully, we'll get something there to show that you were actually on base during Wexford's murder."

"Good. I'm telling you, someone has to have electronically tampered with the file."

"Okay. I'll be back soon. Just know I'm doing everything I can and then some."

"I know, ma'am. And I can't tell you how thankful I am for what you're doing for me. I'll forever be in your debt."

"No, you won't. You're innocent, and it's my job to prove it."

As she exited the building, her cell rang, and she frowned when she saw who was calling.

"Hello," she answered.

"Hey, it's Derek."

"What do you want?" It came out a bit more harshly than she had intended.

"Can we meet in person?"

"I thought we agreed on only strictly professional communications from here on out." She hated being like this, but it was better to keep up the walls and draw the lines while she had this case. Her client would always be her top priority.

Derek sighed loudly. "We did, and unfortunately this is strictly professional. But I'd like to talk in person."

"All right." She didn't really have a choice, given the circumstances.

"Are you available now?" Derek asked.

"Yeah. Where are you?"

"Meet me outside the Dupont Circle Metro station. I'll be waiting for you."

Lexi ended the call and made her way to the Metro. About twenty minutes later she was exiting the Dupont Circle station, and she saw Derek standing outside as promised. She looked up at him and tried not to get distracted.

"Thanks for meeting me," Derek said. "Let's take a walk."

"Why all this cloak-and-dagger stuff?" She wasn't sure what Derek was up to.

He looked over at her as they walked. "Once you hear me out, I think you'll understand."

The seriousness of his tone let her know that this meeting had nothing to do with their almost-romance. This was all business. And at this juncture, that concerned her. "I'm ready whenever you are."

They walked another minute in silence as Lexi's heartbeat began to speed up. She didn't know what Derek was about to drop on her, but it couldn't be good. Nothing about this was good.

"I probably shouldn't be talking to you about this, but I have to," he said.

That warning made her even more curious. "Go on."

"Something very strange is going on in relation to the Rogers case." Derek's jaw tightened. "I've gotten some direct pressure on my end to push Kappen's prosecution."

"Why? And from who?" Her mind went into overdrive.

"That's the thing. It's coming from my boss, but my boss isn't the one really pushing this. He's getting pressure from someone else. Someone who isn't in our office."

Her stomach turned. "Do you know who?"

"I have my suspicions." He ran a hand through his hair. "And the thing is that they want me to offer your client a deal."

"What?"

"Yeah. Exactly. Something is wrong with this entire picture. They want Kappen to be put away for this, but they don't want a trial. And they want it done, like, yesterday."

"Why are you telling me this?"

He grabbed her arm. "Because I don't think your client did this, and I believe someone powerful has a vested interest in making him the fall guy."

The touch of his hand threw her off. She had to focus. "And you think you may have a lead on who is behind this?"

"I have a suspicion, but nothing concrete."

"Something you can share?"

"Not yet."

"Then why bring me in?" Her frustration level was high.

"Because I'm concerned about you."

"You think *I'm* somehow in danger over this?" She found that highly unlikely.

"I'm not sure about anything right now. I just know my instincts are telling me there's a problem, and I don't want to take any chances—especially where you're concerned. I think you understand how I feel about you, even if we've had to slow things down because of this."

Lexi's breath caught at his honest admission. "I feel the same about you, but I'm not sure how we're going to get to the bottom of this mess." Another thought occurred to her. "Are you actually extending an offer for a plea deal here?"

He stopped and turned toward her. "Yes, but I don't expect your client to accept it. If I don't do as my boss asks, though, they'll just put someone else on the case. I need to stay on. Now that red flags have gone up, I have to stick this out."

"Thanks for telling me about this. I realize this is a highly unorthodox situation." She couldn't let herself think about the possible implications of his actions, but if he was right that something fishy was going on, he was probably entirely justified in what he was doing.

"Lexi, I'm not in the business of prosecuting innocent people. That's not my calling. I'll do whatever I can to figure out what the truth is here."

"Then you need to watch your back too. Your warning goes both ways."

"Understood. I'll keep you posted." He gave her hand a squeeze that lingered an extra moment.

As he walked away, she was more determined than ever to succeed in her quest for justice.

◆

After another long day of visiting contractors, Izzy was feeling a bit defeated. Nothing they found out seemed to be helpful.

Jay had insisted on grabbing dinner and then drove her home after they finished eating.

"You know, you didn't have to come up to my apartment and check on me," Izzy told him.

"I'm here, and it makes me feel better. I can't help but think we should all be looking over our shoulders these days."

His parental tone made her smile. She hadn't wanted him to go out of his way, but on the other hand, she was super appreciative to have his protection. In fact, she hadn't told anyone about her recurring nightmares since leaving Arlington PD. The emotional impact of seeing the sergeant was much stronger than she had anticipated.

"I can practically hear you thinking," Jay said as he finished his walk-through of her small apartment.

"It's nothing."

"And now you're lying. Come on, let's sit for a minute and talk." Without waiting for her to respond, he took a seat on her beige couch and patted the cushion beside him.

She sat down but didn't say anything, waiting for him to go first.

He looked directly at her. "We're basically partners on this case. And in my book, partners don't hide things from each other. That's the worst thing you can do."

"Why do you think I'm hiding something?"

"Izzy, I've spent enough time with you to read your tells. With all that I've seen over the years between my experience in the Army and what I've lived through with CID, I can read people. Something is up with you."

She looked into his kind brown eyes and felt tears well up in her own. She hated to cry, especially in front of colleagues, but she couldn't help it. "You're right. I'm having a tough time, but I'm not ready to talk about it."

"Then I won't push you," he responded softly.

She brushed a tear away. "I've been having nightmares, so it's been tough sleeping. I'll get past it. I always do." Her voice started to tremble. Jay didn't know the story. Because she hadn't told him—or anyone.

"I'm here to help in any way that I can. I don't know what's troubling you, but the Navy has counselors you can talk to. Trained people who understand PTSD and psychological trauma."

Izzy looked down as thoughts flitted through her mind. "I don't know. I wouldn't want Marco to find out."

"It should be completely confidential."

She looked up into his eyes again and knew that he spoke the truth. But there was one more thing to consider. "I also think I'm going to church this weekend."

"Is that unusual for you?"

"I haven't gone since right after my father was killed. That was eight years ago," she said softly.

"And whatever it is you're currently struggling with makes you want to reconnect with your faith?" he asked.

"It's hard to explain, but yes." She paused. "I'm just a mess right now."

"No, you're not. And if you want, you're welcome to come with me and my family to our church this weekend."

Izzy couldn't believe how kind Jay was. "That would be really nice." She missed that connection with her family. After her dad's death, her mother had never really been the same. Their relationship remained cold and distant. Izzy had always been closer to her father anyway. And when she had decided to go into law enforcement, it had been hard on her mother. "I don't know how to thank you."

"Don't doubt yourself, Izzy. You'll get through this. Whatever it is. And I'm here if you want to talk. Sound good?"

"Yes, thank you." After the past week, she needed to accept this help.

"All right. How about I see you in the morning bright and early for a run? Okay?"

"Sure thing." Izzy hoped she'd finally find a small measure of peace tonight.

◆

Bailey had accepted Marco's invitation for an early dinner at his place. Their plan was to eat and then review as much of the data from the USB drive they'd gotten from WSI as they could. She really felt like they might find some of the answers they were looking for.

But now, a few hours into it, she was beginning to lose hope.

She sighed as she clicked through the next set of documents on her laptop.

"That bad, huh?" Marco got up from his chair and took a seat beside her on the sofa.

She'd read so many documents that had absolutely nothing to do with the case. "I'm sorry. Just frustrated."

"More pasta? That makes everything better."

She turned and smiled at him. "Your pasta was amazing. Your mom would be proud."

"Hers is *so* much better. Maybe I can take you over to visit one day."

As Bailey typed on her laptop, she thought about his offer. "That would be nice." She stopped typing and looked at him. "Do you think we're barking up the wrong tree here?"

"No, I don't. I think we're missing some pieces, but we'll figure it out. I'm just trying to keep my frustration level in check."

She smiled. "At least you don't bottle up your feelings."

He laughed, which lightened the mood a bit. "I wear all my emotions on my sleeve. There are pros and cons to that. But at least people know exactly where they stand with me."

"So where do I stand?" she asked playfully.

He stopped smiling.

"What's wrong?" She didn't know why their lighthearted conversation had taken a serious turn.

Marco leaned in closer to her but didn't say a word. As she looked into his big dark eyes, she tried to figure out what he was thinking.

"I might be easy to read, but you're not," he said softly.

It had taken her a moment, but now Bailey realized where this might be going. "I'm not trying to hide anything from you."

He placed a hand on the back of her neck. "Am I off base thinking there is a spark kindling between us?"

A chill shot down her arms, but there was no fear. Only anticipation. While normally Bailey would have overanalyzed every angle, she didn't. She just stared into Marco's eyes. She heard herself sigh as he drew her closer. Bailey had never wanted to be kissed so badly. His gentle touch made her put everything else on pause. No overthinking. No stressing about next steps or worrying about the future and the losses that would inevitably come. She was just thinking about Marco.

She closed her eyes, wanting to feel his lips on hers.

But a loud knock on the door made her jump back away from him.

Marco mumbled something under this breath and got up from the couch.

"Are you expecting anyone?" she asked.

He looked over his shoulder. "No." He grabbed his side arm from the table and walked to the door.

She heard the door open a moment later, then voices followed by footsteps.

"Lexi, what're you doing here?" Bailey stared at the JAG lawyer who was now standing in Marco's living room.

"I've got evidence that the guard gate logs at the base were hacked. Tobias now has an alibi for the murder of P. J. Wexford."

CHAPTER
FOURTEEN

Lexi had taken a risk by visiting Marco's house, and she hadn't expected Bailey to be there. But it looked like they were still working, as there were papers and laptops strewn across the living room area and kitchen table.

"You tracked me down, so this has to be good," Marco said. "Come on in and have a seat."

"Yeah. It wasn't that hard to find you in the employee database I have access to," Lexi said. "And I thought, given the nature of this case, that you wouldn't mind an evening interruption—especially when a SEAL's life and livelihood is at stake."

"Why don't you just get to the bottom line?" Marco said.

Lexi looked at him and then Bailey and couldn't help feeling like something was off, but she powered ahead. "I hired a private investigator who is a tech guru. Top of the line. He was able to determine that the base security records were hacked. He was also able to retrieve the original data, which clearly shows that my client was on base. There is absolutely no way he could've murdered P. J. Wexford." She opened her bag and provided them both with copies of her findings.

Lexi watched as they reviewed the pages. Silence filled the room as the long seconds ticked by.

After a minute, Marco looked at her. "If this can all be validated, then I think you have a strong argument, but we still have to deal with the forensic evidence tying Kappen to murders one and two. And given how aggressive Arlington PD has been on the Rogers case, I doubt this will be enough for them."

Lexi was prepared for that point. "Yes, but if someone was sophisticated enough to do this hacking, then they could've planted the evidence for the first two murders. My client is innocent. I'm not expecting a quick fix. I just want the truth to come out and Tobias's name to be cleared."

"We'll work on verifying this right away," Bailey said.

"Thank you." Lexi decided to push for more. "Have you made any headway on the list of defense contractors we provided?" She knew good and well that they'd been working on it, but she had no idea what they had.

Marco arched an eyebrow. "We're working through it, but if you have any other information that could help us, now is not the time to hold back."

She made the strategic decision to open up further. "I've talked with my client, and we believe that of the possible options, WSI is one you should really focus on."

"Why?" Bailey asked.

It appeared she had Bailey's full attention, and that told Lexi something. "Through our own investigation, we've gotten some tips that make us think they would be one of the most likely, if not *the* most likely, employer of the victims. They are known for hiring special-ops guys, and the type of work they do focuses on higher-risk overseas missions, including security details and other protective services." She stood up. "That's all I have for now, but we're continuing to drill down on everything we can. I hope this good-faith effort of full and unfettered cooperation helps demonstrate my client's innocence."

"Thank you for sharing with us." Marco walked her to the door. "We'll be in touch soon."

"I appreciate it." Lexi had taken a risk tonight, but she felt like this one might pay off.

◆

An awkward silence filled Marco's living room after Lexi left. He hoped Bailey would say something first, but she sat silently and twisted her watch around her wrist.

"I think we need to talk about what just almost happened." There, he'd said it.

"Nothing happened, did it?" Bailey looked away.

She was shutting down. The moment they'd shared was over, and he feared his window had closed. At least for now.

"Don't push me away, Bailey. I don't think that's what either of us wants, is it?"

Her shoulders slumped, but she didn't respond to his question. It was time for him to put his feelings on the table. There was no point in playing games. He wanted her to understand where he stood.

"I wish we hadn't been interrupted." He scooted closer to her on the couch.

Bailey looked up at him. "Maybe it's for the best. We have so much on our plate right now. We should be putting all our time and energy into cracking this case. Can we really afford to be distracted by whatever this is?"

"I understand." He wanted to argue with her, but he felt

he needed to pick his battles. Even if he was disappointed, he didn't want to be negative.

But man, he had really wanted to kiss her. He hadn't gone into the evening with that game plan—not at all. But as he looked into her eyes, he felt a growing connection that he couldn't deny. A fire inside of him that not only wanted to be with her, but also wanted to protect her. To keep her safe. To make her his. But if he started to make that kind of grand pronouncement right now, he would scare her off, and that was the last thing he wanted.

Bailey stood. "I should be going. We have another early morning tomorrow."

Even as disappointment filled him, he kept a straight face. He was more determined than ever to win Bailey's heart. Even if he had to do it one step at a time.

◆

The next morning Lexi stood in the Arlington courtroom in front of Judge Bain and steadied herself. She'd decided to revisit Tobias's bail. Tobias had been brought in for the hearing and was seated at the defense table. She'd instructed him not to speak unless directly asked something by the judge. He had promised he would be on his best behavior.

"Lieutenant Todd, what do you have for me today?" Judge Bain asked.

Lexi glanced over at Derek, who was at the opposite counsel's table. Her palms were sweating, but she put on her game face. This was much bigger than her own nerves. She had to fight tooth and nail for Tobias. "Your Honor, you initially denied bail for my client, Petty Officer Tobias Kappen. I have new evidence I'd like to present to argue for him being released with bail."

"Mr. Martinez, anything from the state so far, or shall we proceed?" the judge asked.

Derek stood. "No. I'm ready to hear the defense's argument."

The judge nodded. "Very well. Please proceed, Lieutenant."

Lexi walked up to the podium, but she didn't take any of her notes with her. Everything she was going to say was emblazoned in her memory. "Your Honor, to refresh your memory, my client is being held for the murder of Michael Rogers. NCIS and the FBI are investigating Rogers's murder as part of a larger case involving the murder of two other men—one a Navy SEAL and the other an Army Ranger." She paused a beat. He seemed to be with her so far. "Given the evidence, law enforcement is treating this case as if the same person murdered all three men."

The judge lifted a hand. "Let me stop you right there, Lieutenant. I don't see how any of this is helpful to your client, because as I understand it, your client is the chief suspect for all three of these murders."

"He was, Your Honor, but I have new evidence that exonerates my client of the third murder—the murder of P. J. Wexford."

The judge leaned forward. "What kind of evidence?"

She glanced back at Tobias, who sat expressionless. "Base logs showing that my client was on base at Little Creek during the time of the third murder. But that's not all, Your Honor. The base records were initially falsified to show that my client was off base. I was able to get a technical expert to show that the base's security system had been hacked so that this alteration could be made."

"What exactly are you saying, Lieutenant?" Judge Bain asked.

"Your Honor, first, I am going to provide you with the evidence demonstrating the alibi for the third murder, but secondly, I ask you to consider, given this new turn of events, that my client has been framed. I don't have to prove all of that to you today, but I believe what I have brought to this Court more than supersedes the bar for granting my client bail." She bit the inside of her cheek as she waited for his response. It was difficult not to keep talking, but she didn't want to lay it on too thick.

"Please approach and show me the documents, Lieutenant." The judge put on his glasses.

Lexi walked up to the bench and provided him with a copy of the base records and the certified statement by the technical expert. The judge took his time reading everything. Lexi felt a drop of sweat roll down her back. After a few minutes, she began to second-guess herself and feared that this might not be enough, but there was nothing she could do about it now.

Finally, the judge looked up from his papers. "Mr. Martinez, what does the state have to say about all of this?"

Derek stood. "Your Honor, the state isn't prosecuting Wexford's murder at this point. This case is about Rogers, and we still intend to continue with a vigorous prosecution. Having said that, I will leave it up to the Court to determine if bail is appropriate, given the latest information provided."

Derek was playing this masterfully. He wasn't opposing her position, but he also wasn't endorsing it. The end result, she hoped, would be the judge agreeing with her.

Judge Bain cleared his throat. "I'm comfortable under the circumstances, and given the new evidence provided, with setting bail at two hundred fifty thousand dollars. But your client must stay within the state of Virginia. No exceptions. And he'll need to surrender his passport as a condition of bail."

Lexi exhaled. "Thank you, Your Honor." With a final nod, Judge Bain left the courtroom, and the hearing was over. Lexi walked back to the table and took a seat beside Tobias.

"He had me worried there for a minute." Tobias ran his hand

through his hair. "My parents said they can work with a bail bondsman to make bail. Can you help with that?"

"Absolutely. I'll get on it right away, and hopefully we'll have you released later today or tomorrow. There's one more thing I wanted to tell you in person. The prosecutor has offered a plea deal for the Rogers case only, and they're offering manslaughter instead of murder one."

Tobias's eyes widened. "Why would I take a plea deal? I've done nothing wrong."

"Of course not. I would never advise you to take it, but it's my ethical duty as your attorney to convey any offers to you and explain that manslaughter is a lesser charge than murder in the first degree. So it would carry a lighter sentence, and there'd be no risk of the death penalty."

Tobias leaned in closer. "You can tell the prosecutor no deal. I have to win back my good name, and I'd never admit to a murder I didn't commit. Never."

"I hear you loud and clear. I will let him know that you've rejected his plea deal." There were no surprises there. Lexi would have never wanted him to take it.

Tobias's eyes met hers. "I know I've said it before, but I can never thank you enough for all you've done for me, Lexi."

It was the first and only time he had ever used her first name. They had developed a friendship through this awful ordeal, one that would last a lifetime. "I'm just doing my job. But, Tobias, know that I plan to fight with all I have in me to clear your name."

"You really do believe me now, don't you?" His voice cracked.

Lexi couldn't believe the raw emotion she was seeing from this battle-hardened warrior, and she had to fight to keep her own emotions in check. She placed her hand on his arm. "We're going to get through this. You're going to be exonerated, and then you're going to get back out there doing what you do best—defending this country."

"Yes, ma'am." He looked down. "That's what I want more than anything. The only way I can do that is if I'm completely cleared of all wrongdoing."

"Keep your head up, Tobias. You have absolutely nothing to be ashamed of. I will do whatever it takes to prove that."

"Thank you." He gave her a small smile as the officers came to escort him out.

"I'll see you very soon, Tobias."

After he was removed from the courtroom, Lexi gathered her things and walked out. Derek was standing in the atrium.

"You did well back there," he said.

"Thanks. I appreciate you not opposing bail."

"It was the right thing to do." He sighed.

"You should also know that we are formally rejecting your plea deal."

"No surprise there." Derek leaned up against the wall. "Lexi, I'm still not sure what is going on here. I can't make any promises as to how this will all pan out."

"I know you can't. But I do believe that you're a man who seeks the truth, and that's what I intend to find, no matter what."

◆

After a long day in the office finishing up reviewing everything in the WSI files, the team had a couple of leads they were going to follow up on the next day.

Bailey had accepted Marco's offer of giving her a ride to and from the office. The hotel room was basically home now. She missed her own place, but the memories of her attack were still associated with it.

They'd received word from Lexi that she'd gotten the judge

to grant Kappen bail, and he was now out of prison with certain restrictions in place. Bailey was more motivated than ever to solve this case. In her mind, Tobias Kappen was an innocent man set up to take the fall while the real culprits were still on the loose.

"Earth to Bailey," Marco said, as they started the short drive to her hotel.

"Sorry. Just trying to wrap my head around everything. I feel like we're on the edge of something big. And if we can exclude Kappen, then we have a killer or killers still on the loose. What if they decide to strike again?"

Marco glanced at her before turning his attention back to the road. "We're doing all we can."

Bailey hoped and prayed that was true. She looked at Marco, and her stomach clenched. There was no doubt in her mind she was starting to have feelings for him. The way he had been by her side since the attack had touched her. At first she thought he was just a flirtatious, overly confident federal agent, but now she had experienced a more sincere and caring side of him. The real Marco was a genuine guy with a huge heart. She'd told him they had to focus on the case, and that was true. But a piece of her just wanted him to kiss her good night and wrap his strong arms around her.

That was just wishful thinking. She'd tapped the brakes, and she was sure he wouldn't push things.

"I can hear you thinking, Bailey. Is there another angle you think we should pursue?"

"I wasn't actually thinking about the case," she said softly.

"Oh."

It was like he knew where her thoughts had gone.

He glanced over. "Is there anything else for us to say on that topic?"

Bailey stared out the window. "No. Things are still the same. I think that's best. Don't you?"

"If you're worried that we'll be distracted if we go down that road, then don't you think we're already distracted?" Marco laughed.

She couldn't help but smile. "You have a point."

They sat in silence for a moment. She was trying to determine if she should continue this conversation. Maybe they were crossing into dangerous territory.

Bailey was caught off guard by the bright headlights coming at them from the other direction. The large SUV sped up and started to cross the center line of the road.

"Marco!" Instinctively she braced for impact, fearing the worst—a head-on collision.

Marco quickly turned the wheel to avoid the oncoming SUV, but that action caused them to spin out of control.

The sound of crashing metal was the last thing she heard before her world went dark.

CHAPTER
FIFTEEN

Marco awoke with an intense headache. For a moment he thought he must have overslept, but then the reality came crashing back to him in waves.

He sat up with a start and saw Izzy sitting in a chair in the corner of the room. "Where's Bailey?" he asked.

Izzy stood. "Lie back down. Bailey's getting an X-ray."

"Is she okay?" His mind raced with disaster scenarios. "What're they x-raying?"

"Her arm. They think it's probably just bruised but want to make sure there isn't a fracture." Izzy took a deep breath and stepped up next to Marco's bed. "Bailey is going to be just fine. You're the one they were worried about, with possible head trauma. I'm so glad you're awake. How do you feel?"

He touched his temple. "A massively bad headache." He tried to gather his thoughts. "How long was I out?"

"I'm not sure when you got here tonight, but it's about eleven fifteen now. I know the doctor will be glad you're lucid. They weren't sure how hard you'd hit your head in the accident."

Everything flew back at him. "That's the thing, Izzy. I don't think this was an accident."

Her eyes widened. "Are you serious?"

"Unfortunately. The SUV came straight at us, crossing lanes. It was deliberate. And in my mind, that means we may have stumbled onto something and are one step closer to the truth. Someone doesn't want that truth to come out."

Izzy crossed her arms. "But the million-dollar question is who?"

"Who what?" Jay walked into the hospital room and made his way to Marco's other side. "How're you doing, man?"

"Been better, but thanking God that I'm alive."

"Tell me everything," Jay said.

A few minutes later, Marco had recounted the ordeal to Jay and Izzy.

"You're right," Jay said. "This seems like a targeted attack against one or both of you. Since Kappen is out of jail, we need to check to see if he has an alibi."

Marco shook his head, and the pain struck him. "I don't think it was Kappen."

"Regardless, we'll tie that off," Izzy said.

Jay frowned. "I think we're going to have to be more aggressive with WSI. Go to the corporate executives—the board, if we have to—and start exerting some pressure. Someone there or connected to them is most likely dirty and responsible for all of this."

Marco closed his eyes for a moment to try to focus on Jay's words, but the pain in his head was killer. He didn't want to let on just how bad it was, but it was some of the worst pain he'd ever experienced.

A moment later the doctor came in to check him out, and Izzy and Jay stepped outside.

"How're you feeling, Mr. Agostini?"

Maybe he should be honest with the doc. "Honestly, I've never felt pain in my head like this before."

The doctor nodded. "I'm going to get you into a CT scan right away. Just hang tight."

"Don't worry, Doc. Not going anywhere."

The doctor smiled. "Good to see you have a sense of humor. That's a positive sign. Someone will be right in to take you down for testing."

"Thank you. And, Doc, are you also treating the woman who came in with me? Bailey Ryan?"

"Yes. She's just finishing up in X-ray, but she should be fine. Even if there's a fracture, that's not the end of the world. Could've been much worse for the two of you, but we'll know more about your status after the CT scan. No need for you to be too concerned at this point."

"Thank you."

The doctor turned to walk out and then stopped at the door. "Ms. Ryan has also been asking about you." He smiled before leaving Marco alone.

Marco closed his eyes in prayer to thank God for protecting them.

◆

"Bailey, this is two hospital trips too many." Viv stood to her left beside the bed. "What in the world is going on?"

Bailey grimaced as she shifted in the hospital bed. The X-ray told her that nothing was broken, but her entire body ached, especially her left arm. "You know I can't go into specifics."

"We know that." Layla stepped in. "But you have to give us something. Is there any way we can help? That I can help? I know people I could ask for assistance."

The last thing Bailey needed was the CIA all up in their business. They had enough problems as it was. "No, thanks, Layla. I appreciate the offer, but believe it or not, we have things under control."

"No offense, but it certainly doesn't look like it," Viv said.

"I know how it looks." Bailey blew out an exasperated breath.

"You need security," Layla said. "I assume the FBI will step up and get you what you need, right?"

Bailey didn't want security. She wanted answers. "The FBI will provide whatever I request, but it's not about me right now."

Viv shook her head. "Bailey, you always have a great head on your shoulders, but right now you're taking too many risks. Your personal safety does matter. You can't break open this case if you're dead." Her friend's kind eyes pinned her to the hospital bed.

"I'm just frustrated because we're so close." She didn't know how to make them fully understand. "Has either of you heard an update on how Marco's doing?"

Layla shook her head. "Our first priority was seeing you."

Bailey frowned and hoped that the last update she'd gotten from the nurse still held up.

"What's the deal between the two of you?" Viv asked.

"What do you mean?" Bailey asked quickly. Too quickly.

Layla leaned toward her. "C'mon. We've known each other for years. You're not fooling either one of us. You're starting to like this guy, aren't you? Like, really like him."

Bailey sighed. "I don't know. All my feelings are jumbled up right now. And my first priority is catching a killer, not having some schoolgirl crush."

"What does Marco think about this?" Viv asked.

"We're still trying to work through it." Bailey paused. "Is it really that obvious that I have feelings for him?"

Viv squeezed her hand. "Don't worry. No one else has probably noticed, but we know you better than anyone."

"Good." That was the last thing she needed.

There was a light knock on the door, followed by Izzy walking into the room. "Bailey, are you all right?"

"Hi, Izzy. Yes, the arm isn't broken."

Izzy moved farther into the room.

"Izzy, these are my friends Viv and Layla. Izzy works at NCIS."

They exchanged pleasantries for a moment.

"Have you heard any updates on Marco?" Bailey asked.

Izzy nodded. "He's getting a CT scan right now, but I'm hopeful that everything will be okay."

"Have you spoken to him?" Bailey asked, needing more reassurance.

"Yeah. He was able to have a normal conversation with me. No signs of memory loss or anything like that. They're just being cautious because his head hurt so badly."

Bailey hated to hear that Marco was in pain. "Is Jay here?"

"Yeah. He wouldn't let me come by myself."

"Good. We all need to be extra vigilant." Bailey feared that every member of the team was a potential target.

Izzy looked at Viv and Layla. "How do you two know Bailey?"

Viv smiled. "We went to law school together at Georgetown."

Izzy's eyes widened. "Ah, so you're the friends Bailey told me about."

Layla nodded. "Yeah, but I don't actually practice law. Viv and I work at the State Department. Viv's a lawyer, but I'm a political analyst in the Bureau of Near Eastern Affairs."

Bailey noticed how comfortable Layla was with her cover

story. She wouldn't tell someone she was in the CIA even if they worked for NCIS.

"I would love to hear more about your work sometime. It sounds really interesting." Izzy nodded to Bailey's friends and then took a step back. "I'll get out of your hair."

"You're not bothering us," Bailey insisted. "You can stay."

Izzy smiled. "It's okay. I need to update Jay, and then we're trying to figure out a game plan for tomorrow. Viv, Layla, great to meet you."

"You too," they answered in unison.

Izzy left the room with a wave and a smile.

"She seems nice," Viv said.

"Very. She's young and still trying to figure out how to be an NCIS agent. And working for Marco isn't always the easiest thing in the world." Bailey looked up at the clock on the wall. "It's getting late. You two should go home."

"We're actually working tonight," Layla said. "But we had to make sure you were all right. Thanks for texting us. You know you're never a burden."

As the two of them said good night and left the room, Bailey wondered if that was truly the case, but her friends were too nice to say otherwise.

She closed her eyes to rest, and soon she had dozed off and was dreaming deeply. The next thing she knew, she was awakened by a hand over her mouth—stifling her scream.

A man stood over her, his hand pressing down on her mouth and his other hand on her shoulder, holding her down. "Where's the USB drive?"

His blue eyes were ice cold—and familiar. She'd never forget those eyes. This was the man who had attacked her in the garage.

Fear flooded through her body as she realized this man's plan was probably to kill her. She squirmed, but he pushed down harder on her already sore shoulder.

"Where is it?" he asked again. "Did you make copies of it?"

Of course she had, but she wasn't going to tell him that.

He lifted his hand from her mouth for a second so she could speak.

She gasped for air and screamed. If she was going down, she wouldn't let him get one ounce of useful intel from her.

He quickly pressed his hand over her mouth and nose so she couldn't breathe. Frantic, she started thrashing, but he used his body weight to force her flat onto the bed.

Lord, please help me, but if this is it, please forgive me of my sins and welcome me home. She couldn't get any breath, and the room started to close in on her. *Tell my mom and dad that I'll be there soon, Jesus.*

She closed her eyes, trying to conserve her energy for one final attempt to break away from him.

"What are you doing?" A loud female voice rang out.

Bailey's eyes flew open, and she saw a nurse standing at the door. The assailant ran toward the door, barreling over the nurse, who landed on the floor with a thud.

Bailey hopped out of bed, yelling for help. She crouched beside the nurse, who must have hit her head because she wasn't conscious. Bailey screamed again, and after what seemed like forever but had probably been only seconds, a few nurses rushed toward her.

But her attacker was long gone.

◆

The next afternoon Bailey and Marco had both been discharged and were back at NCIS with Izzy and Jay.

Marco cleared his throat. "We know for certain that Kappen

isn't responsible for trying to take us out, since he was with Lexi and another servicemember at the time. Both the NCIS and FBI directors want to be fully briefed by the end of the day. This last series of events has shot this investigation up their lists, and they want answers." That was an understatement, but he was going to have to manage in the same way Bailey would. He turned his attention to her, and she still looked a bit pale to him. "Bailey, let's go over every detail you can remember about what your attacker looked like."

She looked down. "It was the same man from the garage. He was probably under six feet but bulked up. Caucasian, blue eyes, short blond buzz cut. He almost had a military look about him. And as my email indicated this morning, he wanted to know about the USB drive, but I didn't say a word."

"We're having Ryder take a look at the drive to make sure we didn't miss anything," Izzy said. "If this man was willing to take such a big risk and be seen by Bailey, then it had to be of the utmost importance."

"Bailey is sitting with a sketch artist in a few minutes," Marco said. "Jay, what do you have?"

"I coordinated with hospital security and local PD, but no one is optimistic that this guy is going to emerge again. And his description is generic enough that he could be anyone."

"No distinguishing marks or features?" Marco asked Bailey.

She shook her head. "No. I got a great look at his face, though. I'll never forget those eyes. Hopefully the sketch artist can capture that." She looked up at him. "There has to be something on that USB, or at least they think there is. WSI has to be knee-deep in this. That's where we should focus our energy."

"Agreed. We need to see if we can figure out what WSI is really hiding."

Marco sat on his couch with Bailey by his side. He'd insisted that she hang out a bit tonight because he wasn't convinced that her head was fully in the game after the attack at the hospital. As if the car wreck hadn't been enough, she'd almost been smothered to death. He shuddered to think what would have happened if that nurse had been only a few seconds later. That thought made him thank God yet again for protecting Bailey. She was a woman of faith, and she would need it to get through this. They both needed their faith right now, because if he was honest with himself, he was more than a bit concerned over how quickly things had escalated. The sketch artist had rendered a great image that they were trying to match, but so far they had come up empty.

"Talk to me," he said to her.

"I think I'm talked out." She leaned her head back against the couch. "How're you feeling?"

"The headache has finally started to subside, so I'm thankful for that. I'll feel a lot better if Ryder tells us that he found something on that USB drive." The names of the victims were not in the data that had been readily apparent to them, but Ryder could do amazing things with technology. Marco was still holding out hope that Ryder would bring this thing home.

"We need to talk to Cullen Mink again," Bailey said.

"I completely agree. He is either hiding something or is being played by someone in his organization." This had become highly personal to Marco. A person he cared about had been targeted, and that got under his skin. "Do you want to talk about what happened in the hospital?"

She looked over at him. "We've already done that, haven't we?"

"Yeah, about the logistics of what happened. I'm asking

more about how you feel about it. You've had two personal attacks against you now. That can't be easy to process."

Bailey laughed, but it was clearly out of frustration, not humor. "Yes, I'm a federal agent who has been attacked twice and hasn't been able to do anything about it—or protect the nurse who came in to help me. Of course that makes me feel bad. Helpless. And even more than that—angry. Angry at myself for not being able to do more."

"That is not what I was trying to get at by bringing this up. You cannot blame yourself here. You had just been in a car accident. You weren't expecting someone to come into your room and hurt you at the hospital."

"But I should have! Don't you see? We said we were being more cautious, but once we had one curve ball thrown at us, we let down our guards."

"And that's not going to happen again. It could have just as easily been me if I hadn't been having those tests run." It tore him up to see her struggling. He placed his hand on hers. "We're going to get through this, Bailey. I promise you that."

"I don't know how you can be so confident." She sighed.

"We'll fight another day. That's what we do."

"At least we're not fighting alone." Her eyes misted up. "There were a couple of moments when I thought I was praying my last prayer, but the Lord was there for me in ways I never even realized were possible."

He understood exactly what she was talking about. "This has been a faith builder for me too. We always talk about believing that the Lord is on our side, but having to call on Him for help and strength and seeing it materialize right in front of your eyes is something totally different. I don't even remember reacting when that SUV came straight at us, Bailey. But what I do remember is God's grace protecting us."

She smiled at him, and he wanted to wrap his arms around her. So that was exactly what he did. He pulled her close to him, and she placed her head on his shoulder. He didn't fall easily, but when he fell, it was usually headlong.

What he didn't know was how Bailey would feel about that. Right now she needed safety and someone she could trust. She also needed a friend who would be able to comfort her. He wanted to do all of that and more, but she'd told him before that the case had to come first. Not one to hold back on anything, he turned toward her, looking directly into her pretty green eyes.

"I know this case is our focus, but I also know that, sitting here with you in my arms, nothing has ever felt more right."

Her eyes widened, but she didn't immediately respond. So in typical fashion, he kept talking.

"You're special, Bailey, and I find myself thinking about you and wanting to know if you're thinking of me too. We aren't guaranteed our next breath. The events of the past couple of weeks have made that crystal clear, and I don't want to have any regrets where the two of us are concerned."

She looked up at him. "I don't either."

That was all the encouragement he needed. He pulled her in closer and pressed his lips against hers. He was a ball of nerves, but the moment their lips touched, it was like Fourth of July fireworks went off around them. There was no doubt that he'd thought about kissing her for a while now, but nothing could have prepared him for what that actually felt like.

Not wanting to push things, he pulled back after a minute and looked at her. Fear struck him at first, wondering if she had felt what he had. But when she smiled, he knew they were both on the same page. He couldn't help himself as he gave her one more kiss.

He was crazy about Bailey Ryan.

———————◆———————

At four o'clock the next morning, Bailey lay awake, staring at the ceiling. She'd been up for about half an hour and was unable to go back to sleep. Fluffing the pillow, she shifted onto her side. Her thoughts were on a seesaw—back and forth between the kiss last night and the fear that someone might hurt her again.

She tried to focus on the good thoughts. Yeah, she'd told Marco they needed to wait to explore what was between them, but that was before a brush with death. His words had rung so true to her. She didn't want regrets either. Marco was an amazing guy, and even though she wouldn't normally let someone in, it wasn't that difficult to think about opening up to him. She just hoped she wasn't getting ahead of herself. From what she could gather, Marco seemed like he could be a ladies' man. She didn't think he was a player, but she was worried that he might be the type to quickly jump into something before really thinking it through.

She, on the other hand, was the ultimate queen of thinking things through. Analyzing things from every angle—and she'd lived long enough to know that sometimes the heart made decisions that didn't make logical sense. She told herself that she would just take things one day at a time.

Closing her eyes, she thought about what it would be like for Marco to kiss her again.

Bailey dozed off but was awakened by the loud shrill of the hotel phone. She'd put her cell on vibrate, and only a couple of people had her hotel information, so she knew it had to be bad news.

"Hello," she answered.

"Hey, it's me," Marco said. "I'm on my way to get you, so if you can, start getting ready."

Her stomach dropped. "What happened?"

"Bailey, I hate to tell you this."

"What?"

"Tobias Kappen is dead."

CHAPTER
SIXTEEN

Bailey had jumped in a two-minute shower, not even bothering to wash her hair, and had been ready when Marco got to the hotel. Now they were arriving at the crime scene—the condo in Arlington that belonged to Kappen's parents.

"You ready?" Marco asked her.

She nodded and opened the SUV door. This wasn't how this was supposed to play out. They flashed their credentials and gained entry to a scene already abuzz with NCIS, FBI, and local police. Izzy and Jay had beaten them to the scene.

"What's the deal?" Marco asked Izzy.

"The body is in the master bathroom. He was already cut down." Izzy seemed to run out of words and turned to Jay.

"Kappen hanged himself in the bathroom," Jay said flatly. "Or at least that's what it looks like on first blush."

"Any note, any indication of forced entry?" Bailey asked.

"Neither," Jay responded.

"Who found him?" She walked farther into the condo.

175

"One of his teammates. In fact, that's who cut him down," Izzy said.

"Is he still here?"

"Yes. He's in the living room with the FBI. I told them not to let him go anywhere. I figured we'd want to take him in for more extensive questioning," Izzy added.

"Good move, Izzy," Marco said. Then he turned to Bailey. "Let's go take a look."

Bailey followed Marco down the hallway and through the bedroom before arriving at the bathroom.

Kappen's body lay on the floor, where the ME and another NCIS agent were working. Bailey felt like she'd been sucker-punched in the gut as she looked down at his lifeless body, but she kept her composure.

"What can you tell us?" Bailey asked the ME.

"I'd put time of death as early as twelve hours ago and as late as eight. We'll know more after tests. I'll be running the full tox screen plus anything else you may want me to look at."

"Does this look self-inflicted to you?" Marco asked.

"My first assessment would be yes, but that's always subject to change upon further examination. The scene was a bit contaminated by his friend's presence and actions."

"Yeah, we're going to talk to him," Marco said. "Anything else?"

"No. I understand from the other agents that this is a hot one, so we'll expedite the best we can."

"Thanks, Doc," Marco said.

They walked out of the bathroom and stood by themselves in the corner of the bedroom.

"I don't have a good feeling about this," Bailey said.

"You don't think it's suicide?"

"Think about it. He gets out on bail and then kills himself?

That doesn't seem likely to me. Do we want to talk to Kappen's teammate here or at HQ?"

"Let's get him back to HQ. I'll leave Izzy and Jay here in case anything else comes up."

A little over an hour later, with a large and much-needed cup of coffee in hand, Bailey prepared to question Petty Officer Clark Chandler.

"Who's taking the lead?" she asked Marco.

"Why don't you? That'll give us room for me to escalate if needed."

Bailey took a sip of coffee. "You think Chandler could have something to do with this?"

Marco shrugged. "I really hope not, but everyone is suspect right now. This whole thing screams foul play. And remember, he wasn't even supposed to be close to these guys. He's a loner."

She locked eyes with him. "We'll get to the bottom of it."

"After you."

He let her lead the way to the interrogation room. She took a deep breath. *Lord, please give me discernment to help find the truth.*

She opened the door to find Petty Officer Chandler sitting on the other side of the table. He immediately stood at attention as they walked in.

"You can sit down," she said. "I'm Special Agent Bailey Ryan with the FBI, and this is Special Agent Marco Agostini with NCIS. We need to talk to you about what happened last night."

The SEAL had long dark hair and a full beard—as if he was either getting ready to deploy or had just returned. "Yes, ma'am. I'm not even sure where to begin."

"When's the last time you spoke with Tobias Kappen?"

"Yesterday afternoon. He said he'd gotten out of prison on bail and that he needed to talk. He said he wanted to do it in person because it had to do with Battle's death, and he needed my help. And he was adamant about his innocence."

"And were you friendly with either man?"

"I'm friends with everyone on the teams, but I was closer to Battle. Kappen is a hard nut to crack, but he was a heck of a sniper, ma'am. It's a huge loss. Now we've lost two members of SEAL Team 8 stateside. That's just not how things are supposed to work."

So far Chandler seemed sincere. He was making direct eye contact and showed no sign of nervousness.

"Are you in Battle's or Kappen's platoon?"

"Neither. I'm in a different platoon altogether. I just got home last week. That's when I found out about Battle's murder." He ran his hand through his hair. "I still can't believe it. And now Kappen." Chandler's jaw tightened. "Kappen kept saying he didn't do it, but now I'm even more confused. Do you think Kappen killed himself because he felt guilty for murdering Battle?"

"I'm actually much more interested in what you think," Bailey said. She noticed that Marco was laser focused on Chandler but hadn't yet said a word.

"Honestly, if I hadn't found Kappen myself, I wouldn't have believed it. But there was no one else there. His door was open, but I just figured he wasn't one to lock the door while he was at home."

Bailey made a note of that fact.

Chandler laced his hands together on the table. "Kappen asked me to come meet him. I'm struggling, trying to figure out why he wanted me to find him. Maybe he thought I wouldn't come unless he acted like he had some real information about Battle's death, but his suicide was the information. Maybe that was his confession?" He cracked his knuckles. "I know I'm rambling, and that's not like me. I'm just at a loss."

"And I'm sorry, and I know it seems like we're pushing you here, but you may have answers that you don't even realize you have." Bailey was taking a soft approach so far. Chandler was talking a lot, and she wanted to keep that going. "Let's go back to your conversation yesterday afternoon. Did he sound depressed at all?"

"No. Not at all."

"How did he sound?"

"If you're asking if he sounded like a man who was going to take his own life, I'd say definitely not. He seemed on edge. Maybe a bit paranoid. Although that's a common characteristic among SEALs. But he also seemed determined, and it really sounded like he thought I had a role to play in all of this. That's why I'm confused."

On a whim, she asked, "What do you know about WSI?"

Chandler cocked his head to the side. "Why?"

"Just answer." Marco spoke for the first time, his voice deep and commanding.

"They tried to recruit me about a year or so ago."

"And why didn't you take the job?" Her pulse thumped loudly at this newest revelation.

Chandler looked into her eyes. "I'm not doing this for the money. I do it because of a duty and a desire to serve my country. My father and grandfather were both Navy men."

"And Kappen knew about WSI's efforts to get you to join them?"

"Yeah. It wasn't a secret. Companies like WSI make lucrative offers to SEALs and other elite military men on a pretty regular basis. Our résumé is a helpful way to get them more business, which in turn makes the fat cats more money. As I said, I have no interest in that gig."

Bailey looked at Marco as her thoughts ran a mile a minute.

Then she focused back on Chandler. "Do you know whether Battle had any association with WSI?"

He shook his head. "No. I never heard about that. So if he did, it would be news to me."

"Would you be able to ask around and find out? Do you have other contacts at WSI?"

A flash of concern crossed Chandler's chiseled face. "No, but why do I feel like I'm missing something big here?" he asked. "There's something I must not know, because the two of you seem to be on the same page."

She obviously hadn't kept a good poker face.

Marco stepped in. "We appreciate all of this. We're just trying to put together the pieces in a very complicated and high-profile case. As long as you keep cooperating, you don't have anything to worry about."

Chandler's dark eyes widened. "Wait a minute. You never said that I was being investigated here."

"You didn't ask," Marco responded quickly.

Bailey knew what Marco was doing. He was trying to throw Chandler off his game to see how he reacted. To see if Chandler would break a sweat or reveal some key piece of information.

"Do I need a lawyer?" Chandler asked.

"That's completely up to you," Marco said.

"Unbelievable," Chandler mumbled. He sat quietly for a moment, and no one said a word.

Bailey wondered if Marco had been too rough on him. Her instinct was that Chandler was innocent.

"Look, I'm not in the wrong here. I don't need a lawyer." The SEAL's shoulders slumped. "Sorry for getting defensive. I just hate being so in the dark, but if you think I can somehow shed some light on what's going on, then I'm willing to do whatever it is you want."

"We'll take you up on that. But before we go there, did you notice anything out of place or strange when you got to the Kappens' condo?"

Chandler shook his head "No, but to be completely honest, I'd only been to his parents' place once, about three years ago. So I can't speak to how it usually looked. But there were no evident signs of foul play or a struggle or anything like that, if that's what you're driving at."

Bailey encouraged him to go on. "How long was it between you talking to him and you going over there?"

Chandler thought for a minute. "I'd say about five or six hours."

That was long enough for the real killer to put a plan of action into place.

Marco stood up. "Give us a few minutes, and we'll be back."

"Yes, sir," Chandler responded.

Bailey and Marco exited the room and turned to each other. Bailey spoke first. "I think someone heard that conversation between the two of them."

Marco nodded. "Kappen's line might've been tapped. Both the government and sophisticated defense contractors have that ability."

"Then whoever is responsible had access to the conversation and was afraid enough of the two men talking that they killed Kappen and made it look like a suicide?" Bailey asked.

Marco moved toward her. "What if the plan had always been to kill Kappen like that, and this conversation just accelerated the timing? Kappen's existence was going to be a problem as long as he was alive. Maybe the perpetrators were caught off guard when he was released on bail and started to get squirrely. Whoever is behind this didn't want him to start talking to other SEALs. Think about it. Kappen told us to focus on WSI. With

181

more time and communication with his teammates, he could've presented a threat. They could have figured that suicide might seem like the most plausible scenario, given what he was accused of and his past psychological struggles."

"Those are all good points." She tried to gather her thoughts. The need for more coffee was palpable. "We have Kappen's cell phone, but if we're right that he didn't kill himself, I have a hard time imagining we'd find anything useful on it. The killer would've scrubbed it."

"Let's just take it one step at a time. Including amping up the pressure on WSI."

◆

That afternoon Lexi sat in an NCIS conference room feeling entirely numb. She'd cried after getting the phone call. Then she'd toughened up when she arrived at the scene, but seeing his body had almost undone her. Had he really hanged himself?

He'd promised her he wasn't currently struggling with any emotional issues beyond the stress of being wrongfully accused, and she had believed him. She always believed him, because she didn't think Tobias had ever lied to her.

There was no note that they could find, but NCIS, FBI, and local PD had swarmed the scene. She'd been promised they wouldn't stop until they got answers. She could only hope they were telling her the truth.

As she sat, anger started to boil up inside of her. No, she did not believe that Tobias had killed himself. Not for one single minute. He was a man on a mission to prove his innocence and clear his name. He wasn't a quitter and wouldn't have taken his life while the allegations hung over him. This was all part of a twisted game, and she had to find out who was pulling the strings.

She thought back to the stirring conversation she'd had with him at the courthouse, and then to how happy he'd been when he'd been released on bail. Her body started to shake. It was almost too much to bear.

After leaving her waiting for far too long, Marco and Bailey entered the conference room.

"I'm so sorry," Bailey said.

Lexi thought Bailey actually meant it. The FBI agent seemed completely sincere. The jury was still out on Marco.

"I've been told you got a briefing at the scene but that you wanted to talk directly to the two of us," Marco said.

"Yes." Lexi clenched her fists, fighting back her bubbling emotions. "Tobias did not kill himself. We were working to clear his name. He'd just gotten out on bail. I saw zero indication that he was suicidal. This is all . . ." She started getting choked up. "All part of whatever this mass conspiracy and cover-up is." She leaned back and waited for them to try to refute her point, but neither of them said anything. Finally, hating the silence, she said, "What?"

Bailey looked at her. "We think there could be foul play here as well, but we're still working through all of that."

"What can I do to help?" Lexi offered without hesitating.

Marco and Bailey exchanged troubled glances.

Lexi needed to plead her case. She'd already laid all the necessary groundwork. "Look, my client is dead—most likely murdered. There are no ethical obstacles to overcome here. I'm a JAG officer, and I'm offering my help to NCIS. I've already cleared it with my boss. He'll loan me to NCIS for the duration of this investigation. Please." As she met Marco's dark eyes, she thought he was going to shut her down.

"Welcome to the team," he said.

Lexi let out a breath. She hadn't expected him to accept her so easily. "Thank you." Now was the time to show that she had something meaningful to bring to the investigation. "I know the prosecutor who was assigned the Rogers case. I think he knows more than what he's told me, so I'm going to follow up on that immediately."

"What did he tell you?" Bailey asked.

"He thought something was off with how he was being directed to handle the case. I think I'll be able to get more insight now . . ." *Now that Tobias is dead.* But she didn't have the heart to say the words.

Bailey placed a hand on Lexi's shoulder. "I know this is extremely difficult for you, but you're still fighting the good fight and trying to get to the truth. There is value in that, even if we can't change what happened to Tobias."

Lexi knew Bailey was right. "It's just hard to accept that he's really gone," she said softly. As the words came out of her mouth, she realized she had to do better by Tobias. It was time to put her emotions aside and get answers. "I'm going to get to work. I'll let you know what I find out from the prosecutor. I know my way out."

She left NCIS headquarters with a sense of purpose and a determination to get to the truth no matter the cost.

◆

Bailey's heart ached for Lexi's loss. She feared Kappen had been a pawn in this deadly game and was completely innocent of all wrongdoing. But they had more questions now than ever.

Bailey watched Marco pounding the keys on his laptop and wondered where his head was at.

The conference room door opened, and Ryder walked in, carrying a folder and his computer. His eyes were bright. "I've got something for you."

"Good news, I hope?" Marco asked.

Ryder tilted his head. "It's news. It's up to the two of you to figure out if it's good or bad."

"Give it to us."

Ryder took a seat at the table with them and opened the manila folder. "I've examined the USB drive you received from the WSI employee. At first glance, as the two of you gathered, there's folders of employee rosters, and that's where you didn't find any names you were hoping to find."

"Right," Bailey said. "I personally went over every file and name one by one. None of our guys were on the list." She knew there was going to be more to this story.

Ryder leaned forward in his seat. "You're absolutely right. You didn't miss anything."

"I'm sensing a *but* coming," Marco said.

"Yes. The person who put together this file pulled everything down in folders, but whether he knew it or not, there's a hidden encrypted file that I was able to ferret out. It took some effort, but I was able to unlock a separate list of names."

Bailey's pulse thumped. "Let me guess. Our guys are on that list."

Ryder nodded. "Your guys *are* the list. All three of them. I can tell you that the three victims have been on the WSI payroll for over a year. Looks like their pay was being wired to an offshore bank account in the Cayman Islands. These accounts wouldn't have come up in your searches of their finances. They're completely off the grid."

"That's why we couldn't find any paper trail of payment. And a year is longer than I expected," Bailey said.

Marco nodded in agreement. "What in the world were these guys up to? How did they keep it a secret for so long?"

Ryder slid copies of the list in front of each of them. "You'll have to figure that out yourselves." He stood. "I've got to get back to the lab, but let me know if you need anything else."

"Thanks, Ryder," Marco said.

"Anytime."

After Ryder left, Bailey looked at Marco. "I guess this explains why that guy attacked me in the hospital. They didn't want us to have that information on the USB drive because it's hard evidence linking all three of the victims to WSI. Don't you think it's time we bring in Cullen Mink for questioning?"

"He'll be lawyered up, no doubt."

There was no avoiding that. "Yeah, but we can at least read his body language if his lawyer shuts things down. WSI employed these men. I refuse to believe that's just a coincidence."

Marco stood. "This means Mink will find out we aren't the DoD auditors."

"Don't you think he figured that out already?" she asked.

They headed toward the door. "Yeah, you're right," he said.

She put her hand on the door handle, but before she could open it, he placed his hand over hers.

"You okay?" he asked.

"Yeah. It's just been a long twenty-four hours."

"Unfortunately, it's going to get worse before it gets better."

"I know. But we've got work to do. Let's get Mink in here for questioning."

CHAPTER
SEVENTEEN

Lexi had texted Derek, and he wanted to meet that night at his house in Alexandria. Relying on her GPS, she arrived in front of Derek's modest home and took a deep breath.

Ever since she'd gotten the call about Tobias, she'd had a sick feeling in the pit of her stomach. There was something very sinister at work here, and she hoped they could find the perpetrators before someone else got hurt.

But she also couldn't deny her very real feelings for Derek and what he had shared with her before Tobias's death. They had to figure out how this was all interconnected.

Lexi wouldn't consider herself a particularly religious person. She only attended church services on holidays, but sitting alone in her car outside Derek's house, she felt like she needed God's help to get through this.

Closing her eyes for a moment, she started to pray. It wasn't eloquent at all, but deep down she believed in God, and she hoped that He would help her now. She'd often heard that some people turned to their faith at their darkest hours, and now she understood exactly how that felt. She knew enough to know that God wouldn't judge her for her shortcomings, but she prayed that He would have mercy on her, because she was at a low point in her life like she'd never felt before. Not being able to save Tobias had rocked her. Now she had to do everything she could to clear his name, even if it was after his death. And she was convinced that she couldn't do it alone. *God, please, I need you.*

When there was a knock on her car door window, she jumped in fear. She opened her eyes and saw it was just Derek, and she let out a sigh as she opened the door.

"Were you planning on staying out here all night? What were you doing? Taking a quick nap?" Derek smiled.

She shook her head. "Actually, I was praying."

He stopped smiling. "Are you okay?"

"Sorry." She got out of the car. "Everything has just kinda hit me at once."

He pulled her into a hug, catching her off guard. But once his arms wrapped around her, she couldn't hold back her grief any longer, and she let the tears flow freely.

Derek didn't say a word. He just held her tightly while she bawled. After a few minutes, she tried to pull herself back together.

"Let's get you inside," he said.

She nodded as she brushed the tears off her cheeks. Derek led her up his front steps and into his home. He took her by the hand, and they went into the kitchen. He poured a cup of coffee for her and then one for himself before he joined her at the table.

She sniffled, trying to regain control over her emotions. "I'm sorry I made such a scene."

"That's nonsense. If you weren't upset right now, I'd be worried about you. You're having a perfectly human reaction to an awful tragedy."

"Tobias did not kill himself, Derek. I know that as surely as I'm sitting here with you right now."

"I believe you." He took a sip of coffee. "We both know there's something big and dangerous going on here. So dangerous that I've started to question whether you should just step back and let NCIS and the FBI do their jobs."

"What?" Her voice cracked.

He ran a hand through his hair. "I never should've brought my concerns to you. This isn't like a standard case. Nothing here has been normal, and that tells me there is a much bigger play happening here. These people are willing to kill to protect their secrets. I can't bear the thought of you being next or that I somehow had something to do with it because I fueled the fire."

She clenched her fists. "You know I can't just run away from this. My client lost his life."

Derek grabbed her hand. "And I don't want you to be next."

"Why would they come after me?" Her heart started to race.

His dark eyes narrowed. "If you start digging and snooping around, they might. I'm telling you, Lexi, we have to start assuming this is a massive cover-up for powerful people."

Lexi was a naval officer. Even though she was also a lawyer, she wouldn't shirk this obligation. "I think you realize how this is going to end."

He leaned back in his chair. "I do, and that's what scares me. If you're going to do this, let me help you."

"Now it's my turn to tell you to stay out of it. I'm going to be working directly with NCIS. It makes sense. But you can extricate yourself from this. Now that Tobias is dead, you won't need to touch this thing."

"I still think I have information, and maybe I can work my

sources to get even more. I'm not saying I'm going to be running anything on the ground, but let me do what I can. Use me and the information and connections I have. Please."

His plea hit her in the gut. There were so many dark and awful things happening, but Derek was a ray of sunshine. She reached for his hand and squeezed. "Thank you. Not just for that, but for everything you've done tonight. Your friendship means so much to me."

For a moment they just stared at each other before she pulled her hand away and picked up her coffee mug.

"So, can we talk about what you have?" she asked.

"Sure."

Given the change in circumstances, there was no longer any pending prosecution. She planned to get all the information from Derek that she could. "All right. When we spoke before, you said your boss was pushing you on the case, but you thought he was getting external pressure."

Derek nodded. "Yeah. And I can't say for sure, but I think the person putting in calls to him is high up at the DoD."

She hadn't expected that turn of events. "Why do you think that?"

"Just based on the conversation with my boss and what I was able to sweet-talk out of his assistant."

"All roads lead back to WSI," she muttered.

"What is WSI?"

"It's a defense contractor that we believe all three men were secretly working for."

Derek's eyes lit up. "Maybe we're dealing with a dirty defense contractor and someone on the inside at the DoD who is in on it? Someone who had enough of a vested interest to make pointed calls to the DA's office."

"Yeah." She started to think out loud. "What if the victims

were going to be whistle-blowers about some illegal activity? WSI got wind about it and had them killed."

He leaned in. "And they needed Kappen to take the fall to make it look like it was a SEAL gone rogue. Kappen was completely unconnected to WSI. It places the attention squarely on his shoulders while everyone tries to unravel how he could be connected."

"And if that wasn't enough, then they murdered him and made it look like a suicide." She fiddled with her watch to distract herself from getting emotional again.

"A convenient way for them to tidy up their mess. Because if Kappen had lived and was prosecuted for any of the three crimes, then at some point there would've been a possibility that his innocence could be proven. Which would mean everyone would know the real killer was still on the loose, and the investigation would have to continue. They couldn't let that happen. But once he was dead, then they would think there was no reason to push the investigation any further." Derek shook his head. "This is so much bigger than we could've imagined."

Lexi felt sick to her stomach thinking about this heinous possibility. "Especially if someone powerful at the DoD is involved."

◆

Marco sat with Bailey by his side in the interrogation room across from Cullen Mink and his high-priced attorney, Theo Channing.

"My client is here voluntarily in the spirit of cooperation, so please be mindful of that," Channing said. His sparkling gold cuff links were probably more costly than Marco's best suit.

"We appreciate you taking the time," Bailey said.

"I must say I was a bit surprised to find out that the two of you are *not* DoD auditors," Mink said. "But I assume you have a very good reason for that little charade."

Arrogance dripped off him. Mink clearly thought he was untouchable, but Marco had another plan. "Mr. Mink, I know you're a busy man, so we'll jump right in and get to the heart of our questions."

"Thank you," Mink said.

Bailey leaned forward. "Mr. Mink, we believe that three men who were employed by WSI have been murdered."

Mink's icy blue eyes widened. "What?"

Marco pulled out pictures of the three victims and placed them in front of the WSI VP. "These three men, two of whom were active US military personnel, have been killed. But I believe you already knew that, because a man like you would be up on current events, and the stories of their deaths have been on the news."

Mink looked at his attorney but didn't speak.

Marco didn't have time for his games. "We have tangible evidence that they all worked for WSI. There's no use denying that. What we don't know yet is why they were killed, and that's where we need your and WSI's full cooperation."

"Can I confer with my attorney for a moment?" Mink asked.

"Of course," Bailey responded. "Take the time you need."

Marco was interested to see how Mink was going to play this. Would he claim ignorance or actually bring something useful to the discussion?

The two men spent a minute whispering back and forth. Marco looked at Bailey, but her expression remained stoic.

When the conferral ended, Mink turned back to them. "I can tell you that all three men were indeed WSI employees. What I can't answer for you is why they were murdered."

"Why didn't you come forward when you knew three of your employees had been killed?" Bailey asked.

Mink looked at her. "I didn't want to cause any trouble for

their families. I understood that they were operating off book and without telling their commanding officers. I was afraid that it might impact their benefits from the military. That's the last thing I would ever want, so I kept silent. Nothing I said would bring them back, but if I did talk, the ramifications to their loved ones could be huge. I didn't want that on my shoulders. These men knew the risks they were taking and the need for ultimate discretion. I was trying to respect that."

"What about Rogers?" Marco asked.

The WSI executive looked down. "I just thought it best not to say anything about any of them, given my concerns. I couldn't have spoken up about Rogers in a vacuum. It's all connected, as I'm sure you see now."

Marco remained highly skeptical of what Mink was saying, but he needed to push forward. "When did you recruit them?"

Mink arched an eyebrow. "What do you mean?"

"When and how did you bring these men in to work for WSI?" Marco didn't know how much clearer he could be with the question, but by the confused look on Mink's face, he had to be missing something.

Mink looked directly at him. "WSI didn't recruit any of them. They came to us."

"What?" Bailey jumped in. "You're saying WSI didn't reach out to them? Tell them how much money they could make in the private sector? Give them the sales pitch? Come on. We've heard how WSI and other defense contractors try to entice special-ops guys with a different kind of life."

Mink shook his head. "None of that. We have and do recruit men who are in the military, and there's absolutely nothing wrong with that. But these men came to us."

"Do you have any documentation to show that?" Bailey asked.

The executive pulled out his cell phone. "I think there are

probably emails between me and our CEO and then our head of HR." He started to scroll through his phone, and his lawyer reached over.

"Let's just wait a minute." Channing lifted his hands. "My client won't be turning over his emails without a subpoena."

"Don't worry. You'll be receiving one right away," Bailey said. "But I want to get back to the point. Did all three men come to you individually?"

A frown pulled down at Mink's thin pale lips. "Actually, no. Sean Battle came to me first. He then recommended the other two men. Rogers didn't have a military background, but Sean insisted that he was a jack-of-all-trades. The recommendation from a SEAL was enough for me."

Marco glanced at Bailey, who was focused intently on Mink. Marco couldn't tell whether Mink was truly trying to be helpful, or if his goal was to lead them astray.

Bailey laced her fingers together on the table. "Let me recap here. You're saying that Battle came to you looking for a job, and then he suggested the other two men would be good hires as well."

Mink nodded. "Yes. I guess I'm missing the point on why you think that's a big deal. We have referrals all the time. The only thing that was even slightly odd was that he came to us, but that's not completely out of the ordinary."

"But Battle wasn't full-time," Marco said. "He still had his SEAL duties. We're going to need a list of every job the victims did for WSI."

"We can put that together, but as you can imagine, some of our work is highly sensitive. So we'll have to get all relevant parties to sign off and the requisite clearances."

"That won't be an issue," Marco shot back. There was no

way he was going to let governmental red tape and bureaucracy throw up roadblocks when they'd gotten this far.

Mink looked down at his watch. "I'm sorry, but we'll have to leave it there for now. I've got a meeting that I can't reschedule."

Marco highly doubted that, but he would let Mink go for now. They had a lot to follow up on and dissect.

Bailey stood. "We'll be in touch today with the document subpoena."

"Of course." Channing led Mink out of the interrogation room.

Bailey turned to him. "I wasn't expecting that. Battle went to WSI?"

"It's strange." The closer it seemed they got to the truth, the murkier things became.

CHAPTER
EIGHTEEN

After the Mink interrogation, Marco had called an all-hands-on-deck meeting to regroup and go through everything. The team had expanded by one member with Lexi's presence, which Bailey welcomed. She was a firm believer that having more voices in the room could be a good thing on complicated investigations like this. But there was no mistaking that Marco was still the team leader.

He was becoming a lot more than that to her. As much as she was trying to move slowly where her heart was concerned, it was apparent that was going to be easier said than done. The two of them had already been through so much together. She didn't know how they could ever turn back the clock and reset the relationship to try to make it begin in a normal way.

On the other hand, in their line of work, relationships were often tested and many failed. So maybe it was worth taking a chance on someone who understood the demands of her career. But then, she'd suffered a devastating loss with her parents' untimely deaths. Could she give her heart to someone who faced danger on a daily basis?

Hearing Marco start talking, she forced herself to refocus.

"Lexi is joining our team as we continue this investigation. Lexi, do you have any updates?"

Lexi nodded. "Actually, I do. And for everyone in the room's benefit, I'll tell you everything I have from the beginning. I met with Derek Martinez. He's a senior prosecutor in the Arlington DA's office and was working the Rogers case. Before Tobias's death, he was going about his normal process as he would on any other case, but he started getting phone calls from his boss. His boss wanted him to strike a plea deal and do it quickly. Derek thought it was strange that his boss would intervene and not provide him with much context or rationale for his direction. Of course, Tobias wasn't going to agree to a plea deal for something he didn't do. So I communicated that back to Derek."

"Is it really that odd for a prosecutor's boss to encourage a plea deal?" Izzy asked.

"It isn't abnormal, but it was more how he went about it." Lexi turned to Izzy. "Even when NCIS told Derek that Tobias was no longer looking good for the murder, Derek's boss still pushed him."

"Yeah, that doesn't sound right," Jay said.

"There's more, isn't there?" Bailey asked.

"Yes. Derek was naturally a bit suspicious about how this was playing out. He believes someone outside the prosecutor's office was pressuring his boss."

"Who?" Marco asked.

"Derek doesn't have a name, but he believes it's someone from the DoD."

Bailey straightened. "That could make sense. WSI has substantial government contracts for the DoD."

A muscle in Marco's face twitched. "Maybe someone at WSI was calling in a favor from their friends at the DoD. Trying to get the entire case closed through a plea deal so there would be no further investigation into WSI. The deal would guarantee that this would be wrapped up and no one would look at it further."

"Only the deal was rejected by my client, and now he's dead," Lexi said flatly. "My getting him out on bail may have signed his death warrant."

Silence fell over the room for a moment.

Marco stood and went to the whiteboard. He jotted down notes from what Lexi had said and drew a diagram including the DoD, WSI, and the victims. "We know that the victims worked for WSI. According to Mink, Sean Battle came to WSI looking for work. He then recommended his two friends."

Jay jotted something on his notepad before speaking. "I've verified again with Wexford's commanding officer that he had no clue that Wexford had any off-the-books job—much less with one of the country's biggest defense contractors."

Bailey knew there was more to all of this, but they hadn't quite found that missing link yet. "Let's assume, just for a moment, that Mink is telling the truth. Yes, employment at WSI is going to be more lucrative than many other opportunities, but as Mink said, it wasn't a full-time gig. He's supposed to be getting us everything that the victims worked on, but could there be another reason beyond money that they made the choice to work there?"

"What about some type of revenge?" Lexi suggested.

"How so?" Bailey asked.

"I was reading through the mission files, and about three years ago, Battle's team got ambushed and one of their own was killed. What if he thought he could settle the score by working for WSI?

He recruits two of his buddies to help him track down those responsible for the ambush, because he'd have to do that off book, since the military wouldn't sanction that kind of mission."

"Not a bad theory," Marco said.

Bailey spun it out in her head and then spoke up. "Maybe in their quest for revenge, they crossed the wrong people, and it got them killed? What if WSI isn't directly responsible?"

"I think we have to consider all scenarios," Marco said. "Both the option that WSI had them killed and that as part of the work they were doing for WSI, they got themselves into some kind of trouble."

"If they were in trouble," Bailey said, "then wouldn't they have gone to someone else for help? And after Rogers was killed, why didn't the other two put up their guard?"

"Remember," Lexi said, "Battle was killed only three days after Rogers. It's possible they didn't even know Rogers was dead. It wasn't until after both Rogers and Battle were killed that Wexford should've really been on high alert."

"Izzy and I will take another stab at tracing Wexford's steps after Battle was killed," Jay said. "We might want to take another trip down to Fort Benning now that we have all this additional intel."

"I think that's a great idea," Marco said. He turned to look directly at Izzy and then Jay. "Even though you'll be out of state, the rules we've set up still apply. No rolling solo. You need to be each other's shadow."

Lexi leaned forward in her seat. "You all are that worried about your own personal security?"

It occurred to Bailey that Lexi wasn't privy to everything they'd endured. She took a minute to get Lexi up to speed.

"Wow," Lexi said. "I thought Derek was being a bit overzealous and overprotective, but I see now that he was probably right."

"Yes, everyone needs to be on alert," Marco said. "That means you too now, Lexi."

Bailey wondered what Lexi's relationship with Derek was. Based on Lexi's comment, it seemed that Derek and Lexi were at the very least on friendly terms.

"I'll be careful," Lexi said.

Marco started pacing the front of the room. This case was taking its toll on all of them. "Let's talk later, because we may need to bring in someone else to work with you to make sure you're covered. I don't want anyone investigating alone. Whoever is behind all of this has shown that they have no problem not only with murder, but also with threats and intimidation tactics. We need to be buttoned up on that front."

"Understood. I could get another JAG to help out, if needed. Could be a good training experience."

Marco nodded. "Sounds good."

They took the next twenty minutes to map out their plan in detail as to who was going to do what and with whom. As the meeting finally broke up, Bailey rubbed her temples. She could really use another cup of coffee.

Everyone scattered, leaving her alone with Marco.

He took a seat beside her. "Are you all right?"

She nodded. "Yeah, just feel a big headache coming on. Nothing that more caffeine can't cure."

He smiled. "Coffee is the answer to many of our problems."

She looked up into his dark eyes. There was no doubt in her mind that he was starting to care for her, and the feeling was mutual. "I guess we should get back into our WSI and Mink files. I'm ready to go through the background check."

"Do you think he'll be clean as a whistle?"

"Well, I don't think he is. Whether the files will support that or not is another question. Men like him have many ways to cover their tracks." She straightened her shoulders. "But I told my FBI colleagues that we needed everything they could get." She looked down at her phone. "They've sent me the links to the encrypted files for us to review."

"We got the subpoena served on Mink for documents. We'll see how long it takes his lawyer to turn things over. I think we need to push him aggressively."

"I'm all for that." Now wasn't the time to hold anything back. "We should also try to get the CEO, Rex Barnett, in for questioning. I'm sure he'll be even more lawyered-up than Mink, but we need to see what he has to say for his company."

◆

The next morning Lexi walked through the door of the Arlington DA's office. She had told Marco that she'd find another JAG to assist her, but there was only one person's help she really wanted, and that was Derek's. She didn't report to Marco, so she felt like she could make the judgment calls she needed to. The most important thing was getting to the truth.

She'd talked to Derek last night to develop their plan of attack. And that was exactly why she was here right now.

After a few minutes, Derek came downstairs to greet her with a warm smile. He looked particularly handsome, and as his brown eyes met hers, her stomach clenched. She'd done a good job managing her emotional connection to him because of the case, but now that they were no longer adversaries, she didn't have to worry about that.

"How're you doing this morning?" Derek stood beside her.

"I actually got some sleep for the first time in a while, and I feel like we are at least doing something instead of just waiting for something else bad to happen." She was a woman of action, and today she planned to get answers.

"Right this way. We'll go into my office and talk, but I can't guarantee that the plan we cooked up is going to get results."

They walked up the stairs and down the hall to Derek's modest prosecutor's office. His law school diploma hung on the wall, and there was one picture on his desk—she assumed it was of him with his mother, given the resemblance. His desk was clean, with only a few stacks of papers and file folders neatly organized on its surface.

Derek was right that their plan might not work, but they were still going to try. Although she did worry about whether he might get in trouble with his boss.

"I wanted you to sleep on it," she said. "Are you sure you're okay doing this? The last thing we need is for you to get fired." Yes, she wanted answers, but there were other ways if the repercussions would be too big.

Derek closed his office door and walked over to her, taking her hands in his. "I did sleep on it, and I'm more convinced than ever that I need to do this. I'm not going to be an ostrich here and take the easy way out."

She looked up at him. "And if your boss decides to give you the boot?"

He shook his head. "He wouldn't do that. I know where too many of his skeletons are, if you know what I mean. He has bigger political aspirations than this office. I don't want to play dirty, but if he threatens me, then I'll play hardball right back."

She wasn't used to seeing the more aggressive and tactical side of Derek, but she appreciated his zeal in this instance. They were on the right side here. "Then I'm ready whenever you are. Are we just dropping in on him unexpectedly?"

"Yes and no. I talked to his assistant first thing this morning. She knows I'm coming."

"What about me?" Lexi shifted her weight.

"You'll be a surprise." He smiled.

She followed Derek down the hall, up one more flight of steps, and into a reception area, where Derek chatted with the assistant for a moment before the two of them were ushered into a conference room.

A couple of minutes later, a tall blond man walked into the room. Lexi rose to her feet.

The man stretched out his hand. "I'm District Attorney Perry O'Shea."

"Nice to meet you. I'm Lieutenant Lexi Todd with JAG."

Perry firmly took her hand, and she could see flecks of gold in his hazel eyes. She also saw confusion as to why she was in his conference room.

"Please have a seat and tell me what can I do to help JAG today," Perry said.

Lexi glanced at Derek. They'd decided it was best for him to take the lead, since he worked for Perry.

Derek cleared his throat. "This is actually about the Rogers case."

Perry frowned. "Isn't that case closed now that the suspect is dead?"

"It's a bit more complicated than that," Lexi said.

"How so?" Perry raised an eyebrow.

"You should know that Lexi was the suspect's attorney," Derek said. "She's now working with NCIS and the FBI as they investigate a string of murders that includes Rogers as well as the two military personnel who were killed."

"I get all of that, Derek, but what does any of this have to do with me?" Perry asked.

Lexi waited to see how Derek was going to play this out.

"Perry, I know you were talking to someone at the DoD about

the Rogers case. I remember the heat you put on me about it, and given all the circumstances, including what we believe now is a murder made to look like a suicide, we need to know what you know."

Perry crossed his lanky arms. "I have to say that I don't appreciate your accusatory tone. Maybe it's best that you and I speak alone without Lieutenant Todd in the room."

Derek shook his head. "There's no reason to be defensive. We just want to get to the truth—something I know that you, as the DA, care about very much. You could have critical information to the case and not even know it."

"Then shouldn't I talk to those doing the investigating and not you?"

Derek pushed forward. "We came to you first, but I know the two lead agents would be happy to talk to you. I thought it might be easier to have the conversation with us, though. I know you would never do anything to jeopardize anyone's safety."

"Who is in danger?" Perry asked.

Lexi spoke up, as she wanted Perry to understand how high the stakes were. "Pretty much everyone who has touched this investigation."

A deep frown pulled on Perry's lips. "I think you're assuming I know things that I simply don't know."

"Anything, however small, might be able to help us." Lexi hoped that being encouraging would help their cause.

"Why don't we start with who at the DoD called you and what they asked you for?" Derek suggested.

"All right. That's easy enough. The person who called from the DoD is Alex Gomez, but he told me he was calling for someone else."

"Do you know who?" Lexi asked.

Perry shook his head.

"That's a lot of layers." Lexi thought about the implications of a further cover-up.

"And what was Alex's request of you?" Derek asked.

Perry leaned back in his chair. "He wanted to know how the Rogers case was going. He said that someone at the DoD was asking him to check into the status and to push for a quick resolution—one that made the guilty person pay. He suggested a speedy plea deal would be best for all parties."

"Did you wonder why the DoD would care about a civilian construction worker?" Derek asked.

Perry looked down at the conference table before answering. "Honestly, I didn't think that much about any of it. Alex and I served on a nonprofit board together a few years ago and became friends. So once he made the ask, I went directly to you, as the lead prosecutor on the case, and conveyed the request. After that, he followed up with me again, and that's when I went to you a second time to ask for an update. But once I heard about the suspect's death, I thought that none of this would matter."

"And you didn't think any of this was strange?" Lexi couldn't help but ask.

Perry gave a shrug. "In my job, I get calls all the time about cases. It just goes with the territory. So I treated this the way I would treat any request, but maybe more seriously since it was from a trusted friend who worked at the Pentagon. I had no reason to read anything nefarious into it—just the opposite. I thought both he and I were helping reach the best solution for everyone."

He seemed like he was being forthright and honest, and there was really no reason he'd have a direct role in any of this. But Perry's story only made Lexi more suspicious about how deep the conspiracy and cover-up might go.

"If I'm reading this situation right, you two think there is something nefarious going on here?" Perry asked.

"Unfortunately so," Derek said. "But we have a million questions and very few answers."

"I'm happy to connect you with Alex." Perry pulled a card out of his suit jacket and wrote on it. "This is his direct line. If something bad is going on here, I'd have a really hard time believing Alex has anything to do with it. He's a straight shooter. A real stand-up guy."

"It's possible he was just a conduit. We're seeing a lot of that," Lexi said.

Perry stood. "Well, if you two will excuse me, I have other matters I need to handle. Derek, please keep me informed. I want to do my best to protect this office from any blowback."

What he really meant was to protect *himself* from it. Spoken like a man with real political aspirations, just as Derek had told her.

Derek rose from his chair. "Will do."

"It was nice to meet you, Lieutenant," Perry said, turning to her.

"Likewise, sir."

Perry exited the conference room, and silence filled the space. Her heartbeat thumped. "We need to talk to Alex Gomez." She turned to Derek. "I can get us into the Pentagon. We just have to hope that he'll talk to us."

"Well, if Perry was telling the truth about his friend, then it shouldn't be a big deal."

Lexi nodded. "I guess we're about to find out."

◆

Marco walked into the interrogation room with Bailey at his side. Barnett had quickly responded to their request for an interview. And while he'd brought his attorney, that was to be expected. It was also not a surprise that Barnett had a different lawyer from Mink.

The attorney rose and stretched out her hand. "I'm Evie Leonard, and I represent Mr. Barnett."

They all exchanged pleasantries and had a seat.

"Mr. Barnett, thank you for taking time out of your busy schedule to come in today. Have you spoken with Mr. Mink about the investigation?" Marco knew the CEO almost certainly had, but he had to ask.

"Yes. He debriefed me after you spoke to him."

"Good. So you understand the situation we have here."

Barnett looked at him. "I'd still like to hear it from you directly. Sometimes, as CEO, I get a sanitized version of events."

Bailey shifted in her seat. "It's pretty simple, actually. We have evidence showing that the three men who have been murdered were all employees of WSI—but not in the traditional sense. They were working secretive or off-book jobs. Now they're all dead. We're trying to get to the bottom of that."

Barnett shook his head. "It really is a tragedy. I hate to lose anyone. Even though the type of work we do at WSI is high risk, losing someone stateside is even more difficult to come to grips with."

"Let's start at the beginning," Marco said. "Mr. Mink told us that Battle came to him seeking employment. Is that how you remember it?"

Barnett rubbed his chin. "Yes, I believe that's correct. I remember because we were excited about the opportunity to work with someone of his caliber. Then he suggested two of his friends, and we took them all on."

"And you did that knowing two of them were full-time military?" Bailey's tone was one step shy of accusatory.

"I realize it's a bit unorthodox, but truth be told, we weren't that concerned about it. If these men wanted to take on additional work, we were happy to have them. How they handled the military was up to them."

"And you wired them cash payments to an offshore bank account?"

"Don't answer that," Evie interjected.

"We aren't trying to come after you for tax fraud, but we are very interested in their murders, because there are three men dead, and they are all connected to your company, sir." Bailey was more fired up than Marco had ever seen her.

"Agent Ryan, I don't appreciate your tone." Evie's hazel eyes narrowed.

Barnett held up his hand. "No. I respect Agent Ryan's passion on the topic, but I will also take my counsel's advice on that last question. I think what you're really trying to get at is whether I have any information about their deaths, and unfortunately, I don't. If I had anything, I would've come forward immediately."

Marco took a moment to size up Barnett. Was this man telling the truth? "What about speculation? Any theories about what could've happened to them?"

Barnett clasped his hands on the table. "You know, I've thought a good deal about it, and maybe they crossed the wrong guy or organization. They were willing to take on extra work even though their superiors surely wouldn't have allowed it. That tells me these men were risk takers, and that type of man usually engages in behaviors that might not always be on the up-and-up."

"Like what?" Bailey asked.

Barnett let out a loud sigh. "This is pure speculation, but I heard that Rogers was quite a gambler. So maybe the three of them got wrapped up in something like that and then crossed the wrong guy when they couldn't pay up. We paid them well, but given they only did side jobs for us, it wouldn't have been enough to cover large debts."

Marco glanced at Bailey. She frowned but didn't say anything.

"Do you know where Rogers liked to gamble?" Marco asked.

Barnett shook his head. "I don't. Like I said, I'm basing this off the rumor mill, not any specific knowledge I have. And . . ."

"Go on," Bailey said.

"There is a chance that what happened to these men is tied to their work for us. I would hate that to be true, but I'm putting it out there because I know you'll be asking about that."

"That gets us to what their assignments were. We got pushback from Mr. Mink on that."

"I know, and I got the proper clearances to be able to provide some information on that subject." Barnett nodded to his attorney.

She opened her briefcase, pulled out a piece of paper, and slid it across the table.

Marco skimmed the page. "This is short on details."

"We still have active ongoing operations all over the globe. I'm sure you can appreciate our need for discretion, but at the same time we wanted to provide you with what we could."

"And I'm afraid that's all the time we have for today." Evie touched her client's arm. "Mr. Barnett needs to get back to his schedule. We already pushed some meetings around to accommodate this."

Marco wasn't going to make a scene about asking more questions. They needed to dig into what Barnett had provided. "We'll be in touch. There's someone outside the door to escort you out."

Once it was just Marco and Bailey alone in the room, he turned toward her.

"Before you ask," she said, "I'm going to check back with Organized Crime again on the gambling angle."

He nodded. "What do you think of this list?"

Bailey ran a finger down the page. "It gives us the type of work, which we already knew was personal security services. Then it provides dates and regions or countries. But it's not very specific. For example, the March entry says France. It doesn't go beyond that."

"That doesn't give us much to go on."

"I know we probably think he was just blowing smoke, but what if we're wrong and it actually does have something to do with one of these jobs?"

"Then we have even more work to do than we thought."

CHAPTER
NINETEEN

Izzy took a cat nap on the quick flight down to Georgia. They were making their second run at P. J.'s commanding officer and anyone else they thought they could talk to and get information from. By the time they got on base, Izzy was filled with energy and ready to go.

"This is going to be a lot different than our first meeting. I'll just tell you that right now," Jay said.

Izzy was glad they were back. She felt there was still more they could uncover. "We didn't get very deep with Colonel Hayden last time."

"Well, that's going to change." There was determination in Jay's eyes.

Izzy wasn't so sure that the colonel would be excited to see them again. "I guess we'll see how he takes a second visit."

Once they got through the base bureaucracy, they were met once again by First Lieutenant Shi, who got them settled into a conference room.

"How long do you think the colonel will make us wait?" Izzy asked Jay.

"Not sure. It may depend on how much of a pain in his side he thinks we are. On one hand, I think he'd welcome our presence and our desire to solve the murder of his own man, but sometimes that can all go sideways, especially if the truth is inconvenient."

"You can't really think that the colonel had anything to do with this?" She had to keep holding on to the belief that there were good guys out there. There were far too many evil aspects to this investigation.

"Probably not, but at this point, I'm not taking anything off the table. People could be pawns in a deadly game and not even realize it." Jay's eyes softened. "Looked like you were able to nap on the flight."

"Yes. No nightmares." Izzy stared out the window. She'd thought long and hard about whether she wanted to tell Jay what was behind her strange behavior. She'd taken his advice and started seeing a counselor. Her counselor had suggested that it would be helpful to open up to him as a trusted friend. "Jay, there's something else."

He turned to face her. "What is it?"

"I think I'm ready to talk about what has been bothering me." Her breath caught.

Jay looked right in her eyes. "Izzy, it's completely up to you how much you want or need to share."

"I know. The counselor thought it might be good to talk to you. Since you're one of the only people I trust." In the short time they'd known each other, she'd come to rely on Jay. "In fact, I just spoke about this for the first time ever with her, and that's when she urged me to tell you. I think she knows that we've become close and that I feel safe with you."

He placed his hand on her shoulder. "Izzy, whatever happened to you, you're safe now. And I have your back no matter what. Whatever it is, I'm here to listen."

She believed Jay was telling the truth. There was no doubt in her mind that he was trustworthy. Although that didn't make what she was about to say any easier. "There's no good way to say this."

A frown spread across his face. "I'm used to difficult. It's best just to get it out there. If you want to, that is."

And she did. As she looked into his kind eyes—he reminded her so much of her father—she knew he would be there for her once she revealed her darkest secret. "When I was at Arlington PD, I was assaulted by one of the senior officers."

Jay's eyes widened, but he didn't say anything.

Izzy sighed. "It could've been even worse if I hadn't been successful in fighting him off." She paused. "I know it seems unbelievable."

Jay's eyes narrowed. "Izzy, I believe you. Don't ever doubt that."

His affirmation was just what she needed to be able to continue. "I was an idiot. He told me he wanted to talk about my career, that he had some ways he thought I could improve as an officer. I was naïve and met with him alone in his office late after hours. He said that was the only time he could meet." As the words came out, the memories gripped her in fear. But she knew she didn't have anything to fear from Jay. He was an honorable man, unlike the heinous man who'd attacked her. "The next thing I knew, he was putting his hands all over me. At first I was in shock, but then as things escalated, he became more violent and aggressive. My survival instincts must have kicked in, because I fought him like crazy with everything I had. I was scared to death at what I thought he was going to do to me. Thankfully, I got away. But I knew after that night that I could never stay at Arlington PD."

Jay looked her in the eyes. "Izzy, don't for a minute *ever* blame yourself for this. It is not your fault at all. It's the monster who did this to you. He's the one in the wrong. You were completely innocent."

"I appreciate you saying that," she responded softly.

"It's the truth, and don't ever doubt it. Did you report him?"

Ashamed, Izzy shook her head. "No. I know I should've, but I felt so insecure and afraid. I thought no one would believe me. He was a highly respected sergeant, and I was a nobody. And it looked so bad. Why did I go to his office so late? I wanted to try to protect my reputation. I see now that was a cowardly thing to do, and I've been carrying around that baggage." Her voice cracked, but she fought to keep it together.

"What's his name?" Jay asked.

Fear shot through her. "You can't do anything about it. If I'm not willing to testify, then nothing will ever happen to him."

Jay shook his head. "That's not entirely true. Please, Izzy. The name."

She didn't even know if she could say his name. Speaking it made it seem even more real. "Sergeant Henry Tybee."

"The man we met at Arlington PD." Jay blew out a breath. "I'm so sorry you had to face him. If I'd known anything about this, there's no way I would've let you within a hundred feet of that sorry excuse for a man." Jay jotted down the name on the back of one of his business cards and put it back in his pocket.

Gratitude and relief swelled within her, lightening the fear and shame. "Jay, I can't thank you enough for having my back. After this case is over, I'd really like to stay in touch. I hope you take this in the most positive way possible, but there aren't a lot of men like you out there. Especially someone who would mentor a young woman like me and do it with such integrity." Jay's moral compass was undeniable. She was coming to realize that his faith probably had a lot to do with that. On that front, she was still a work in progress.

"Izzy, I'm so sorry that man hurt you, but I wouldn't be a very good friend if I didn't tell you that there are still good men out there. Men who will fight to protect you and never do you harm. You have to search harder to find them, but they are out there. I can assure you of that."

Those words made her smile. "A lot harder."

The door opened, and they rose to greet the colonel. His cool blue eyes actually went to Izzy first and then to Jay.

"Agent Graves, Agent Cole, I would say it's good to see you again, but I figure this is far from a social visit. Please sit down."

They took their seats, and Jay started in. "You're right, Colonel. Thanks for meeting with us again on such short notice."

"What is it I can do for you two?" The colonel sat up straight in his seat, shoulders back.

"Colonel, sir, we've been able to unearth more information since the last time we visited, and we need to run some things by you."

So far Jay was being mild mannered and deferential. She wondered how long that would last.

"Proceed," Hayden said.

Jay pushed onward. "We have evidence that Wexford was working at Whitfield Security International along with the two other men who were killed—as you'll remember, one of whom was a SEAL. Did you know anything about that employment?"

The colonel's expression didn't change. "Absolutely not."

"Are you sure?" Izzy took a chance by asking and waited for the fallout.

Hayden's eyes zeroed in on her. "Agent Cole, I would have *never* approved one of my Rangers working for WSI. That's just not how we operate around here. It is completely out of the question. End of story."

"So, Colonel, if Wexford had come to you seeking permission, you would've denied him?" Jay asked.

"You bet I would." The colonel's voice got louder with each word. "We're the US Army. We're not a for-profit company. WSI does some good work, and they serve an important purpose, but it is far different from the mission of the Army."

"Do you have any idea what he could've been doing for them?" Jay asked.

"Wexford was a highly skilled Ranger. He could do just about anything he put his mind to."

"Let me lay this out for you, Colonel, and get your thoughts." Jay leaned in. "We've learned that the Navy SEAL went to WSI looking for work and then specifically recommended Wexford and the civilian to be hired as well. What does that sound like to you?"

Hayden looked down for a moment before resuming eye contact. "It doesn't sound like anything good."

Izzy had to ask. "And if anyone in the Army had told them to seek out such a job, you would've known about it?"

Blotches of red crept up the colonel's neck. "Of course I would have. No one would blatantly ignore the chain of command like that."

Izzy wondered how Hayden could be so sure of that fact. On a hunch, she continued. "What if the direction had come from the civilian side at the DoD?" She'd gotten an update from Lexi last night that they were following a lead there, so why not throw out a flyer?

"I still think I would have been consulted, but I can't guarantee it once you get outside the direct Army chain of command." His face continued to redden. "And I can guarantee that I would not take kindly to that type of blatant circumvention of authority."

"Then we'll be asking for your assistance to help us try to figure out what these men were up to, because whatever it was, it most likely got them killed," Jay said flatly.

"What can I do?" the colonel asked.

"Honestly, we're open to hearing your theories. What do you think they could've been doing? And whatever it was, would it have been enough for the orders to come from WSI? There has to be a reason these three men were murdered."

"What about the suspect you had in custody?"

Jay looked at Izzy, so she responded. "Tobias Kappen is dead. They are still looking into his death because although it appears to be a suicide, we all suspect foul play."

Jay picked up the thread. "So as you can imagine, that has only raised more red flags for our investigation. Kappen had an alibi for Wexford's murder, but that was only because we were able to show that base records had been hacked—initially they showed that Kappen was off base during the murder, but that definitely wasn't the case."

"Let me get this straight. You believe someone set this other SEAL up to take the fall, and then killed him but made it look like a suicide?"

Jay crossed his arms. "I know it sounds farfetched, but the facts are leading us in that direction."

"And what is WSI saying?" the colonel asked.

"Not a lot. NCIS and the FBI have interrogated the CEO and

VP. They are being somewhat cooperative so far. The VP is the one who claimed WSI didn't recruit these men."

Hayden rubbed his chin. "Something doesn't add up."

Izzy tried to stay calm. "Our thoughts exactly."

"If there is something more sinister going on here, I doubt my phone calls are going to get any confessions out of anyone. But I'll do my part and see what I can find out. I assume you'll be making WSI tell you what our guys were working on?"

"Yes, sir," Jay answered. "They threw up some initial security clearance roadblocks, but here is the list we do have. It's not very detailed, but it's something." He slid a piece of paper across the table.

The colonel didn't immediately respond, taking a minute to read the list. "I'll look into this. I'll also circle back up with the SEAL's CO and see if the two of us can put our heads together and come up with anything."

"Thank you, sir."

"Whatever you need. At first I thought this might just be an awful coincidence, but after hearing everything you've told me, this sounds rotten to the core. And it happened on my watch to one of my men. That's unacceptable, and I'm here to provide the full support of the Army in this investigation."

After they spent the afternoon reinterviewing other Rangers on base, Izzy and Jay boarded the plane home.

Izzy felt a wave of fatigue come over her. "I feel like this afternoon was a waste of time. Nobody had anything new."

"But at least we've covered our bases."

"Who is pulling the strings here? Do you think it's Mink and WSI?"

"Hopefully Marco and Bailey are closer to finding that out."

Bailey sat in the NCIS break room, eating a chocolate donut she didn't need while Marco was in NCIS Director Mercer's office, briefing her on the case.

"Agent Ryan?"

Bailey looked up to see a tall blond man in a dark suit standing in front of her.

"Yes, that's me."

He stretched out his hand. "I'm Julian Mayfield from the DoD. I work with Alex Gomez's team."

Ah, this was the part of the case that Lexi had been working on tirelessly. "Nice to meet you."

"There have been some late-breaking developments related to your investigation. I was told to come pick you up and take you to a classified briefing at the Pentagon."

Finally they were getting somewhere, but she didn't say that out loud. She didn't want to seem ungrateful. This guy was just the messenger. "That's great. We just need to wait for Agent Agostini to finish briefing the director."

Julian shook his head. "I just checked with the director's office, and he's going to be a while longer. My boss doesn't want to delay the briefing. We're starting to get pressure from all sides on this and need to stop the bleeding ASAP before this thing gets completely out of control."

"I understand that." A surge of energy went through her at the thought that someone at the Pentagon might be able to tell them what was going on. Maybe this nightmare was about to be over. She gathered her things and followed Julian out of the room.

They walked down the long hallway, and then Julian turned to the left.

"Wait, Julian, the exit is this way." She pointed down toward her right.

"Oh, there's another exit this way. The service exit. Haven't you used it before?" he asked.

"No. I've only gone in and out the main way." She was pretty set in her routine.

"This is quicker. I promise. That's where I'm parked, so we'd have to walk around the entire building if we went out the main door."

Not wanting to argue, she followed him, anxious to hear what the DoD had to say for itself in this mess. She wondered if Gomez was going to explain his involvement and how it was all linked to WSI.

They rounded the corner, and she noticed that Julian had started to sweat. It wasn't that warm inside. She took another look at him, and a warning bell sounded in her head.

"Who did you say you worked for again?" she asked.

"Alex Gomez."

When his blue eyes made contact with hers, she knew he was lying about something. About what, she didn't know, but it was enough to make her want to stop and talk this out.

But before she could do anything else, he drew his weapon and pointed it at her.

"You're not going to shoot me in NCIS HQ." She said the words with more confidence than she felt.

"I don't want to shoot you, but I will." He pulled her in front of him and pressed the gun into her back while at the same time dislodging her weapon from her side and taking it.

"If you're not going to kill me, then what do you want with me?" She stumbled a step forward, purposely trying to move as slowly as possible.

"I need information from you."

She looked over her shoulder. "Then you'll have to kill me, because I'll never talk."

Julian squeezed her shoulder and leaned down. "That's not my call."

His breath in her ear sent a chill down her back. "Who do you really work for? Is it Cullen Mink? Someone else at WSI? Someone in the Pentagon?"

As Julian took a right and started down another long hallway, two people entered the hall from the other end.

"Don't even think about it," Julian whispered.

Bailey feared for her life, but she was more worried that if she spoke up, Julian would kill the two unsuspecting people walking toward them. So she let them pass without saying a word.

"Good girl," Julian said.

She wanted to punch his lights out, but she couldn't let her anger overtake her. There had to be a way out of this. They were still inside NCIS HQ, but pretty soon they'd be taking this service exit that she'd never even seen.

Bailey believed that someone had to be monitoring that area, especially if it was where NCIS took deliveries. She should have insisted on waiting for Marco, but she'd been so anxious for a break in the case that she'd just assumed this guy was legit. He'd gotten into NCIS, which meant he had credentials—whether they were his or stolen remained to be seen.

"When we get to the exit, we're both going to flash our credentials to whoever is working the area. If you don't, you die along with them. And I've read your file, Agent Ryan. You're not the type to put others in harm's way."

"Who are you?" She looked back at him.

"We'll have more time to get acquainted once we get out of here. Then you can tell us all your secrets."

Why did he think she had some special insight? The look he gave her sickened her. She had to do something. "How did you get into NCIS? How did you get credentials?"

He flashed her a sinister smile. "It isn't that hard to steal from someone if you know what you're doing. And once you're inside, if you act with authority, people will just tell you what you want to know. It worked out well that you were alone. Even better than expected. If I'd had to take both of you with me, I would have, but this is much cleaner."

She didn't like the sound of any of that. This man had carefully planned this.

When they reached the service exit, Julian opened it, and she walked a few steps. She saw the loading dock where a few people were working. It was clear that Julian—or whoever he was—didn't think she would make a move. That gave her the upper hand because he'd be caught off guard.

Lord, I really have no great plan here. Please protect all of these innocent people from harm and give me the strength to get through this.

Taking a deep breath, she spun around. "Gun!" she yelled as loudly as she could.

She slammed the heel of her hand into Julian's nose and heard a crunch. She'd probably broken it. It was a move she'd practiced a thousand times, but she'd never done it with as much force as at that precise moment.

Someone in the loading dock had pressed the alarm, because it started to blare, indicating a security breach. She could tell there was bustling around her, but everyone was confused about where the threat was coming from.

Julian lunged toward her, and she sidestepped him. Unfortunately, he had her side arm.

A man came running out of the building, distracting her, and Julian lunged again. She tried to grapple with him, but he was too strong and was able to regain a tight hold on her. He pressed his weapon against her head.

"Everyone back up, or I will kill her," Julian barked.

She had to buy time. "Come on, Julian. This isn't going to end well. Just let me go so we can talk."

"I will shoot her!" He ignored her words but tightened his grip.

Lord, help me. How was she going to get out of this alive?

CHAPTER
TWENTY

Marco had just finished briefing the director and was on his way to find Bailey when the security alarm sounded. The blaring noise gave him an instant headache.

He wasn't sure what was going on, but it had been a few months since the alarm had sounded, and that had been a drill. He didn't think this was a drill, or as a supervisor, he would have been notified.

After the brief wave of annoyance passed, his mind immediately went to worst-case scenarios. Marco ran down the hall and almost mowed over another agent.

"Sanchez, do you know what's happening?"

Sanchez nodded. "Yeah, there's word of a hostage situation at the loading dock."

Not wasting a second, Marco sprinted down the hall to the stairway, then took the steps three at a time. Maybe this had nothing to do with their case, but he wasn't taking any chances.

Once he reached the main floor, he ran through a maze of

people heading in the opposite direction. As he neared the loading dock, he saw a swarm of security personnel.

"You need to stay back," one of them told him.

"Who is the hostage?"

"A blond female. We don't have identification yet."

Marco's stomach dropped. "She's FBI. This has to be related to the case we're working. You need to let me through."

After a moment, the NCIS security guard relented. Marco pushed his way through and stood at the open service door.

Outside a tall blond man pointed a gun at Bailey's temple. He had his arm wrapped tightly around her waist. The gunman knew that he was so close to Bailey it would make a shot at him unlikely.

Marco stepped out the door. "Hey," he yelled.

That got the man's attention. "I told you, back off or I'll shoot her."

"I'm Agent Marco Agostini. I work with Agent Ryan."

A flash of recognition flickered through the man's eyes.

"Yes, you know who I am." Marco took another step. "Take me instead of her." Bailey's eyes widened at Marco's statement. He inched a step closer. "It's a good trade and you know it. I can get you out of here in one piece. It's your best chance."

The man laughed. "I'm the one with all the leverage right now, and she's the one I want. So here's how it's going to go. I'm going to take Agent Ryan with me. We're driving out of here. If anyone tries to stop or follow us, I will kill her. It's that simple."

"If you kill her, you're a dead man." Rage bubbled up in Marco like a volcano.

"Then it appears that it's better for everyone to just let us go."

"What's your name?" Marco asked.

"He told me it was Julian," Bailey answered.

"One last chance, Julian." Marco couldn't let this go any further. He pulled his gun.

"You won't take the shot," Julian said. "You'd be too afraid you'd hit your partner."

Marco was one of the best shots at NCIS, but could he risk it? He looked directly into Bailey's eyes, trying to read her. She gave him the slightest of nods. She wanted him to take the shot. She trusted him. And that made him even more fearful.

Lord, I need your mighty hand on me right now. I can't do this on my own.

He made one last plea. "Julian, you can take me."

"No. Enough! I'm taking her."

Marco drew in a breath and steadied himself, blocking out everything around him. Time seemed to stop as he stared the attacker in the eyes and made the hardest decision of his life. He'd trained for a moment like this, but it paled in comparison. One wrong move on his part, and he could kill the woman he'd come to care so much about. But the risk of this man taking her was too great.

Once he'd made the decision, he didn't hesitate. He pulled the trigger.

The bullet hit Julian squarely in the forehead.

Marco exhaled. It had been a kill shot, but he'd had no choice with Bailey's life on the line.

Bailey ran toward him, and he grabbed her in a tight hug, not caring what others would think.

That had been far too close. Bailey could have been killed. He couldn't let there be a next time.

◆

Lexi and Derek had made their way through the bureaucracy of the Pentagon and were waiting to be seen by Alex Gomez, senior advisor to the deputy assistant secretary for Russia. Right before they'd gotten into the building, Lexi had taken a frantic phone call from Izzy. She'd learned of a scary hostage situation at NCIS, and Lexi planned to ask Alex about these new developments. She was more convinced than ever that there had to be some nefarious connection between the DoD and WSI.

A short, stocky man with thick black hair emerged and greeted them, and they exchanged introductions.

"Please come into my office," Gomez said.

They followed him into his office and took a seat at his small conference room table.

"What can I do for you?" Gomez asked.

Lexi started. "I'm working a case involving the deaths of a Navy SEAL, an Army Ranger, and a civilian. I believe you've heard of that case."

Gomez raised an eyebrow. "Yes, I have."

"We wanted to talk to you because we understand that you made a call to the Arlington district attorney about the Rogers case. We wanted to understand why you made that call."

"I made the call because someone else asked me to. I didn't have any direct interest in the case."

Derek leaned forward. "And who asked you?"

"Does that really matter?" Gomez asked.

"Actually, it does." Lexi was about to drop the newest development on him. "We just had someone calling himself Julian Mayfield get into NCIS headquarters and take an FBI agent hostage at gunpoint. He's now dead."

"What?" Gomez's eyes widened.

"Mayfield claimed you sent him."

Gomez lifted his hands. "I can assure you that Julian Mayfield is alive and well. I just saw him not more than ten minutes ago. He's here, right down the hall."

"You should check to see if the real Julian Mayfield's credentials have been stolen."

Gomez nodded. "I'm going to have to make some phone calls before I can reveal any details to you about what I know."

"Can you do that ASAP?" Lexi asked. "People's lives are on the line here."

"Understood. But as you can imagine, I'm dealing with people who have very busy schedules. Leave me all your contact information, and I'll get back to you as soon as I possibly can." Gomez stood.

Lexi knew when she had been dismissed, so she did the only thing she could and shook Gomez's hand before she and Derek exited the office. Once they were out of sight, she turned toward him. "He was hiding something."

"That's an understatement." Derek took her hands in his. "He might even be behind this entire thing, and we just sat there and confronted him. He'll know we're on to him."

"We don't know that for certain."

"We certainly can't rule it out."

She thought for a minute as they made their way back through the maze that was the Pentagon. "Did he seem like a killer to you?"

Derek gave her a scolding look, but he softened it with a smile. "Lexi, we've seen enough in our line of work to know that looks can be deceiving."

"I know. I guess I just don't want to believe that a high-ranking Pentagon official would be involved in this mess."

Derek picked up his pace. "We need to get out of here. If we just rocked the boat, I don't want to be around for the fallout."

After much deliberation, Bailey had relented and was now sitting on the couch with Marco in the living room of an FBI safe house. It was located about twenty minutes north of NCIS in a sought-after neighborhood in the city of Occoquan, known for housing many young professionals. The light blue Colonial-style home was positioned midway through the subdivision. Bailey knew the FBI had picked the location because there were two ways to get out of the neighborhood instead of only one entrance. Given the security issues, you always wanted multiple ways out.

"Until we know exactly what we're dealing with here, this safe house is the best option for you," Marco said for the fourth time. "I know it isn't your first choice, but we have to deal with the situation we have in front of us."

"What's the word on everyone else?" She wanted to make sure they were all okay.

"They're safe. We didn't think we needed to move them, but they all have security present."

"I'm not going to try to play tough here. There have been too many attempts on our lives for us to write this off." She rubbed the back of her neck.

"Bailey, he wanted *you*. Not me. You saw his reaction when I offered myself up. He had absolutely zero interest in me."

Her stomach churned at Marco's statement. "I know," she replied.

He shifted in his seat. "There has to be a reason they are so focused on you and what you know. Julian, or whoever he was, specifically wanted to interrogate you. And he seemed dead set on it no matter the cost. They think you know something, and, honestly, I don't think we've figured out what they believe we have."

"It's almost like he thinks I have some special knowledge." She bit the inside of her cheek. "I wish I did."

Marco rubbed his temples. "Think back. Is there anything in your notes that were stolen that could possibly send them down this path?"

Bailey thought hard. It seemed like a lifetime ago. "I was just brainstorming at that point. Honestly, I don't even have a great memory of what I had written down."

"NCIS security is working on how the Julian poser got inside, but it appears that he stole the real Julian's credentials. Lexi thinks Alex Gomez at the DoD could be involved in this."

"A DoD cover-up of some sort with WSI? But for what?"

"We've served the subpoena on WSI for all of their DoD contracts within the past year, so that might give us some leads if the lawyers play ball. I started the cooperation discussion with Mink's lawyer first."

Bailey knew this song and dance all too well. "We need to be able to sweeten the pot for Mink. Say we'll put in a good word with the prosecutors if he is cooperative, but if he shuts us down, then there will be no leniency at all."

"I clearly planted those seeds with Theo Channing. If he knows what's good for Mink, he'll give us what we need. We have subpoenas out to WSI as a company and to Mink personally. I think you're right that we'll get a lot further with him individually than with Barnett. WSI will be fully lawyered up and will try to drag this out as long as possible."

"I know." She looked up at him, and they held each other's gaze for a moment. "Thank you for what you did today. You saved my life."

Marco scooted closer and held her hand. "I'm not going to lie. I was afraid, but I knew that I couldn't risk him taking you away."

"Is that why you decided to take the shot?"

He nodded. "Yeah. I'll tell you, though, God was really watching over us today. I couldn't have made that decision without Him."

"Do you ever question Him?"

"God?" Marco asked.

"Yeah."

"Of course, but at the end of the day, I have to keep my eyes on what really matters. As awful as this life can get, there's an eternity ahead of us. This is just our temporary situation. A fallen world, and we're all broken people. I know I am."

Bailey let his words soak in. "I like to think that my faith is strong, but sometimes doubts creep in. Like why did those men have to die? Why did my parents have to die?" Her voice started to tremble. "Why did God spare me again today?"

Marco leaned in toward her. "It wasn't time for you to leave this earth, and while we can't claim to know all of God's ways, that's why we have to have faith."

His words rang true to her. "Sometimes that's easier said than done, but the Lord has protected me and held me close since we started this case. I can't deny that. I feel it deeply within. I just don't understand why me and not others."

"I don't have all the answers, but I'm always willing to listen to whatever is on your mind."

"I know you are. I'm used to being so independent and staying inside my emotional cocoon to make sure I don't get hurt again. But it's really hard to go through this life alone." As she said the words, she couldn't believe she was being so blatantly honest.

Marco squeezed her hand. "That's why it's important to have people around you to support and encourage you. To pull you up when you fall, and for you to do the same thing for them when they need you."

Her heart felt like it was going to explode, listening to his earnest words. "I don't know how I could've gotten through any of this without you. Not just you saving my life today, but everything. I couldn't ask for anyone better to be by my side."

Marco dropped her hand and put his arm around her, pulling her close. "When I thought I might lose you today, I was scared there might never be a chance for the two of us. And that reality hit me hard."

Her breath caught as she looked into his warm dark eyes. "I know. I was scared too. I was mad at myself for blindly following him instead of insisting that we wait for you. I was so ready for answers that I didn't question him further."

"You'd have no reason to believe that someone inside HQ would've had an ulterior motive."

"Now we know that's not the case," she said.

"You're safe here. This location is strictly need-to-know."

She rested her head on his shoulder. "As an agent, I'm used to taking care of myself, but being here with you makes me feel safe, and I'm okay with that."

"If you're worried about letting down your guard when it comes to me, I can assure you that this isn't a one-way street."

She smiled. "Marco, don't even try to act like you aren't a ladies' man."

He laughed. "You're concerned I'm some type of player?"

"Am I right?" She lifted her head and made eye contact.

"Oh, Bailey, I'm not. I'm the type of guy it's easy for women to be in the friend zone with, and that's been perfectly fine with me."

If that was the case, then she wanted to know why he had changed his mind when it came to her. "So why don't you want to keep me in the friend zone?"

Marco didn't answer. Instead he leaned down and pressed his

lips to hers. A tingle of excitement shot through her as he deepened the kiss. There was no denying how physically attracted she was to him, but this was about so much more than that. And that was the part that really scared her. It was his kind and protective heart. His smart and witty comebacks. It was him.

He pulled back a little. "That doesn't seem like two people who should be in the friend zone, does it?"

She couldn't deny that, so she didn't even bother. She just rested her head back on his shoulder and enjoyed the moment of peace she felt in his arms.

◆

The next day Bailey sat across from Layla in a small NCIS conference room. They had just finished the lunches Layla had brought in for them. If Marco asked what Layla was doing here, Bailey could just say that the two of them were having lunch and Layla had wanted to check on her. That way there would be no suspicion on his part.

"Thanks for coming."

"Bailey, you never ask for anything from me, so I know this has to be important." Layla's big brown eyes focused on her.

"It is important. This is actually not something I want to do, but I feel like I've run out of options." Bailey had thought through the scenarios a million times as she lay awake last night in the safe house. She couldn't tell Marco, because she couldn't blow Layla's cover without her approval.

Layla placed a hand on Bailey's arm. "No matter what it is, I'll do whatever I can."

"You're one of the best friends I've ever had, and I hate to bring you into this, but I think maybe you can help." Bailey prepared herself for a big request.

"Go on," Layla said.

Bailey gave Layla a quick recap of the case and where they were. Then she pulled the photo of Michael Rogers out of her bag. "This man is a phantom. Supposedly he's in construction, but we know that according to Cullen Mink at WSI, Battle asked that Rogers be hired. There were also some wild rumors about him being a hit man at the construction site. Since we also believe that someone at the DoD could be dirty, I need your help. Can you do some digging and see if you can figure out anything on your end? See if the Agency has a file on Rogers? Anything might be able to help us at this point. I've got his prints too. I know the CIA has files on a lot of people, and if Rogers was working for WSI, I'm hoping the CIA knew about him."

Layla looked down at the picture and frowned. "I'll dig around and let you know. This case has gotten extremely dangerous, and I'm worried about you."

"Thank you." Bailey squeezed her friend's hand. "While I'm making requests, if you can give me anything you have on Alex Gomez from the DoD, that would also be helpful."

"He's the one you think might be dirty?" Layla drummed her fingers on the table.

"Yeah. A man posing as someone working for him is the one who broke into NCIS and took me hostage." She'd already told Layla about the harrowing ordeal over the phone.

"Any luck identifying that man?"

"Not yet." Bailey had to be completely transparent with her friend. The stakes were too high for anything else. "If this is as big as I think it is, you need to be really discreet. I don't want anything happening to you."

Layla leaned in. "I've got this."

Bailey didn't doubt Layla's ability. If she hadn't thought Layla was up for it, she would have never gone to her in the first place. But she was still worried. "I know you're at the top of your game, but I just can't have someone I care about getting hurt because I dragged them into it."

"You haven't dragged me anywhere. I'm going in with eyes wide open. I'll see what I can find out and get back to you ASAP." Layla paused. "You didn't tell your handsome partner about this, did you?"

Bailey shook her head. "You know I wouldn't do that without your permission."

Layla smiled. "I know. You've been rock solid on my cover since we graduated." She picked up her small purse. "How is it going between you and Mr. Smoldering Dark Eyes?"

Bailey felt her cheeks flush. "We're working as hard as we can on the case."

Layla narrowed her eyes. "Bailey, I know you. I can tell you have feelings for him. In fact, this is the first time I've seen you truly interested in someone since law school when you had that crush on the con-law teaching assistant."

"That *never* went anywhere."

"I know. But this—this *could* go somewhere. He seems like a great guy. The total package."

"And you know this how?"

Layla patted her hand. "In my line of work, reading people is key. He's one of the good guys. That much I know." She took a moment, seeming to gather her thoughts. "And, Bailey, I know you've lost so much in this life with losing your parents, but please don't let the fear of being hurt keep you from seeing what possibilities there could be with Marco."

She was spot-on. "It's like you can see right through me."

"And you me. Let's not even get started on how messed up I am in the relationship department. You have a chance at something good here. I say embrace that chance and take a leap."

Bailey desperately wanted to do what her friend was suggesting, but it wasn't easy. "It's scary to put yourself out there."

"It is. But you met Marco at this point in your life. I believe that God can use even this awful investigation to bring about good things."

And the thing was that Bailey did too.

CHAPTER
TWENTY-ONE

Izzy took Jay up on his offer to go to church with his family again and had enjoyed the service. Jay's wife, Georgia, was lovely and welcoming and had invited Izzy over to lunch afterward.

Izzy had tried to help Georgia in the kitchen, but Georgia had insisted that Izzy was a guest, and that was that. So now Izzy sat in the living room, taking in the cute Victorian-style house. When the front door opened, she stood up, not sure who would be coming through the door.

A guy with dark blond hair and brown eyes walked into the living room. She made eye contact and knew at that moment who he was. He had his father's eyes.

"Mom, I made it," he yelled. Then he stepped toward Izzy. "Hey," he said. "I'm Aiden Graves."

"Isabella Cole, but everyone calls me Izzy." She took his outstretched hand and gave it a shake. They connected a beat longer than she would have expected.

Jay walked into the room. "Aiden, I see you've met Izzy."

"Hey, Dad." Aiden gave his father a quick embrace.

"We weren't expecting you for lunch today," Jay said.

"I got off my shift early and wanted to surprise Mom. I didn't realize you'd have company." He eyed Izzy. "Sorry if I'm interrupting."

Jay patted his son on the back. "Nonsense. I'm working a case with Izzy. She's an NCIS agent."

"Really?" Aiden asked.

"Yeah, I realize I don't exactly look the part." Warmth crept up her neck, and she suddenly felt extremely self-conscious.

Aiden shook his head. "Oh no, I didn't mean it like that. I just meant that it's cool you're an NCIS agent. I'm an officer with VSP."

Virginia State Patrol. She should have noticed his cop vibe right off.

"You better go say hello to your mother," Jay said.

"All right. Be back in a few." Aiden smiled at her.

Izzy turned to Jay, who was grinning widely. "What?" she asked.

"I've never seen you blush before."

She wanted to crawl in a hole. Talk about not having any finesse around cute guys. "I'm not blushing. It's just a little warm."

Jay couldn't stop smiling. "I'll get you some iced tea, then. Have a seat."

Izzy sank onto the couch and was thankful that Jay didn't push the issue. She didn't know what had happened when she shook hands with Aiden, but whatever it was, she couldn't show that reaction anymore. The last thing she needed was to crush on a cop. After what had happened to her, she'd told herself she'd never date a cop. Ever.

But after lunch she found herself alone in the living room

with Aiden while his parents insisted on cleaning up the kitchen.

"I've got to ask you something," Aiden said.

"All right."

"What's it like working with my dad?"

That was a safe topic. "It's actually great. He's really good at his job and has been there for me through some tough stuff."

Aiden beamed. "I always knew growing up that I had a special dad, but I realize it even more as a grown man. If I can be half the man he is, then I'll be ahead of the game."

She completely agreed with that statement. "I lost my dad when I was young. He was killed in the line of duty."

"Was he a cop or military?"

"Cop. His death is what inspired me to go into law enforcement. After a year at Arlington PD, I got the gig at NCIS. I'm still a rookie."

"I figured you were about my age. I'm twenty-seven."

"I'm twenty-four. And since I'm petite, a lot of people think I'm still in college."

His brown eyes softened. "That has to be tough. It's hard enough being a rookie in law enforcement as a guy. I see what my female colleagues go through, and it's even tougher. That must mean you've got a strong backbone."

She smiled. "Honestly, some days I'm not so sure."

"Do you enjoy NCIS?"

She took a moment before answering. "Yes and no. I definitely like it better than my previous job, but I can't help but wonder if I'm still not in the exact place I need to be. I figure, regardless, I'm getting a ton of amazing experience that is going to prepare me for whatever I do next."

Aiden looked down at his watch. "I have to run. I'm meeting a buddy at the range who is struggling with his shot." He paused. "But I was wondering if you'd be interested in hanging out sometime?"

Was he asking her out? She didn't even have words to respond as she just stared at him.

"It's totally okay to say no." He stood. "I'm sorry. I'm sure you're already spoken for. I don't know what I was thinking."

Izzy got up. "No, I'm not." She walked over to him and pulled out her phone.

Aiden did the same. "What's your number?"

She rattled off her number, and he put his phone back in his pocket.

"Aren't you going to give me yours too?" she asked.

Aiden smiled. "No. Call me old-fashioned, but I'll be calling you."

There were women who wouldn't have liked his response, but not Izzy. If Aiden was like his dad, then maybe he was a true gentleman. "Sounds good. It was really nice to meet you."

He offered his hand again, and she took it. They lingered for an extra moment, hand in hand, eyes locked, before Aiden said good-bye.

A bit later, Jay took Izzy back to her place. "You know, he will call."

"What?" she asked.

"If Aiden said he'll call you, he will."

"Do you disapprove?" She feared what Jay would think about this entire thing.

"Of course not. But I want to stay out of it. I think my son is amazing, but he's my son, so I'm completely biased. You'll need to form your own opinions about him."

Something was weighing on her. "I didn't know whether you'd want him to consider seeing someone as damaged as me."

He glanced at her. "What? Izzy, please don't talk like that.

You're a strong, smart woman. We all come to the table with our issues and baggage. Some of us more than others."

"I do have one request." This was important to her.

"Sure. Whatever you need, just name it."

"Let me talk to Aiden in my own time about my past. Outside counseling, you're the only person I've ever talked to about what happened to me that night."

Jay nodded. "Please don't worry about that. I would never violate your confidence. What you tell Aiden and when is completely up to you."

She let out a breath. "Thank you, Jay. That means so much to me."

"Like I said, I'm not going to get involved, but I'll put in one plug for my boy, and then I won't say anything ever again. I realize that he's a cop and that may present issues for you, but Aiden wouldn't hurt you, Izzy. I can promise you that. He's a protector."

The thing was that she'd known from the moment she laid eyes on Aiden that he would keep her safe. The only problem was whether she'd just experienced something she never even thought possible: love at first sight.

◆

Early the next morning, Bailey sat across from Layla in the safe house kitchen. She'd had no doubt that Layla would be able to provide highly useful information, but her palms started to sweat as she waited for Layla to provide her update.

Bailey eyed her friend. "I guess I shouldn't be surprised that you located the FBI safe house."

Layla smiled. "I'm good at my job."

"Marco will be here soon to pick me up."

"That's why I wanted to come early, before he got here. I'll make this fast. I still need you to try to keep me out of this," Layla said. "If Marco pushes too hard, then we can revisit the issue, but let's try to keep my cover intact as long as we can. Just tell him you have a source at the CIA who got the info for you. Can you do that?"

"Of course." What Layla was suggesting wouldn't be a lie, and Bailey had to protect her friend, especially after Layla had gone out on a limb for her. "What did you find?"

Layla's eyes widened. "Your instincts about something sinister brewing were spot-on. You were just missing a piece of the puzzle." She paused. "A huge piece."

"What?" Bailey held her breath, not sure what Layla was about to drop on her.

"You're going to have a hard time believing this."

Bailey wondered what her friend had found that was so groundbreaking. "If you tell me, then I'll believe it."

Layla lifted her chin. "Rogers was a deep-cover CIA officer."

Bailey's stomach dropped. "Are you serious?"

"Deadly. I got my boss to sign off on telling you this, and I only got that permission because I told him everything you already knew, and he figured it was only a matter of time before this information came to light."

"Go on." Bailey couldn't believe this latest turn of events.

Layla shook her head. "Unfortunately, I can't. You'll need to go to Langley for a classified briefing."

"How am I going to do that without Marco?"

"You can bring him. I just won't be anywhere near it. That's why I need you to say this came from a CIA source you have cultivated."

Bailey understood the drill. "I'm on it. When does this briefing happen?"

"As soon as Marco gets here to pick you up, you should

head over to the Agency. I don't know all the details myself, but given the reaction I got from my boss, I'd say this is pretty huge. And another reason for you to be careful. I still haven't fully wrapped my head around everything that is going on."

Bailey stood. "Thanks for sticking your neck out for me."

"You'd do the same for me." Layla gave her a quick embrace. "I'll let myself out."

About fifteen minutes later, Marco arrived at the safe house and walked into the kitchen.

"Good morning," he said.

She turned toward him. "We need to talk."

He narrowed his eyes. "What's up?"

"We need to go to the CIA right now."

"Why?"

"Because Michael Rogers was a deep-cover Agency operative."

He grabbed her shoulders. "What? How did you find that out?"

"I have a source at the Agency. They were able to get us an audience with some higher-ups who can shed light on all this. Or at least hopefully they can."

Marco ran a hand through his hair. "I hadn't thought about the CIA being involved in this." He paused. "But you did, or else you wouldn't have gone to them."

She shook her head. "You're giving me too much credit. I didn't think that Rogers was a CIA officer, but I did think that they might have some type of file on him. Especially once we feared that the DoD was involved. It made sense to reach out at least. I'm glad I did."

"We need to get to Langley ASAP."

Marco couldn't help thinking there was more to this story than Bailey was telling him, but he would have to trust her. She hadn't let him down so far, so he would keep pushing forward. This might be the big break in the case they'd been waiting for, and at the end of the day, it didn't matter exactly how they ended up here, just that they'd arrived.

After getting through extremely tight security at Langley, they were escorted up to the seventh floor of the building, where the bigwigs sat. He wasn't sure whether to be glad that they were getting that type of access or terrified.

They were brought into a SCIF and told to have a seat at the large conference room table while they waited. Being left alone in a secure room specially designed for discussing highly classified information didn't help Marco's nerves.

Thankfully it was a short wait. After a few minutes the door opened, and two gray-haired men walked in.

The taller one spoke first. "I'm Jim Smith, and this is my second-in-command, Ned Whelan."

Marco and Bailey introduced themselves, and everyone had a seat.

"Everything we're going to talk about today is highly classified," Jim said. "I've reviewed both of your security clearances and feel comfortable sharing this material largely because you've already ferreted out some of this information. I believe that once you hear everything, you'll understand why I've decided to bring you into the circle. You have developed a need to know."

"We understand," Bailey said. "Any help the Agency can provide on the three homicides we're working would be greatly appreciated."

Ned nodded. "Agent Ryan, we've been fully briefed on your investigation, and yes, we do believe we're at the point where we need to share intel."

"What can you tell us about Michael Rogers?" Marco asked.

"Rogers was a decorated CIA officer, and we hated to lose him." Jim avoided eye contact.

"Then why stay silent?" Bailey asked. "He was murdered along with two other men. All patriots."

Jim frowned. "This is a lot bigger than just one CIA officer. Ned, fill them in."

Ned laced his fingers together in front of him. "You two have done a great job with your investigation. So good that you were able to trace this back to us." He took a deep breath. "The employment at WSI was a deep-cover Agency operation. We had intel that led us to believe that WSI was taking arms shipments that were supposed to go to Saudi Arabia and diverting them to Iran."

Marco let Ned's words sink in. "Aren't those things closely accounted for?"

"Yes, but if your supplier—here, WSI—is dirty, then they can make that happen. They were very smart about it. Siphoning off amounts in small increments instead of large chunks. We only had a hunch this was happening. To know for sure, we put together a top-notch team of operatives: Rogers, Battle, and Wexford. Their cover story was that they were in need of an off-book job to bring in more money, but really they were working for the Agency the entire time. This was never, ever about money for those men. They knew the risks, and they took the assignment willingly and bravely in service to the United States of America."

"And they found evidence of WSI's wrongdoing with the arms shipments, and it got them killed?" Bailey asked.

"Unfortunately, Agent Ryan, it gets much worse than that." Jim looked at Bailey.

"How so?" Marco clenched his fists under the table. It already seemed bad enough.

Jim turned his attention to Marco. "While fulfilling their assignment, the guys believed they uncovered the existence of a mole at the DoD who was working hand in hand with WSI. If they figured out the mole's identity, they didn't get a chance to tell us before they were killed. As far as we're concerned, there's still an ongoing conspiracy here. It's a top priority to find this traitor within the Pentagon. As you know, the official policy of the US government is that we do not under any circumstances sell arms to Iran—they are on the State Department's list of state-sanctioned terrorism. They're on every embargo list we have."

"But why would anyone at the DoD want to work with the Iranians?" Bailey asked.

Jim slammed his fist on the desk. "Greed, pure and simple. We're convinced they're paying him top dollar. And we do think it's a man we're looking for at the DoD."

Marco wondered how best to make the next play. The curve balls just kept coming. As if Rogers being CIA wasn't enough of a surprise. "We don't want to do anything to interfere in your Agency operation, but you also have to understand that we have three grieving families needing answers. These victims were loyal patriots to this country, and their families deserve justice."

"We've also had targets put on our own backs because of this," Bailey added. "So this has become very personal for us."

Jim looked at Bailey. "And I'm sympathetic to that. The two of you are up to your necks in this, and I'm afraid it's only going to get worse if you keep investigating. I can't look you in the eyes and ensure your safety. This case is fraught with risks."

Bailey sighed. "We need to know who actually killed these men and Tobias Kappen—because we don't believe that was a suicide."

"Neither do we," Jim responded.

"How can we help each other get to the outcome that we all want?" Marco asked. He felt it better to ask than to direct them, considering they were the CIA and were going to do whatever they wanted anyway.

Jim tapped his pen on the desk. "Keep pushing WSI. Let us worry about the DoD."

"I have another question," Bailey said. "Were all of their commanding officers in the dark on this?"

Jim nodded. "I realize it's highly unorthodox, but yes. We kept the circle extremely tight. And that was before we realized we had a problem with someone at the Pentagon. To pull off something like this, you have to be hypervigilant. And we were doing well for a while. I'm not sure how the guys were made, but we told them to push hard, and unfortunately we had a bad result."

That was an understatement. Just look at the death toll. But Marco knew the CIA operated under different rules and assumptions. And risks, for that matter. "I assume you're looking at Alex Gomez."

Ned shifted in his seat. "Yes, among others, but we think that part of this matter is best left up to us. You two can figure out who is responsible for the murders. That's clearly your jurisdiction. If we had to guess, we'd say someone at WSI ultimately ordered the hit and then hired someone, but we don't have any evidence for that. Hopefully, with all of this new intel, you'll be able to drill down and get the answers you need to close these cases."

"And we can't reiterate enough how dangerous the work your team is doing will be," Jim said. "Whoever is pulling the strings here is completely ruthless and is willing to kill first and ask questions later. The Iranian connection makes this a lethal powder keg. The fact that there have been unsuccessful attempts on your lives speaks to your abilities."

"And God's protection," Marco said without reservation.

"Well, you're going to need it," Ned said. "It's best if we keep communication to a minimum. Agent Ryan, I believe you have a contact here. Please use that contact as a conduit—strictly between you and the contact. Got it?"

"Yes, sir," Bailey said.

Marco wondered who this mysterious Agency contact was, but he knew he shouldn't be pushing that issue right now.

"Thank you both for coming. We'll have someone escort you out."

The two men left the room, leaving Marco alone with Bailey.

She stepped closer to him as he stood. He leaned down and whispered in her ear. "You don't have a secret boyfriend here, do you?"

She looked up at him. "No. Why, are you jealous?"

Marco grabbed her hand. "Yeah, I am."

"You don't have anything to worry about."

Why wasn't he so sure about that?

CHAPTER
TWENTY-TWO

The next morning Bailey was hoping to get answers. She sat with Marco, waiting on the others to arrive at HQ for their meeting.

"When are you going to tell me who this mysterious contact of yours is?" Marco asked.

She couldn't do that. "It's not something I'm able to share."

"Do you not trust me?"

The hurt showed in his eyes, but she had to stand firm, because this was not her secret to tell. "I'm sorry, Marco. I have to protect this person's need to keep their identity private, given the nature of their work and cover with the CIA."

Marco nodded. "I'll let it go." He leaned forward in his chair, gesturing toward the files spread across the table. "This is everything we have about Mink. On paper, he's looking pretty clean."

She couldn't hold back a smirk. All the sleepless nights were starting to get to her. "Isn't that convenient." She paused, remembering something. "I heard back from my Organized Crime contact on the gambling angle that Barnett brought up. He's run it to the ground, and they have nothing tying Rogers to the gambling scene. Zero. I think Barnett could have been sending us down a rabbit trail. What we don't know is whether it was intentional."

Marco took a breath. "Same thing on the list of assignments we got from Battle's and Wexford's COs. We've had those cross-referenced with the threat matrix, and nothing has been a hit."

She understood the significance. "Meaning nothing major was going on in those places when the men were there for their official missions. Even things under the radar."

Marco nodded. "Our search was comprehensive. Plus the colonel at Fort Benning reviewed the list of ops we got from Barnett, and there was nothing that overlapped with their official work, not even going back as far as five years."

"Two dead ends on that front."

The conference room doors opened, and Lexi walked in, followed by Izzy and Jay.

"Good morning, everyone," Marco said. "Have a seat, and we'll get started."

"I've got some updates," Lexi said.

Bailey was interested to hear what she had found. Lexi was almost obsessed with getting to the truth because of the injustice she'd witnessed with her client. Bailey's heart went out to her. Even if they solved this case, it would never bring back Tobias Kappen.

Marco stood at the whiteboard, ready to take notes. "You go first, Lexi. Then we'll let the group know our latest developments."

Lexi pulled out her notepad. "I went to the Pentagon with Derek, and we paid a visit to Alex Gomez."

Bailey exchanged a glance with Marco. It was going to be

interesting to see how they handled this, given the direction they'd been given by the CIA.

"What happened?" Izzy asked.

Lexi looked around at the team. "Gomez said that he made the phone call to the DA's office because someone asked him to, but that he wasn't at liberty to tell us who."

Bailey shifted in her seat. "And do you believe him?"

Lexi shook her head. "No. Not really. I felt like he was hiding something. He also confirmed that the real Julian Mayfield was perfectly fine and still working at the DoD."

Marco started to write things on the board. "We've got the fake Julian Mayfield, who we've just ID'd as Ross Stanley. We're running him through all the databases to see what we can find on him. And we've got this Gomez angle at the DoD."

Izzy stood and walked over to the board. "Do we know whether Gomez and Mink have any connection? Or Gomez and Barnett?"

"That's one of the things we'll be looking for." Marco added that note to the board.

That was the perfect segue, and Bailey waited to see if Marco would take it.

He stepped forward. "Well, we have some major news. Bailey, you brought in the lead, so why don't you tell everyone?"

Bailey stood up. No need to beat around the bush. "Mike Rogers was a deep-cover CIA officer."

The room was so quiet that the only noise for a few moments was the humming of the air conditioner. Her statement had gotten everyone's attention.

"Are you sure?" Jay asked.

"Yes. We're certain. All three men were working on a top-secret Agency mission." She proceeded to tell them about WSI diverting arms sales and funneling them to the Iranians.

"Who did you meet with at the Agency?" Jay asked.

Marco cleared his throat. "Two men. Jim Smith and his deputy, Ned Whelan. They helped fill in some huge missing pieces for us."

"How does the DoD fit into this?" Lexi asked.

"They think someone on the inside is working with WSI on this deal."

Lexi snapped her fingers. "It has to be Alex Gomez."

"How can you be so sure?" Marco asked.

"Why else would he be connected to this?" Lexi's voice got louder with each word. "His excuse about acting on someone else's behalf seemed weak."

"But not improbable." Bailey didn't want Lexi to jump to conclusions. "Given this new information, we have to examine everything in a fresh light. We have someone at the DoD pulling the strings, and they could be at any level."

"On that issue, though, there is something else." Marco crossed his arms. "We've been told by the Agency to focus on the WSI element of the murder investigations. They want to take point on the rogue DoD employee."

Lexi lifted her hands. "Are you joking? We can't just pretend like we don't know that the DoD is involved here."

"I understand your frustration, but I think we need to tread carefully." Bailey empathized with Lexi but still gave a word of caution. "Our first priority is finding the people responsible for these murders."

"I'm with Lexi here," Izzy said. "We can't look at these incidents in a vacuum. If someone at the DoD is involved, then they could just as likely be behind the murders. It's all interconnected."

"I know everyone has strong opinions on this," Marco said. "We want to be a good partner with the CIA, but we also have a job to do. I think we go wherever the evidence takes us."

Bailey wasn't so sure that was a smart idea, but she didn't voice opposition in front of everyone.

"So do we believe that the victims found out who on the inside at the DoD was part of this illegal arms scheme, and that's why they were killed?" Izzy asked.

"That's our current best working theory, but the CIA can't guarantee that the men actually uncovered the source at the DoD. Maybe they were getting close, and that was enough to have someone take action against them. Or maybe they did find the source." Marco shrugged. "Regardless, their knowledge of WSI's activities is intricately connected to why they were killed."

"Or maybe their cover was blown," Jay suggested, "and WSI didn't want their dirty laundry out there."

Lexi leaned forward. "Am I the only one who doesn't just take everything the Agency is saying at face value?"

"Why the hesitation?" Bailey asked.

Lexi laughed. "Because they're the CIA. They are only telling us what they want us to know, and the version of the facts they want to share."

Lexi's words hit Bailey hard. Were they being naïve? Was her friendship with Layla clouding her judgment?

Marco jotted down some notes on the board before turning back around. "I don't think we have to take every word as true, but the basic premise that this was a CIA operation is key to how we're going to crack this case. So I say we take the information and use it the same way we would any other lead or piece of evidence."

"Marco's right," Jay said. "Let's put this information into the larger narrative and keep pushing."

Marco gestured toward the board with his marker. "And to that end, let's discuss assignments."

Bailey mostly zoned out while Marco assigned each person's responsibilities. She knew that her priority was Cullen Mink. She felt like he could be the key to this entire thing.

When everyone had dispersed, Marco came over to her. "How do you think that went?"

She felt a bit deflated. "I wasn't expecting everyone to be so skeptical."

"Me neither, but after hearing their viewpoints, I get it."

"And you're comfortable with Lexi following this Gomez lead, even given the directive from the CIA?"

Marco tilted his head. "Well, it didn't matter what I told Lexi. You could see it in her eyes. She's going after that lead no matter what we tell her."

He had a point. Lexi was like a dog with a bone.

"Now we have a big decision to make. Do we get Mink back in here and confront him with what we know?"

Marco stared at the board for a minute, thinking. "There are pros and cons to that approach. His lawyer did send over an initial set of documents. I thought that was a positive development. I don't want to aggravate that cooperation."

"I think we have to push the envelope. Look him in the eyes when we make the allegations. We have to determine if he's at the center of this, or if we're on a wild-goose chase and he's just a pawn."

He gently wrapped a hand around her arm and pulled her closer. "Hey, are you okay?"

"Yeah. Why do you ask?"

"You seem preoccupied or something. Just wanted to make sure you were all right."

She nodded. "I'm good. I think I'm just wound up about all of this."

"I understand." He paused. "If you think it's the best move

to confront Mink, I'm all in. You've got great instincts on this stuff, and I trust your judgment."

"Thanks. And I'm sorry if I seem off. I'm not sleeping that well at the safe house." Every time she closed her eyes, there was danger lurking. It wasn't just that, though. She was trying to push through and act on her feelings, like Layla had encouraged her to. But it was tough.

"You're protected there, Bailey. Nothing will happen to you." Marco pulled her even closer to him so he could wrap his other arm around her waist.

They locked eyes for a minute, and then Marco's gaze drifted over her shoulder. She turned and saw Izzy in the doorway before she walked away.

Well, that was going to be an awkward conversation later.

◆

They'd only been driving for a few minutes when Izzy received a text from Marco with a change of plans. He needed them to go to WSI and pick up Cullen Mink. Bailey was pushing to get in front of Mink again, so their orders were to bring him back to NCIS headquarters for further questioning.

Jay changed directions, and Izzy stared out the window.

"Jay, do you think something is going on between Marco and Bailey?"

"What do you mean?"

"Like, romantically?"

Jay shot her a look. "You think there is?" While it was a question, it came out more like a statement.

"Yeah. I guess it's not my business, but I just found it odd. Bailey doesn't seem like the type to get involved with someone she works with."

"Remember, Izzy, Bailey is FBI. She's in a totally separate

chain of command than Marco. So there's nothing wrong with it if something is happening." Jay sighed. "And I'm sorry, but I think that maybe this hits a sensitive issue for you, and that's why you're concerned about it."

There were moments when she wished she hadn't opened up to Jay about her past, but she couldn't do anything about it now. "Maybe you're right."

She saw Jay glance at her. "In the spirit of getting into other people's business, has Aiden called yet?"

She couldn't help but smile. "Yeah, he did. We've talked a couple of times. Our schedules are both crazy right now, but there has been discussion of getting together." She gave him a sidelong look. "I thought you were going to stay out of it?"

Jay grinned. "You can't blame me for being invested."

She shook her head. "Enough of that. I shouldn't have even brought up the Bailey and Marco thing. You're right. I should stay out of it. Let's get back to what we're doing here. I don't understand why we aren't broadening the net. What if Mink is clean? We need options."

"I think the thought is to run down Mink first, given all the signs that point to him, and then branch out if needed."

"You've been doing this a really long time."

Jay laughed. "Thanks for pointing out that I'm old."

She smiled. "No. I didn't mean it like that at all. I just meant that you've seen a lot of things in your career with the Army. Do you trust the CIA?"

"No, not completely," he answered quickly. "I doubt they're giving us the entire story, but they've given us enough to increase our understanding of what happened and help us get answers."

"You don't think they made this whole thing up, do you?" Izzy feared that possibility.

"No, not at all. But with the Agency, there might be other

elements at play that we'll never know about. Our job is to bring the guilty to justice for these three murders, and that's what we'll do."

They arrived at WSI and got out of the SUV.

"I'm guessing Mink isn't going to like this surprise visit," Izzy said.

"He doesn't have a lot of choices. We'll let him call his lawyer so he can meet us at HQ."

They checked in at the desk, and after they'd waited in the lobby for a few minutes, a tall man with gray hair walked up to them.

"Agents Graves and Cole, I presume?"

They rose to greet him. "Yes."

"I'm Rex Barnett. I'm CEO of WSI."

"We're looking for Cullen Mink," Jay said.

"I realize that, but Cullen is not in today."

"Should he be?" Izzy asked.

"I'm not the keeper of Cullen's schedule," Barnett replied.

"Was he here yesterday?" Izzy pushed.

Barnett nodded. "Yes. We were both here late into the evening last night. All I can tell you is that he's not here. Is there anything I can help you with?"

"Not right now. Thank you," Jay said. He grabbed Izzy by the arm, and they headed out of the building.

"What is it?" Izzy asked as soon as they got outside.

"We need to make sure Mink isn't fleeing the country. We've got to make calls now."

"Why do you think he'd do that?"

"Because that's what rich, guilty men who have international connections and power do."

Marco wasn't buying Bailey's excuses. He couldn't get into her head, but there was something going on in there. He wondered if he had said or done something wrong, but they had far more pressing problems right now, based on the phone call he'd just gotten from Jay. They'd put everything into motion, alerting the alphabet soup of agencies that Cullen Mink should not be allowed to leave the country. They were now searching to see if they were too late.

Bailey pulled her phone from her ear. "That's the last one. Everyone has been notified. Now we're just trying to verify that his passport hasn't already been scanned."

"There's also a high likelihood that he could have used a fake," Marco added. He hated to bring it up, but it was a possibility.

Bailey rubbed her temples. "Yeah. Of course he could have. Are Jay and Izzy checking out his house?"

Marco nodded. "They're en route now."

"Guess we have to wait and see what they find." She took a breath. "About earlier, Izzy saw us together."

Izzy was the last thing Marco was concerned about. "I'm not worried about her. We're not doing anything wrong."

"I still might talk to her about it. I think that would make me feel better."

He smiled. "So there's something to talk about?"

She looked away from his discerning gaze. "You know there is."

"Good." Marco was falling quickly for Bailey, and he wasn't even trying to slow down his heart. There was a feeling deep in his gut about her, and he was going with it. "When this case is over, we won't be working together anymore."

"That's probably for the best," she replied softly.

He nodded. "Yes, but it also means we'll have to make time to see each other."

Bailey looked up at him with her bright eyes. "I've learned something over the past few years. If something is truly important to you, then you'll make time for it."

"Have you made time for anyone else while you've been an agent?" The question came out of his mouth before he'd thought it through.

She shook her head. "No, not in the romantic sense. But I have made time for Viv and Layla. They've become my family, and it's critical that I spend time with them. They've shown me what it really means to love and be there for one another. You saw them in the hospital, how quickly they were there when I needed them."

"That's really special to have friends like that in your life. And I agree with you. We'll make the time. I am making that commitment to you now. I just don't want you to overthink things."

Bailey laughed. "What ever gave you the idea that I would overthink?"

"Pretty much everything about you, but I'm spontaneous enough for the both of us. How does that sound?" He hoped he wasn't pushing too much too fast, but for some reason he needed a measure of validation from her that she was in this too. He couldn't deny that his feelings had only been amplified by the dangerous situation they'd found themselves in, but nonetheless he still knew what he wanted. He wanted Bailey.

"Let's get this case wrapped up, and then we'll have plenty of time to make plans."

Bailey had made it clear from day one that her first priority was the case, and he could respect that. But for him, he'd crossed a line—a dangerous one. His first priority had become her. There was nothing he could do about it except work as hard as he could to close the case.

His phone rang, and he answered it. "Jay, Bailey's here too, and I've got you on speaker."

"We're here at Mink's house, and I can say with certainty that he hasn't left the country."

"How do you know that?" Bailey asked.

"Because Cullen Mink is dead."

CHAPTER
TWENTY-THREE

That night at the safe house, huddled up on the couch, Bailey eyed Marco as he finished a cup of decaf coffee. They had both agreed that they didn't need any more caffeine, as they were already running on fumes.

"Someone murdered Mink to stop him from talking to us," Bailey said. "The only problem is that I'm not sure we can just tie this all up neatly with a bow and assume that one big bad monster is behind everything."

Marco set down his cup. "I completely agree with you. What if the CIA wanted Mink dead?"

That got an eye roll out of her. "C'mon, Marco. Do you really think they'd kill an American citizen on US soil?"

"I hope not, but we know how messy this has gotten. You need to reach out to your phantom CIA contact and figure out what's going on."

She'd already thought about that. Hopefully Layla could shed some light on things. "I will."

"Is that a phone call you can make, or is there some secret bat signal you send out?" Marco asked.

"I can make a call, but I'm not sure I can have this discussion over an unsecure line. I'll reach out tonight, though, and then we can figure out how to connect tomorrow."

"Good."

She could sense that Marco was still worried that her contact at the Agency was a guy. In a way, she had to admit it was cute, but she didn't want him to worry for no reason.

"Marco, I can't tell you who my contact is."

"I know that."

She placed her hand on top of his. "But I promise it's not anyone you should be worried about."

He smiled. "Are you saying that because you're not interested in him, or for some other reason?"

Bailey hesitated, trying to figure out how much she could or should say. "I'm not interested. It's not like that. I promise."

Marco brought her hand to his lips. "I believe you, Bailey. I trust you. I'd trust you with my life."

Her breath caught—not just at the honesty of his statement, but also the magnitude. "I don't really have the words to respond to that."

"Sometimes words aren't necessary."

She couldn't agree with him more as she reached up and pulled him in for a kiss.

◆

Lexi stared into Derek's dark eyes. She was plotting and planning and hoped that he wouldn't think she was crazy.

"You look like you're on a mission," he said.

"I am." Her nails dug into her palms. She couldn't give him the details of what she knew, and that made this much more difficult. Derek had invited her over to his place to discuss what their next steps would be. And unfortunately, she could only give him bits and pieces of the truth she had learned about the CIA's involvement in this mess.

Everyone had their own agenda. She wasn't forgetting her own.

"This is personal for me, Derek. Tobias was loyal to this country to the end. He put his life on the line defending our freedoms. I have to clear his name. That is my duty, and I can't just let it go."

Derek's eyes softened. "I know this is a tough spot to be in. I absolutely hate operating in the dark. As a prosecutor, the need to know all the facts and get to the truth is at the core of my DNA." He paused. "But I realize we're living in a very unusual situation, and it's not of your making. I'm saying all of this because if that means I have to go outside my comfort zone, I will. I want to help you in whatever way I can."

Lexi knew deep in her gut that he was trustworthy. She didn't know how this case was going to impact their chance at romance, but he was offering her help, and she wasn't going to turn it away. "You're right that I can't give you a full debrief, but maybe that can be a positive. You aren't constrained by what I know. We can keep digging into Gomez until we get real answers."

"I want that too, but I'm also worried about you. The fact that you're having to hide critical information from me only amplifies my concern. We have to be smart about how we're going to do this, because I don't want to arrive at a crime scene and find you there."

Those words made her throat feel tight, but she couldn't live in fear. She had a job to do. "We start by doing some recon."

"On Gomez?"

"Yes. We obviously can't monitor his moves inside the Pentagon, but I want us on the rest of his comings and goings."

"Then we need to figure out where he lives."

She pulled a piece of paper out of her bag. "Already got it."

"Stakeout?" he asked.

It wasn't like she was going to be able to sleep anyway. "Yeah."

"I'm in."

Lexi had never been on a stakeout, and by the time they had settled in Derek's car not far from Alex Gomez's house in Arlington, she wondered if this was a waste of time. She figured they didn't really have anything to lose.

"So now what?" she asked.

Derek laughed. "We wait."

Lexi looked down at her watch. It was almost midnight. "We don't know whether he's already at home or not."

Derek turned toward her. "This will help us form a baseline for his behavior."

"You don't think this will be resolved quickly?" It was a half question, half statement.

"I doubt it. So it's best for us to log what we see so we have an accurate record."

She studied him. "Why do you sound like a stakeout expert?"

"I'm not, but I have been on several as part of cases I've worked over the years. I also shadowed a PI years ago because I thought it would be a good experience. I picked up some pointers along the way."

"Well, at least one of us has a clue what we're doing." She was only half joking. She was an experienced lawyer, but this was a bit out of the box for her. Given the circumstances, though, she didn't think she had any other choice. While Derek seemed to think this could be a long, drawn-out process, her gut was telling her otherwise. She felt like things were going to come to a head very quickly.

After a couple of hours, she felt her eyelids start to get heavy. But that was when motion at the front door caught her attention. "Derek, look."

"I'm on it." He pulled out his phone and started snapping pictures.

A man she didn't recognize was leaving Gomez's house. "We should follow him."

Derek looked at her. "That wasn't the plan. We stick to Gomez. What if we chase this guy and then it's a dead end?"

She bit her lip as she considered their options. "All right. We should find out who he is first. We don't need to be wasting our time. Send me the pics, and I'll get them to the team."

He pressed a few keys on his phone. "Sending now."

Maybe this mystery man was just the break they needed.

◆

Early the next morning, Bailey was surprised when Layla showed up at the safe house, knowing it was time for Marco to pick her up. She was more shocked that Layla would make herself known to Marco, but it appeared she intended to do just that.

Standing in the kitchen, Marco wore a deep frown. "Layla," he said. "What're you doing here?" He turned to Bailey. "I thought we agreed to keep this location from everyone—even our friends and family."

Layla gestured toward the kitchen table. "Maybe it's best for us all to sit down so we can talk."

Marco raised an eyebrow. "Why do I feel like I'm missing something here? Bailey, what's going on?"

Bailey sat at the table. "Because you are missing something. We'll explain."

They all took their seats, and Bailey nodded to Layla. She would let her take the lead.

"Bailey didn't tell me the location of the safe house. I found it on my own. Marco, I'm about to tell you something that you have to keep in confidence. No one else on the team can know. Do you understand?"

"Yes," he said. "Just give it to me straight."

Bailey exchanged another look with Layla.

"I'm CIA," Layla said flatly.

Marco's eyes widened. "Okay. Wow. Just when I think I can't be shocked by anything else on this case."

"It's actually a good thing that you're surprised," Bailey said. "It's really important that Layla keep her cover as a State Department analyst."

Marco turned to Layla. "Your secret is safe with me. I would never do anything to endanger your work or your safety."

Layla smiled. "Thank you. Now that we have that out of the way, I understand there's some stuff we need to talk about."

"Cullen Mink's death," Marco said. "Is there any way the Agency was behind it?"

Layla shook her head. "No, that wasn't us. But I am authorized to tell you that the CIA does think Mink was a player in this, but that he wasn't the ringleader. He probably got in over his head and then couldn't find a way out."

Marco whistled. "That's why he was willing to turn over those documents."

It made sense now. But that left a bigger issue to resolve. "Then who killed Cullen Mink?" Bailey asked.

Layla looked down. "Unfortunately, we don't know. So we're all in the dark here. If whoever is behind this was worried that he could be a weak link and flip, then they'd want to take him out just like they took out the other men. I just don't know whether someone at WSI or the DoD is pulling the strings or who put out the hit."

"Why all the secrecy?" Marco asked. "What is the Agency hiding?"

Layla shrugged. "There's always a more complicated story than what appears on face value. I could make some guesses as to what else is going on here, but that is all they would be. At the end of the day, this was an Agency-led operation, and now three highly valued men have been killed. Someone is trying to shift the blame or pass the buck to make sure they don't take the hit if this ever gets out."

"That's not a satisfactory response, and you know it." Bailey wouldn't cut her friend any slack.

Layla's dark eyes met hers. "But it's the truth. I could sugar-coat it, but I won't. Not with you."

"So where does this leave us?" Marco asked.

"From the Agency's standpoint, the powers that be still want you focused on the murder investigation, but if you can find out what happened to Mink, that would be good too."

"And they still want us to stay away from the DoD and Gomez?" Bailey asked.

"Yes. They want to handle that internally. These things get really dicey when you're talking about interagency power plays. I'm not sure who is ultimately calling the shots on my side, but whoever it is has some grave concerns about what is happening at the Pentagon."

Marco looked at Bailey and then Layla. "Since you're Bailey's friend, I assume you know that neither she nor I will just let that go."

Layla lifted her hands. "I'm just the messenger."

Bailey needed to say something. "I'm sorry, Layla. I brought you into this, and it isn't even something that should be on your plate. I don't want to cause you any more stress and trouble than I have already."

"I told you before, you never ask for help. I'm glad that I could be here when you needed me. I don't want you to think another thought about me. I can handle it. Focus on your safety and solving this case." Layla stood. "Watch your backs. Both of you. No one really knows how deep and wide this could go."

Those words gave Bailey pause. "I'll walk you out." She escorted Layla to the door and gave her a fierce hug. "Thank you again."

Layla squeezed her shoulders. "I meant what I said back there. I don't have a good feeling about this."

"We'll be careful." Bailey watched as Layla walked out the door. She took a moment to gather her thoughts before rejoining Marco in the kitchen.

He looked up at her from his chair. "Now I feel like a complete idiot for worrying about your CIA contact."

"There's no way you could've foreseen that. And I appreciate you understanding the importance of Layla's cover."

"Absolutely. But you know I have to ask if Viv also works there." He laughed.

She shook her head. "No. She really is a State Department attorney."

"You're not some type of undercover agent, are you?" He smiled.

"No. Although this case makes me feel a lot more like one than I'd like." Her phone started buzzing. She picked it up and saw a message. "One of my FBI analysts was able to identify the man who visited Gomez last night. It was a bigwig."

Marco raised an eyebrow. "Who?"

"Deputy Assistant Secretary Oliver Patterson. He's Gomez's boss."

"Good grief. Are the analysts going to run a background check?"

"Already in process."

"We're closing in," Marco said.

"Are we? I feel like we take two steps forward and then another back. Mink's murder doesn't feel right to me. Beyond the obvious that it's a murder."

"I hear you, but we'll get to the bottom of this." He looked at his watch. "You ready to get out of here?"

"Yeah." It was going to be another long day.

They were about to head out the door when Marco stopped. "Let me grab a travel mug. I think I'm going to need it today. I'll be right behind you."

Bailey picked up her bag and exited the front door of the safe house.

A loud crack pierced the air. It was the unmistakable sound of a gunshot. And they were gunning for her.

◆

When Marco heard the first gunshot, he dropped his mug in the sink and ran toward the front door. As the shots continued to ring out in rapid succession, he prayed that he wouldn't find Bailey's dead body riddled with bullets on the other side of the door. *Lord, please help her.*

He pulled his weapon and opened the door for a quick look before taking cover again. Bailey was crouched on the ground, hiding behind the short brick wall surrounding the flowerbed. Her arm was bleeding.

"Bailey, are you okay?" he called.

"Yes, I just got grazed."

Another rapid set of gunshots rang out. Bailey returned fire.

"Let's get you back in here. I'll cover you." He popped off a few shots.

Bailey stayed low and ran back into the house. He slammed the front door shut, but it wouldn't provide much protection.

Marco looked her over, making sure she was truly okay. "We've got extra firepower in the basement. One of us should go down and get it."

"I'll go. You keep them at bay. Call for backup!"

Marco pulled out his phone and took cover in the living room. He started calling as Bailey ran toward the basement. He asked for immediate assistance. "ETA is five to ten minutes," he called to her.

"How many shooters do you think there are?" she yelled from the basement.

He popped up to look out the living room window. "I count two, but there could be more. They've taken cover behind a large black van."

After a minute, Bailey returned with two more handguns and some extra magazines from the small armory. The two attackers kept firing shots at the house.

She crouched beside Marco in the living room just as the large windowpane shattered at the impact of another bullet. They both ducked reflexively. The gunshots continued, and they returned fire through the gaping window.

One man ran out from behind the van while the other provided cover. The one on the move hid behind the large oak tree in the front yard, changing angles and trying to flank them. He was dressed in camo and moved as if he had expert military training.

"They're getting closer," Bailey yelled.

"I know." *Lord, please help us.*

"I'm out!"

He slid one of the extra guns to where she was hunkered down, and she grabbed it.

The sound of sirens started to sound in the distance. "I think our help is coming," he said.

More shots exploded through the air. "Not fast enough," she said.

"We're going to make it, Bailey." He was saying those words as much to encourage himself as for her. He rose up and got off a few more rounds.

This time there was no return fire, and the sirens blared loudly, moving ever closer to their location.

He looked over at Bailey, who remained crouched down with a gun in her hand.

"Sounds like our backup is here," she said.

"Where was your external coverage?" Marco asked.

Bailey shook her head. "I don't know."

There should have been two FBI agents on the street outside of the safe house. Marco feared the worst. That they were dead.

CHAPTER
TWENTY-FOUR

Later that day it was all hands on deck at NCIS HQ. Bailey didn't want to admit it, but she was still shaken up after the harrowing events of the morning. The two FBI agents on her security detail were dead, and she was having a major guilt trip. They were innocent people caught in the cross fire while protecting her. And now their families would never see them again. The thought made her sick.

She fought back tears as she listened to Marco tell the rest of the team what had happened at the safe house.

"We have a security breach," Jay said. "I don't know which agency, if any, we can trust right now."

Marco nodded. "I think the only people we can trust are those of us sitting in this room."

Bailey didn't feel like adding any comments, so she just sat there as the others went through status updates on the investigation.

"Bailey, you hear anything on Patterson's background check?" Lexi asked.

The direct question broke her out of her malaise. "Still waiting, but it shouldn't be much longer. Although considering Patterson's a deputy assistant secretary at the DoD, I doubt we'll find anything on paper. They vet for those positions very stringently. He never would've gotten the job if he had major dirt that could be traced."

Lexi stood and went over to the whiteboard. "We've been working on the organizational structure of Gomez's office. Gomez has a team working under him, including the real Julian Mayfield. But Gomez reports to Patterson. He's very well thought of and is at the top of his game. Patterson's area of expertise is in Russian and European affairs. He visited Gomez in the middle of the night, but we have no idea what that was about, and we can't rule out that it was work related and on the up-and-up. At this point, we're looking at the whole team and trying to connect the dots with any possible associations to WSI."

"Good work, Lexi," Marco said.

"Don't thank me yet. We still need answers," she replied.

"Izzy and I are working through the background files for the rest of the WSI executive team," Jay said. "Izzy, tell them what we found last night."

Izzy stood up. "The chief financial officer, a guy named James Jameson, or J. J., went to college with Gomez."

"Really?" Lexi's eyes widened. "That's interesting."

"It doesn't mean that J. J. is dirty, but the connection is still something we want to dig into."

"What about Barnett?" Marco asked. "We're still trying to figure out his angle in this."

"Clean so far, but we're still searching," Izzy said. "No major red flags. He's very wealthy, but that's to be expected in his position. He gets a crazy salary and bonus as the head of one of the biggest defense contractors. It appears he is not a micromanager and gives his employees a lot of autonomy."

A thought struck Bailey. "Is it possible that WSI would engage in this type of activity—stealing and selling arms to a country we don't do any business with—without the CEO's blessing?"

"I find that highly doubtful," Izzy said.

Marco nodded. "Izzy, run everything about Barnett to the ground. Make him priority number one."

"Will do," she responded.

"There's one more thing we need to think about." Marco crossed his arms. "For some reason, Bailey is being targeted more than any of the rest of us."

Her head snapped up. "We don't know that for certain. You've been under attack too." That sounded weak even to her, but she didn't want to believe that she was being singled out.

"But I think that's just because we happen to have been together. You might have some link to this case that we don't know about. We need to figure out what that is."

"Easier said than done. We were never supposed to have found out the truth about this operation."

"Now that we have, we'll just have to deal with the consequences."

"And hopefully stay alive."

◆

Izzy thought Marco and Bailey were acting strange, so when she got a minute alone with Bailey in the break room, she had to ask about it.

"Bailey, what's going on with you and Marco?"

Bailey sighed. "I wondered how long it was going to take you to ask me about what you saw."

Izzy laughed. "I actually wasn't talking about that."

"Oh." Bailey sucked in a breath. "Then what?"'

"Something is off. I don't know what it is, but I've worked with you two long enough now to know that something is wrong."

"We're just stressed. The shootout at the safe house is hard to deal with."

"And that's it?" Izzy was skeptical.

"Yes. That's it."

Izzy didn't believe Bailey for one minute. She and Marco were hiding something, but Bailey clearly wasn't going to tell Izzy what was going on.

"And, Izzy, about the other thing, you're probably wondering whether that's even appropriate. In a perfect world, I would never get involved with someone I work with, but we both realize that this is only a temporary assignment. I don't report to him, and he doesn't report to me."

Izzy lifted a hand. "You don't need to explain yourself. I get it."

Bailey tucked a strand of hair behind her ear. "But I do want to explain, because being a woman in law enforcement is hard, and I realize I may not be setting the ideal example for you."

"You can't help who you fall in love with," Izzy said.

Bailey's eyes widened. "Wait a minute. I didn't say anything about love."

"You didn't have to. It's obvious to anyone who sees the two of you that you've developed a special bond." Izzy hoped to find that connection with Aiden if she got the opportunity.

Bailey closed her eyes. "Nothing about this investigation has been normal, and with all the danger thrown at us, I think Marco and I will need some time once this is over to figure out where we really stand."

Izzy smiled. "Okay. If you need to tell yourself that." She paused. "But seriously, you're sure there's nothing else going on? If there is, the rest of the team is here to help. You know that, right?"

Bailey nodded. "Yes. Let's just keep pushing as hard as we can."

"One more thing," Izzy said. "In the full spirit of transparency."

"Okay."

"I'm going on a date with Jay's son."

Bailey blinked. "What? How did that happen?"

"Jay invited me to church with his family, and I met Aiden afterward. I don't think there's any issue with it, but since you confessed about Marco, I wanted to be open."

Bailey smiled. "You really like this guy. I can tell by how your face lit up. If Aiden is anything like his dad, then he's a good one."

"That's what I'm hoping to find out. But like you said, our first priority right now is this case."

"Thanks for sharing, Izzy. I'd really like for us to stay in touch once this is over."

"I'd like that too."

Izzy felt like she'd found a friend in Bailey, and it had been a long time since she'd had a true girlfriend. She just hoped they'd all make it through this investigation alive.

The last thing Lexi had expected was to receive a phone call from Alex Gomez. He'd been very cryptic, just asking to meet with her alone at a coffee shop in Dupont Circle. She'd debated what to do with Derek. She didn't want to risk spooking Gomez, but on the other hand, given the level of danger involved, she had ended up bringing Derek with her. She hoped it was a decision she wouldn't regret.

They'd only been waiting in the coffee shop for a few minutes when Gomez walked in and made eye contact. Then he motioned for her to come to him.

"I thought I told you to come alone," he hissed.

"You don't get to set the terms here," Lexi shot back.

"Let's take a walk, then," Gomez said.

Derek remained silent, and they followed Gomez out of the coffee shop and down the street. Lexi reminded herself to breathe as she waited for Gomez to speak and make the first move. Her stomach was in knots.

"Lieutenant Todd, at first I was really annoyed by all your questions and the insinuation that I was somehow involved, but I couldn't help myself and started fishing," Gomez said.

"Really?" Lexi's pulse thumped.

He glanced her way but then turned his attention forward again. "Yeah. If I'm wrong about this, I'll be canned, but I couldn't take the risk."

"What? What did you find?" Was Gomez providing critical intel or playing them?

"I have serious concerns that my boss is mixed up in this WSI debacle."

"Oliver Patterson?" Her voice shook.

"Yes."

She grabbed his arm. "What do you have on him?"

Gomez stopped walking and turned to her. "Patterson met with WSI employees on multiple occasions. I was able to access his calendar. He met with Cullen Mink and the CEO, Rex Barnett." He looked over his shoulder before continuing. "Also, you should know that I went to college with James Jameson. I know he's clean."

She already knew about the college connection, but at least Gomez had affirmatively told her. Maybe that was a sign that he was sincere. "How can you be so sure about Jameson?"

He shrugged. "Because I just am. Trust me." He started walking again.

She followed with Derek glued to her side and let Gomez keep talking.

"I reached out to J. J., and he said that Barnett is acting squirrelly. And that even though he's not supposed to know, he's seen Patterson and Barnett together, working on something hush-hush."

"Did he have any idea what it was?" Derek asked, breaking his silence.

Gomez shook his head. "No, and he was sticking his neck out by answering my questions, given he could lose his job over this. But J. J. doesn't want anything to do with trouble. He fears that some people at WSI have crossed over to the dark side. He's actually looking for a new job now, but that can take time."

Lexi let all of this new information sink in as she glanced at Derek, who remained expressionless.

"Another thing you need to know," Gomez continued. "Patterson is the one who told me to call the DA's office. I had no idea that there was anything nefarious going on. And unfortunately, before I realized what was really happening, I told Patterson that NCIS was asking about that phone call."

That wasn't good. "So he knows that we're potentially on to him."

"I'm afraid so. At the time, it never occurred to me that he would be capable of something like this. He told me not to tell you anything, that it was all part of some highly classified project, and that I needed to keep my mouth shut for security reasons. I'm sorry."

"It's all right. Like you said, you had no reason to disbelieve him. He's your boss, a well-respected person, and a high-ranking official in the Pentagon."

Gomez ran a hand through his hair. "I'm afraid now that I've put you and your team in more jeopardy."

"You've also put yourself in danger," Derek said. "If Patterson finds out that you've been snooping around, then you've put a target on your back."

Gomez stopped again. "Don't worry about me. I can take care of myself. But I couldn't live with myself, knowing what I know now and keeping quiet. I still don't understand exactly what Patterson is up to and how it interplays with what happened to those men, but I know there is some connection."

Lexi felt herself softening toward him. "Thanks for trusting us with this information."

Gomez looked down at her. "Stay safe. It's probably best that we not meet again like this. I'm worried someone might be watching."

A chill crept down her spine as she looked around the crowded streets and wondered if they'd already been found.

◆

Bailey sat on the couch of the new FBI safe house with her laptop, reviewing documents they'd received from Cullen Mink's attorney. They'd gotten a debrief that afternoon from Lexi on her meeting with Alex Gomez. Bailey felt like they were nearing a turning point in the case, but there were still missing pieces.

The second safe house was in Dale City, where many military and civilian government employees lived. The split-level house had a cozy feel and was decorated with a homey touch, but Bailey couldn't help but feel an ominous cloud hanging over her.

Along with moving to a new safe house, she and Marco

had taken extra precautions by dumping their cells and getting burner phones. They'd provided the burner numbers only to the team and Layla.

Marco walked into the room carrying two cups. "Decaf."

"Thank you." She took a sip of coffee. "If we believe Gomez is one of the good guys, then we have this narrowed down to Patterson and probably the CEO, Barnett. Mink's involvement probably got him killed."

"We're getting close, Bailey. I can feel it."

"Close isn't good enough."

He placed his hand on hers. "We'll get there."

She sighed and closed her eyes for a second.

"You're exhausted," Marco said. "Maybe we should call it a night."

She looked into his warm eyes. "I am tired, but I really think we might be able to find some answers in these documents."

"They'll still be here in the morning."

"Time isn't on our side, Marco." The statement came out more harshly than she'd intended.

"I get that," he said softly.

She hated that she'd snapped at him. "I'm sorry. I don't want to take my frustrations out on you. It's not fair."

He moved closer to her. "I want to make things better, and it's hard when I can't do that, because I've come to care so much about you."

"I care about you too." She rested her head on his shoulder. "I wish I could just close my eyes and be away from all of this."

He wrapped his arms around her. "If I had it my way, I'd whisk you off somewhere completely safe."

"But we both know that's not possible." Although for a minute she wanted to pretend like it was.

"Bailey, I know we've both been under tremendous stress

and it's not an ideal way to start a relationship. But now that I've gone through all of this with you, I can't imagine my life without you in it."

She sucked in a breath at his declaration.

"I don't want to scare you off, but being honest about how I feel is just the guy I am, and I want you to know exactly where you stand with me. I can only hope you feel at least close to the same way."

She looked up into his eyes. "You know I do. It's just not as easy for me to show it." She wanted to tell him that her heart felt like it was about to explode, but the words didn't come. Instead, her fears came out. "I'm just afraid of losing you. I can't deal with another major loss. I just can't." Her voice cracked as she spoke. "Losing you would be unthinkable."

"I'm not going anywhere."

"We both have dangerous jobs," she said, trying to make her point. "This case is the perfect example."

"Yeah, we do, but we're in God's hands. Just look at how He has protected us over these past few weeks. He has a plan for us, and I truly believe He brought you into my life for a reason. Not just to solve this case, but for so much more than that."

Did she believe the same? "I definitely don't understand all of God's ways, like why He chose to take my parents, but I try to put my faith and trust in Him. When I was grieving their deaths, my faith was the only thing that got me through. Even when I kept crying out and asking why, knowing that He heard those cries gave me the strength to face the next day. I can't claim to know if God put us together for a greater purpose than this case." She paused, wondering how much she should say. "But getting to know you has opened up my heart."

"You're an amazing woman, Bailey. I know this has probably

281

moved much faster between us than you would've wanted, but my heart is yours. Where the future will lead us, I don't know. But I know how I feel sitting here with you now."

She couldn't match his eloquence, so she didn't even try.

"I hope that wasn't too much?" Marco asked.

She shook her head. "No. It was just right."

"Good." He gave her a quick kiss. "I know you want me to shut up now so you can get back to work." He laughed.

"Just one more hour. I think I've got that in me."

"That's a deal."

She turned her attention back to her computer and the documents from WSI. About half an hour later, something caught her eye.

"Marco, look at this."

"What is it?" He leaned over.

"An email from Patterson to Mink. Patterson is telling him not to worry about anything. That Patterson had talked to 'NW' and it all was under control."

Marco read the email chain. "Who is NW?"

They sat in silence for a moment, and then it hit her. "It can't be."

"What're you thinking?" Marco asked.

She looked up at him. "Ned Whelan. CIA."

Marco sucked in a breath. "Man. Wouldn't that be something."

"Think about it. He was the one pushing us not to focus on the DoD angle. It could be because he's in cahoots with Patterson."

"This is major. What if it doesn't stop with Whelan? We don't know who at the CIA we can trust."

"Except Layla. I know she'd never do anything like this."

Marco was quiet for a moment.

"I know my friend, Marco. That's off the table." Bailey would defend her friend no matter what.

"If you're right, then she could be in danger, given her involvement in this."

"And I'm the one who brought her into this mess." Bailey shook her head in frustration. "What do we do now?"

"Take this to our directors."

She clenched her fists. "What if either of them is involved?"

"C'mon, that's highly unlikely. I think this stops at the CIA. If, God forbid, something else happened and we didn't tell them, that would put us and them in an awful position. It's just a risk we have to take to try to bring this case to a head."

She knew deep in her gut that he was right, but that didn't make it any easier. "Do you think we call a joint meeting?"

"Probably better for us to handle this together as opposed to separately."

Her phone rang, but she didn't recognize the number. "I don't know who this is."

"You shouldn't answer it," Marco said.

"I have to." She accepted the call.

"We've got a problem," Layla said.

"I didn't recognize your number," Bailey replied. "I've got you on speaker."

"I'm also on a burner."

"What's going on?" Marco leaned in.

"Someone has been using the CIA database to run checks on Bailey. They know we're friends."

"When did these searches start?" Marco asked.

"Soon after the second murder," Layla responded.

"What're you not saying?" Bailey asked.

"The reason you might have been singled out is because of your association with *me*. When you started working the case, they probably did a background investigation into both of you. When they found the connection to me, that might have set off alarm bells. Whoever is behind this might've thought you know more than you do—or that I know it, for that matter. Someone has been fishing for a long time and using CIA resources to do it."

Bailey and Marco exchanged glances. But he shook his head. He didn't want her to tell Layla their suspicions about Whelan.

"And there's one more thing. I ran Ross Stanley, aka the fake Julian Mayfield, through our system, and it's not good news."

Bailey prepared herself for the worst.

"Stanley was a CIA hired gun. He doesn't work for us anymore, but this only makes me more worried about the Agency connection."

Bailey agreed. Layla only knew part of the story. "Thanks for telling us, Layla."

"You two need to be careful. I haven't been able to locate your new safe house. That's good, because hopefully that means no one else can either. Let me know if there's anything I can do."

"Will do," Bailey said. "Thanks again." She ended the call and looked at Marco. "Whelan could've hired Stanley. The full picture is starting to come together."

"It was too risky to tell her about Whelan," Marco said. "For her own safety. That wasn't a secure line. If Whelan is involved in this, then the less Layla knows, the better."

"You're right. But how are we going to get the goods on Whelan?"

"We need more than that one email. We have to keep looking."

◆

A couple of hours later, Marco took Bailey's hand. "How're you holding up?"

She sighed. "I've been better, but I have faith. The Lord has protected us this far. He'll continue to do so." Her voice held her sincere conviction.

"I couldn't agree with you more." He probably hadn't prayed enough for their safety, but Bailey's point was an excellent reminder that God was still in control. Plain and simple. He'd known women of faith throughout his life, but Bailey's faith was different because it was battle hardened. She'd faced down one of the worst losses a person could deal with and come out stronger on the other side. He not only respected her for that, but he was also drawn to her by it. "I'm not saying we should be reckless, but we need to keep looking."

"Marco, there is a real chance that something could happen to us, and it seems like they're more focused on me. You could let me do this on my own. I don't want to jeopardize your life unnecessarily."

"Are you crazy?" He leaned toward her. "You know I would never leave you. Never. So don't even bring that up again."

"It would be safer for you."

"But not for you. Even if I didn't have feelings for you, I wouldn't leave you. That's not how I operate. We're in this together no matter what. Understood?"

She let out a breath. "Yes."

"I'm serious, Bailey. I am not cutting and running. Ever."

"Thank you," she replied softly.

He squeezed her hand. "Stick with me. We'll make it through this together."

CHAPTER
TWENTY-FIVE

The next morning Izzy conferred with Jay and Lexi in their conference room. "I got a cryptic message from Marco saying that he and Bailey are following up on a lead and asking us all to remain at HQ. I don't have a good feeling about this." She was anxious to get their reactions. After her strange conversation with Bailey, in which she knew Bailey was holding back, and now this message from Marco, her antenna was up. Everything was telling her that something was wrong.

"Let me give the FBI a call and see if we can get a check-in from the security detail stationed at the safe house." Jay pulled out his phone. A minute later he looked at Izzy. "They're going to call me back when they have something."

"I hope Marco and Bailey aren't planning to go off on their own. We're a team, and we should stick together." Fear bolted through Izzy at the prospect of something bad happening to them.

Lexi stood. "I know they were reviewing the WSI documents. Maybe they found something and are trying to chase down a lead before looping us in. Is there any way for us to get into the database and look at what they were seeing?"

Izzy nodded. "Yes, and if I can't, Ryder can."

About an hour later, the team was huddled around a screen, reading the emails that Bailey's user log showed she had been reviewing the night before. Izzy focused on the words, hoping for a clue.

"Who is 'NW'?" Lexi asked. "Do we know anyone with those initials?"

The room was quiet for a minute.

"Beats me," Izzy responded.

Then Jay cleared his throat. "Ned Whelan. The CIA deputy."

Lexi gasped. "If you're right, then the CIA created this top secret mission *and* is behind all of this?"

Izzy thought through the options. "It might not be the Agency. Maybe Whelan has gone rogue. Let's see what else we can find. We'll run searches in the database and go back to all the background checks of WSI employees. We need to figure out who at WSI was involved with Whelan."

They spent all morning dividing up the documents and searching to find any additional references to Whelan. They found a couple more and printed off copies, placing them on the whiteboard. A story was starting to take shape. A very troubling story that reached into the heart of the CIA.

Izzy finally felt like she was coming into her own as she stood at the board. This was the first time in her career that she actually felt like a leader. And Jay, to his credit, was not trying to jump into the spotlight.

"Here's what we know," she said. "Look at the timeline. Whelan didn't come into the communication picture until later. What we don't fully understand is the role Whelan played. Oliver Patterson and WSI were working together on the scheme to illegally divert the arms shipments. At a bare minimum, Cullen Mink was an operational player, and that probably resulted in his death. He knew the truth."

"Doesn't that mean the WSI CEO, Barnett, is also at risk?" Lexi asked.

The room fell silent before Izzy spoke again. "Barnett's on the emails. So I think that's your answer."

"Motive?" Jay asked. "Why make the deal with the Iranians in the first place?"

"Money. Political favors," Lexi suggested.

"Or what if the Iranians have some dirt on Patterson? They forced him to act," Jay said.

"It wouldn't be the first time that someone has been leveraged," Lexi said.

"What do we know about Patterson's stance on Iran?" Izzy asked.

Jay looked down at his laptop. "Iran isn't his area of expertise. But in the past, he's been more pro-engagement, wanting to focus on diplomacy." His phone rang. "It's the callback from the FBI."

Izzy waited anxiously, as she could only hear Jay's side of the conversation, which wasn't much.

When he hung up, Jay turned back toward her and Lexi. "The two of them left the safe house this morning, but the agents said they seemed calm and composed. There was no sign of danger."

"I guess we'll just have to wait for them to show up here," Izzy said.

They spent the bulk of the afternoon trying to build out all the facts. When the conference room door opened, Izzy's eyes widened. It was NCIS Director Nadine Mercer. Her gaze immediately landed on the whiteboard.

"I see you all have figured out what I was just briefed on by Agent Agostini," Director Mercer said.

"So he's all right?" Izzy asked.

Director Mercer nodded. "Yes. He and Agent Ryan are following up on some other leads."

Izzy let out a sigh of relief.

The director turned toward Izzy. "We have a team of agents bringing in Barnett right now. Izzy, I want you to take the lead on interrogating him."

"Yes, ma'am." Izzy suddenly felt sick. Could she do this?

Director Mercer crossed her arms. "We need to get him to flip and give up Patterson and Whelan. We're willing to work out a highly favorable deal. But we won't budge an inch unless he's willing to flip. Not a millimeter until we get what we want."

Izzy didn't immediately respond, so Jay jumped in. "Understood, ma'am. We'll be ready when he gets here."

Director Mercer exited the room, and Izzy exhaled the breath she'd been holding. "I guess we've got an interrogation to prepare for."

◆

Bailey and Marco met Layla at the National Mall near the Washington Monument. They'd chosen that spot since it was a major tourist area and there was a summer festival taking place that day, so they felt they could get lost in the crowd.

"What's going on?" Layla asked.

They walked through the crowd, staying close together as they made their way down the grassy lawn.

Bailey readied herself for this conversation. "We couldn't say anything last night on the phone, but we now believe we have evidence tying the CIA to these crimes."

Layla's brown eyes widened. "I was worried about that once I found those searches for you. Who is it?"

"Ned Whelan," Marco responded.

"This was his operation. Well, it was ultimately Smith's operation, but Whelan was involved in planning the op and running it day to day. It just doesn't make sense that he'd sabotage his own plan." Layla frowned.

"We think it's more complicated than that," Bailey said. "The timeline we've come up with doesn't show Whelan getting involved until soon before the first murder."

"Do you have a theory?" Layla asked.

Bailey and Marco had spent half the night poring over documents, trying to create a plausible scenario and build out a timeline.

Marco nodded. "We do. What if the guys figured out that Patterson was the DoD turncoat? They reported that back to Whelan, since he was running the op. Let's say Whelan confronted Patterson and, instead of ratting him out to Smith and the rest of the Agency, Whelan made a deal with him."

Layla bit her lip. "Maybe Patterson paid Whelan off for his silence?"

"How much do you know about Whelan?" Bailey asked. "Could you see him selling out?"

Layla didn't immediately respond.

"Is that a yes?" Marco asked.

"Whelan is old-school. He grew up in the Agency during the Cold War. He's respected but cagey. Although you don't get to be a top spook without being like that. But sometimes people do get corrupted by money. Also, I know that someone inside the CIA was digging around about Bailey. That would line up with this." She paused. "And there's no evidence of Smith's involvement?"

"None," Bailey said. "Not a single thing."

"That's good. I would've been shocked if he was involved. But regardless, this would mean that Whelan is responsible for the deaths of our own because of money. I guess the only way to bury the truth would be to kill them all." Layla stopped walking and looked up at the sky.

Bailey touched her arm. "I know it's awful."

Layla's dark brown eyes focused on her. "If Whelan is willing to kill his own operatives, then no one who knows the truth is safe. And that includes Barnett and even Patterson."

"You think Whelan would turn on Patterson?" Bailey asked.

Layla nodded. "I have no doubts, given this context."

Marco started walking again. "We jointly briefed our directors by phone on a secure line before we came here. They want to handle Whelan. But we're going to focus on Patterson and Barnett."

"You need to lie low, though, Layla, until Whelan is neutralized. He may try to come after you."

"I'll go dark. The two of you need to be careful too. I checked this morning, and I still couldn't find the location of your safe house. I think it's clear. I'd either stay at NCIS or the safe house until this is all buttoned up if I were you."

"Will do," Bailey said. "And I'm sorry again that I've brought you into this. I never intended to put you in danger."

Layla pulled her into a tight hug. "We're in this together." With a nod to Marco, she turned and started walking toward the monument, disappearing into the crowd.

"We need to get out of here," Marco said.

Bailey nodded. "I hope this nightmare is almost over."

◆

The past twenty-four hours had rushed by in a blur, and now Izzy sat with Jay in a room at WSI, about to watch a meeting between Rex Barnett and Oliver Patterson. To Izzy's surprise, it hadn't taken much to flip Barnett. He clearly wanted out of this mess. They'd learned a lot from him singing like a canary.

According to Barnett, he'd done it for the money and had zero expectation of any dead bodies—much less the mounting body count. He'd been told at the beginning that this was a lucrative deal with almost zero chance of getting caught. Barnett viewed it purely as a business deal, a transaction.

But once Battle and his fellow undercover agents started to figure out what was really going on, things got dicey. When Barnett found out that their operation had been exposed and Patterson had brought in Whelan, Barnett was boxed in. He had no power anymore.

Barnett said that he never put out any of the hits, and it was all about Patterson and Whelan and what they wanted. But regardless, under the law and any ethical norm, Barnett was still accountable as part of this conspiracy, and that was enough to get him to cooperate. Izzy had put everything on the table for Barnett—including that he was expendable and a liability to his buddies.

His full cooperation included bringing Patterson into WSI for a meeting that would be fully recorded so they would have the evidence they needed to turn over to the relevant prosecutors. Given the facts, they'd easily secured a wiretap warrant.

"I just hope we can trust Barnett not to tip off Patterson," Izzy muttered.

Jay looked at her. "Barnett wants to save his own hide. You saw what a weakling he was when we started pushing him in the interrogation. We told him that if there's any doubt, all deals are off the table. He'll play the game."

Izzy hoped Jay was right, because this was their best and only chance that she could see to successfully solve this case.

"Game time," Jay said.

Izzy watched the screens as Barnett shook hands with Oliver Patterson.

Barnett was in his early sixties with a full head of thick gray hair. Oliver was younger, only in his fifties, and wore a suit that was probably too rich for his government pay grade.

"I wonder if Iranian money bought that designer suit and fancy gold cuff links," Izzy said.

Jay rolled his eyes. She knew it wasn't at her but at Patterson.

"Thanks for coming, Ollie. Please have a seat," Barnett said.

Patterson took a seat, and Barnett did the same. "You said it was important." Patterson unbuttoned his suit jacket.

"Yes. I've got the Feds breathing down my neck. I need your help managing this situation before it escalates even further."

Patterson leaned forward. "You've got nothing to worry about. We're completely clean in all of this. If they had anything on us, we would've heard by now. So just relax."

"How can you be so sure?" Barnett pushed.

Patterson's light blue eyes glistened. "Don't get cold feet. Stay the course."

This was the opening Barnett needed. "Let's see how good an actor our CEO is," Izzy said.

Barnett slammed his fist on the table. "This is my company. My life. My livelihood. I need more than just your bare assertion that everything is going to be okay."

"Easy." Patterson smiled and placed a hand on Barnett's arm. "Believe me. Our last problem is about to be solved."

"What do you mean?" Barnett's voice cracked.

"The FBI woman. The one working with the CIA. Whelan is taking care of her and her boyfriend once and for all."

Izzy gasped. "They're going to try to kill Bailey and Marco!" She turned to Jay. "We have to get more information."

He nodded. "Just give Barnett a second. I'm sure he'll follow up."

"So you found her?" Barnett asked.

"Close enough. Whelan has a team closing in, and this time there's no chance they'll get away."

Barnett raised an eyebrow. "How can you be so sure? She's evaded others and continues to be a thorn in our side."

Patterson cleared his throat. "Because these aren't the two hired guns we've been using. We called in help from Tehran. It's the end of the road this time."

Barnett's mouth hung open. "Iranian assets?"

"Yes. They'll find out what she knows and then close up all the loose ends for good. If anyone else is too close to the truth, they'll find out through the interrogation, and then they will eliminate them. You've got absolutely nothing to worry about. Once the Feds are out of the picture, this will all just fade away. The CIA has too many skeletons to come after us. We'll exert leverage if we need to, but this should be the end to this mess. And regardless, we're airtight. With Cullen dead, there's no one on earth who knows our secrets except us. We're rock solid."

"You don't think we should back out?" Barnett asked.

Patterson laughed. "Rex, you realize that if we try to back out, we're going to be the ones on the wrong side of the Iranians. We still have shipments to deliver. I'll take my chances with the US government. Let's just keep our heads down, and everything will be fine. Whelan's a pro. He knows how to get things done."

"That he does," Barnett replied. "But, Ollie, we've known each other for, what, almost fifteen years? What if Whelan decides that the two of *us* are liabilities? It's like you said—the circle is so small now."

Patterson shook his head. "My friend, that is not going to

happen. Whelan's with us. He's a rational, business-minded man. You have the connections to make other deals happen. That will be very useful in the future."

"With all due respect, I'm worried that you're going to hang me out to dry."

Patterson's face began to redden.

"Uh-oh," Izzy said. "I hope Barnett didn't push too hard."

Jay held up a hand, urging her to wait.

"That's not true." Patterson's face was crimson.

Barnett leaned in. "I just want to make sure we're squared away. The two of us have gone through far too much over the years to be railroaded by a spook."

Patterson stood. "This will be wrapped up soon, and we can put this sordid ordeal behind us and get back to business. There are still many business ventures we can make happen as long as you don't lose your cool." He walked to the door and slammed it behind him.

CHAPTER
TWENTY-SIX

"**I'll be ready to go** when we get the call." Bailey walked into the living room of the safe house. They'd come back to pack up and clear out. The wheels were in motion, and if everything went as planned, all the suspects would be in custody by the end of the day, and there'd no longer be a need to stay at the safe house. Given the threat level, Bailey had been ordered by the FBI to remain at the safe house until they were given the all clear, which they were expecting at any time. Marco had insisted on staying with her.

A loud knock on the front door startled her. "No one should be here," she told Marco.

They both drew their weapons. Marco stood. "Let me check it out. If something happens, run out the back and don't stop running, whatever you do."

She didn't want to argue with him, but there was no way she'd just leave him in danger. She would back him up just as he'd done time and again for her. Letting him go ahead, she trailed slightly behind.

"Who is it?" he asked at the door.

"FBI," a deep male voice said. "There are two of us at the door. It's no longer safe for you here. There's new intel about an immediate threat to your lives. We need to get you out of here ASAP."

"Who sent you?" Marco asked.

"FBI and NCIS in conjunction with Layla Karam."

Bailey stood beside him. "How do we know you're really who you say you are?" After falling for the Julian Mayfield stunt, she'd learned her lesson.

"Agent Ryan, Layla told us to tell you that she is going to the Georgetown reunion and that you should go too. She said you would know what that meant."

Marco looked at Bailey, and she nodded. "They're legit. No one else would know that we've been talking about that. And she's telling us it's okay to go with them."

"All right. I'm opening the door so you can come in." Marco turned the knob and opened the door.

Loud gunshots cracked through the air.

One of the FBI agents standing directly in front of them fell to the ground. Bailey watched as the life left his body. She tried to process what was happening. The other FBI agent ran inside, and Marco slammed the door behind him.

"We're too late. They're here," the FBI agent said. "I'm sorry."

She didn't understand what he meant. "Who is here?"

"Back up from the door." Marco pulled her away, not waiting for the agent to answer.

"Men sent to kill you." The FBI agent pulled his cell and started calling for backup.

Marco still held on to her arm. "Basement."

"But then we'll be trapped." *Lord, please help us. We need your intervention again to get through this attack.*

Marco shook his head. "If we go outside, we die. It's that simple. We need to take cover and buy time."

Before they could take two steps, the front door was busted down. A group of armed men wearing black masks ran inside.

"Don't move!" one of them barked.

As the words came out of his mouth, Bailey detected a slight British accent mixed with another she couldn't place. Her heart raced as she tried to think of a way out.

Marco lifted his hands. "No one has to get hurt here."

"Enough talking," the man said. He was obviously the leader of the group. "Drop your weapons slowly. Place them on the floor. Any sudden moves, and everyone is dead."

Bailey looked at Marco, and she knew he was trying to figure a way out of this. At her count there were three good guys and five bad ones. Those weren't good odds. There was already an FBI agent down at the front door.

"You want me," Bailey said. "I'm here. Let these guys go." She slowly crouched down and placed her weapon on the ground.

"Bailey, what're you doing?" Marco snapped.

She shook her head and took a step toward the ringleader. "I'll go with you, but you have to let them go."

"What makes you think we're in the mood for negotiation?" the leader replied.

As the words rolled off his tongue and she looked into his eyes, her worst fears were realized. The FBI had been right. These were most likely highly trained men who killed and tortured for a living. "Then what do you want?"

Without another word, the attacker shot the remaining FBI agent in the right thigh, and he crumpled to the ground with a loud groan.

She rushed forward. "No! Don't hurt anyone else—just take

me." She wasn't above begging, if that's what it took. The problem was that she knew that men like this were cold-blooded killers. They'd been sent here on a specific mission—one that obviously included taking her alive for questioning before they killed her. If the order had just been to kill, they would have all been dead already.

The lead attacker grabbed her arm. One of the other men took ahold of Marco.

"You're both coming with us," the leader said flatly.

It was as she had suspected. Her bigger fear was that they would use her feelings for Marco against them. They'd both be tortured to find out what they knew before they died a miserable death. She closed her eyes and started praying, because only the Lord could help them now. They truly needed Him to act in a big way, but she still believed He could do it.

"What're you doing?" the man barked.

"Praying." She opened her eyes and looked directly into his face.

"Your God isn't going to help you now." He pulled her toward the busted front door.

Just as he pushed her through the opening, gunshots fired in rapid succession. The man beside her fell to the ground, but she still stood. Alive.

Who was shooting at them now? She leapt back through the open door to take cover, then turned and looked for Marco.

Another attacker right behind her was leveled by someone with an amazing shot. The fact that she was still alive and he was dead made her think that God had answered her prayer for help. The good guys had arrived. *Thank you, Lord.*

"Marco!"

She watched as a struggle ensued between Marco and one of the attackers. Marco had knocked the gun out of the man's hands, and now they grappled and punched at each other, their arms locked around each other's bodies.

She no longer had her weapon, so she grabbed a gun off one of the dead men on the ground beside her and whirled back toward the fight. She raised the weapon, hoping for a clean shot.

The man pulled a knife and reared back, aiming for Marco's throat. Without taking another breath, she squeezed the trigger. She hit her target squarely in the temple, and he fell to the floor.

The other two men, sensing the inevitable, had already run toward the back door. "We can't let them get away," she said.

Marco grabbed his gun off the floor and was by her side as they ran through the house toward the back porch.

But the two men had stopped short. Their hands were up. Bailey couldn't see who had them cornered until she stepped to the side. "Izzy!"

Izzy stood with her gun drawn, flanked by a couple of other NCIS agents.

Jay jogged into the kitchen from the direction of the front entrance. "Are you two okay?" he asked.

"Yeah," Marco answered, trying to catch his breath.

Bailey threw her arms around Marco. Her heart felt like it was beating out of her chest. They didn't have to say anything to each other as she pulled back and looked into this eyes. A quiet understanding passed between them. They had survived.

"We can give you all the details back at HQ," Izzy said. "But we got Barnett to cooperate, and we have Patterson in custody."

"And Whelan?" Bailey feared the answer.

"He's being brought in as we speak," Jay responded. "This entire operation is about to come crumbling down."

Marco grabbed Bailey's hand and squeezed.

"And Lexi is back at HQ, working as hard as she can on the

legal ramifications of all this—so it was really a team effort," Izzy said.

Bailey smiled at her, proud of how she'd handled this impossibly difficult situation.

"You did a great job, Rookie." Marco patted her on the back.

Izzy beamed. "I learned from the best."

◆

After close to forty-eight hours of interviews and briefings, Marco and Bailey had finally been released.

Marco had insisted on taking Bailey home to her apartment. While rationally he knew that the threat had been neutralized, he couldn't let her go back to her place alone. Not after all that had happened.

They walked into her apartment, and she let out a sigh. "It is *so* good to be home."

He followed her inside and did a quick security check. Everything seemed to be in order. The FBI had done a more thorough check last night of both of their places so they could go home in confidence. But after everything they'd gone through, he couldn't help himself.

"I guess it's really over." He took Bailey's hand, and they sat together on the couch.

"I'm still processing everything." She paused. "And I'm beat. It will be nice to sleep in my own bed tonight. Do you really think we're safe now?" She looked up at him with her bright green eyes.

It was a question he'd asked himself repeatedly. "I do. The secret is out. There's no more need to target our team. Whelan, Patterson, and Barnett are all in custody. And now that everything has been blown open, there is no reason for any foreign agents to be involved. The jig is up."

"But not before the Iranians got their hands on a substantial number of our weapons," she said flatly.

"It could've been worse, though. We have to remember that." It was something he had to keep reminding himself as well.

"And we still have to track down the professional hit men who were hired."

"The FBI has that squarely in hand." They'd learned the initial questioning had indicated that there were two top-of-the-line hit men behind all the killings. The initial three victims, plus Kappen and Cullen. One of them was also responsible for the attacks against Bailey.

Bailey blew out a breath. "I know they told us to take time off, but I wish we could see this thing through to the end."

"We did our part. It's time for us to let others step in and tie it all up."

"What do you think the chances are of the FBI finding those assassins alive?" she asked.

"Slim to none." Marco figured they were already dead—most likely by Whelan's order. "But the FBI will find out. I'm certain of that."

"What are they going to tell the families?" she asked. "Given all the security concerns, I can't imagine they will tell them the truth."

He shook his head. "No. They won't. The government will try to keep this entire thing on lockdown. I just hope they get told something that gives them closure. They deserve that and so much more."

Bailey nodded. "It's ultimately not our call."

The directors of both NCIS and the FBI had made that abundantly clear. It would be against the vital national security interests of the United States for the full story to come out.

Marco had an extra-soft spot toward Kappen now. "Once

Whelan turned, he started digging around and thought he'd found the perfect fall guy in Kappen. It's a shame he got pulled into this because a CIA traitor targeted him."

"Another innocent man dead."

Silence hung between them for a few moments.

Marco pulled her close to him. "You saved my life."

"You would've done the same thing. And I haven't forgotten that you also saved mine." She took a breath. "And the Lord was there for us, Marco. I may not fully understand why I've been spared, but I'm going to do the most I can while on this earth to fight for justice."

Her words touched him. "I'm right there with you. But we have to take things one day at a time."

"That's all we can do."

He brushed a lock of blond hair out of her eyes. "This case was tough, but I have to think that after everything we've gone through, we'll be able to get through anything."

She smiled. "I know. I guess life is going to seem boring in comparison."

"I say we start by going out on a proper date. How about dinner this weekend?"

Her eyes brightened. "I'd love that."

EPILOGUE

Bailey took a deep breath and drank in the humid summer air. Even her usually straight-as-a-board hair had a little wave to it as she stood on Director Mercer's large boat. It was the perfect day to be on the water, and having her new and old friends around her made it even better. She looked over at Marco and gave him a little wave. He smiled at her while laughing loudly at one of Jay's corny jokes. She was enjoying a moment to herself as she stared out at the water and basked in the warm breeze.

The past month had been telling. Her life would never be the same after all she had witnessed. It had been terrifying and uplifting at the same time. She'd seen the worst in people, the death and destruction that accompanied evil. But she'd also felt God's protective hand on her life. He'd never left her side, and her eyes had been further opened to some of the truths that she held dear.

Given a traitor in their midst, the CIA had taken great lengths to keep the entire scandal under wraps. Whelan was currently being held at an undisclosed secure location. Bailey figured it was a black site. Since Whelan was an American citizen, he still deserved due process, and she had been assured he'd get it, but she doubted that would be the case. The Agency had a way of dealing with things that might not be completely constitutional.

Multiple agencies working the case had found direct financial links between state-linked Iranian groups, Barnett, and Patterson. They'd transferred the money using a highly sophisticated shell game, but the dots were being connected. The Iranians had paid the two men directly for the arms deal, using offshore bank accounts. Then Patterson had to go back to the Iranian well to get more funds for Whelan once he was in the picture. The Iranians had then wanted additional shipments in return for the payoff to Whelan.

As Bailey had feared, the dead bodies of the two assassins hired by Whelan were found by the FBI. Whelan had taken them out in his attempt to play cleanup. But little had he known at the time that none of it would matter. They'd also found wire transfers to a Cayman bank account in Ross Stanley's name that connected back to Whelan.

Patterson had been neck-deep in the operational details of the scheme and making the logistics work, including facilitating payment to the hit men. He was locked up in federal prison and would never see a public trial after working out a deal that would keep him behind bars for decades instead of facing the death penalty. Since Barnett had cooperated, his jail time had been reduced, but he would still serve a substantial sentence.

Lexi and Izzy walked over to Bailey, arms linked. "Hey there. How're you?" Lexi's long hair hung loose and blew in the wind, a startling contrast to her usual JAG-approved bun.

"I'm doing all right." Bailey took a moment to soak in the sun. "How about you?"

Lexi raised her sunglasses up onto her head. "I'm not going

to lie. This has been a rough month. But I got to speak to Tobias's family, and they don't believe their son died in vain. They understand the security concerns and the classified nature of the situation, but I was able to share with them that information Tobias provided was key to us solving the case. And while that doesn't bring him back, it's a reminder to them of the type of man and patriot he really was."

"Unlike the cowards who are responsible for all of this," Izzy said. "I have to hold my tongue, or else I'll say things I shouldn't."

Lexi sighed. "Yeah, I hate all the deal making that was done, but I'm hoping Patterson and Whelan never see daylight again. And we still have to deal with the Iranians and the fallout from the arms they were able to obtain."

"We can't solve every piece of this ourselves." It was something Bailey had to remind herself of daily.

Lexi nodded. "Yeah. And I know we've got our best people on it."

"One good thing came out of this." Izzy smiled. "I've met some great people, including the two of you, who I now consider my friends."

Bailey couldn't agree more. "Absolutely. Viv and Layla are throwing me a little girls-night-in party next weekend at my place. I really want you both to come. No guys allowed."

Izzy's eyes lit up. "That'll be so fun."

"Count me in too," Lexi said. "Although at some point we'll have to let the guys come around, since we're in new relationships and they can't stand being without us." She laughed.

"Speak for yourself," Izzy said. "Aiden is so busy with work, we barely see each other." Then she smiled. "But he's worth it. I'm fine with moving slowly. I think it's for the best."

Bailey gave Izzy an encouraging pat on the shoulder. Izzy

had opened up to her about an awful attack she had endured. Bailey had also learned that Jay had confronted the sergeant who was the perpetrator. Bailey wasn't sure what Jay told him, but it had resulted in the sergeant taking an early retirement. At least he was no longer on the police force and couldn't use his position of power to hurt anyone else.

Marco joined them and said hello. Lexi and Izzy excused themselves, and he wrapped an arm around Bailey. "This has been a great afternoon. I love being on the water. Especially with you here."

She leaned her head on his shoulder. "I know. I need to stick with you. All your Navy friends have boats." She laughed.

He turned her toward him and wrapped his arms around her waist. "I hope you'll stick with me even after summer ends. And when all this craziness is finally over and we're back to business as usual with our own careers. You at the FBI and me at NCIS."

She'd given their relationship a lot of thought, and she was certain how she felt. "I'd like that a lot. Remember how we talked about making time for each other?"

"Yeah. I do."

She looked up into his dark eyes. "Well, you should know that I've put you in my calendar as my standing Saturday night date."

He grinned. "Oh, really?"

"But sometimes I do get called away."

"As long as you come back, I'll be fine with that."

"There's nowhere else I'd rather be." As the words came out of her mouth, she realized how true they were and how real her feelings for this man had become.

"Bailey, I know we're just starting on our journey together, but I want you to know how much goodness and light you've brought into my life. You challenge me, you help balance me out, and you are the only woman I want in my life. I love you."

"I love you too, Marco. I can't wait to see what our future holds."

As he leaned down and kissed her under the bright sun, her heart was filled with love. She no longer lived in fear of loss but in hope of what was to come.

ACKNOWLEDGMENTS

I'm so excited to launch the CAPITAL INTRIGUE series and am very thankful for the opportunity to write more books.

To my wonderful agent, Sarah, your love and support mean so much to me. I look forward to all the things we plan to do together.

To Dave, Jessica, Noelle, Amy, and the entire Bethany House family, thank you for continuing to believe in me and my books. I love working with everyone and appreciate all you do. Dave and Jessica—thanks for taking my ideas and helping make them so much better!

Aaron, I love you. Thanks for loving me and supporting my career as an author.

Rachel's Justice League, thank you for not only being avid readers of my books but for being there for me as I walk through this author journey. Thank you for everything.

To my friends and writing buddies Alison, Lee, and Dana, I am so blessed by our friendship. Y'all make me laugh and bring so much joy into my life.

To my entire family, thank you for telling the world about my books and being my cheerleaders. Mama, I love you so much, and I can't wait to hear what you think about this new series.

And without my Lord and Savior Jesus Christ, none of this would be possible. I thank the Lord for blessing me and being so very strong when I am weak.

Rachel Dylan is an award-winning and bestselling author of legal thrillers and romantic suspense. She has practiced law for over a decade, including being a litigator at one of the nation's top law firms.

Rachel is the author of the ATLANTA JUSTICE series, which features strong female attorneys. *Deadly Proof*, the first book in the series, is a CBA bestseller, an FHL Reader's Choice Award winner, a Daphne du Maurier Award finalist, and a HOLT Medallion finalist. *Lone Witness* is the winner of a HOLT Medallion, a Maggie finalist, and a Selah finalist.

A Southerner at heart, Rachel now lives in Michigan with her husband and five furkids—two dogs and three cats. She loves to connect with readers. You can find her at www.racheldylan.com.

Sign Up for Rachel's Newsletter!

Keep up to date with Rachel's news on book releases and events by signing up for her email list at racheldylan.com.

More from Rachel Dylan

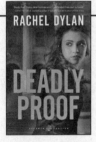

In the intense courtrooms of Atlanta, Georgia, three female lawyers seek truth and justice as they risk everything—including their hearts. As the stakes rise and their worlds are turned upside down, they have to decide who to trust in their pursuit for justice.

ATLANTA JUSTICE: *Deadly Proof, Lone Witness, Breach of Trust*

More Gripping Suspense!

Mystery begins to follow Aggie Dunkirk when she exhumes the past's secrets and uncovers a crime her eccentric grandmother has been obsessing over. Decades earlier, after discovering her sister's body in the attic, Imogene Flannigan is determined to find justice. Two women, separated by time, vow to find answers . . . no matter the cost.

Echoes among the Stones by Jaime Jo Wright
jaimewrightbooks.com

When cybercriminals hack into the U.S. Marshal's Witness Protection database and auction off personal details to the highest bidder, FBI Agent Sean Nichols begins a high-stakes chase to find the hacker. Trouble is, he has to work with U.S. Marshal Taylor Mills, who knows the secrets of his past, and the seconds are ticking down before someone dies.

Seconds to Live by Susan Sleeman
HOMELAND HEROES #1
susansleeman.com

When a Coast Guard officer is found dead and another goes missing, Special Agent Finn Walker faces his most dangerous assignment yet. Complicating matters is the arrival of investigative reporter Gabby Rowley, who's on a mission to discover the truth. Can they ignore the sparks between them and track down this elusive killer?

The Killing Tide by Dani Pettrey
COASTAL GUARDIANS #1
danipettrey.com

◊ BETHANYHOUSE